DEUCE

DEUCE

Joe Yurgine

ISBN-13: 9781517055783
ISBN-10: 1517055784

Acknowledgments

In gratitude to SM for his poetry and to Dr. KJ for his help on medical issues.

CONTENTS

Nineteen sixty-eight was the pivotal year of the sixties: the moment when all of the nation's impulses toward violence, idealism, diversity, and disorder peaked to produce the greatest possible hope—and the worst imaginable despair.
—Charles Kaiser, *1968 in America*

We've only one virginity to lose, and where we lost it, there our hearts will be.
—Kipling

CHAPTER 1

THERE'S SOMETHING HAPPENING HERE WHAT IT IS AIN'T EXACTLY CLEAR

NEW YORK CITY

Monday, March 18, 1968.

IT'S A-COMIN'.

Growing up, this was an expression uttered in our house when dark clouds rolled in from the west, bringing artillery-like flashes and claps of distant thunder on a purple sky deeper than the cape of a Catholic priest I once served as an altar boy. Simply saying the words in our house was enough to send our cat, Hairdo, into deep hiding.

It was Monday, midmorning, and in New York City you need a good pair of legs. I was walking at a fast pace on First Avenue on my way to Central Park, and the wind was picking up.

A storm was a-comin' all right, and it was more than just the weather. The nation was sick. The long hot summer of 1967 with its race riots was over but things were getting worse. In the words of Steve Stills, paranoia was striking deep. Masses of people were rising up in New York City and elsewhere in opposition to the Vietnam War. The country was in the throes of a nervous breakdown.

The Tet Offensive in Vietnam was going into its third month, and today North Vietnamese infantrymen attacked the encircled US marine base at Khe Sanh. Yesterday, Senator Robert Kennedy announced his candidacy for president. Kennedy was unhappy with the war and wanted a change of course. He wanted the president to appoint a commission to study a "necessary" revision of American policy in Vietnam. Meanwhile, in London two hundred youths held an antiwar protest at the US embassy.

Today I was assigned and scheduled to meet the Poet, my friend and fellow FBI agent, in Central Park to cover another Vietnam War demonstration, and I was late, which had to do with a hangover after a raucous day on Sunday at a packed Third Avenue Irish saloon with friends. It had been St. Patrick's Day, the one given day a Catholic can break a fast to celebrate. Unless I was back in Chicago on Division Street, there was nothing quite like St. Patrick's Day in New York City.

I'd known the Poet for only six months, but he was the most interesting and curious person I'd ever met. The Poet was from South Carolina and loved words and poetry, which was why he was called the Poet. When the Poet was on the street, he would carry note cards to record inspirational thoughts of persons and events he observed, which he later expanded to longer prose writings. I had no doubt that his creative temperament would find considerable low-hanging fruit in the mass of humanity we were going to encounter in Central Park.

Our supervisor, who'd sent us on this mission, had a way of downplaying lawless and violent behavior. He anticipated that this demonstration was going to be large in scope and rowdy but non-violent and free of criminal acts, except pot smoking. His words.

To the Poet and me that meant the demonstration was going to be rebellious, with more citizen resistance opposing the government's Vietnam War policy. Hippies and yippies would be out in force. February had been one of the deadliest months in the war's history.

Despite the bad weather that was brewing and the nation's woes, First Avenue was alive with taxies taking well-dressed financial traders down to lower Manhattan. Other urban souls, and businessmen who held lower-paying jobs, were all moving aggressively and quickly to subways for their trips to their offices. Stewardesses in attractive blue uniforms, who always stirred my intense interest and daily lust, were standing by curbs waiting for their rides to the airport. Traffic was clogging the streets and poisoning the air. Everybody moved with purposefulness. Like me, everyone had someplace to get to, someplace to go, and they had better get there in a hurry. Their style of walking was not a walk of the penguins at a glacier's pace but rather the gait of army ants, and the ants and the bustle of activity were reflected in the many glass windows. Jaywalking is illegal, but forget that, and forget the color of traffic lights, because those are criminal offenses or obstacles that should not stand in anyone's way, for they do not make a difference. They will slow you down. This is New York. This morning it was business as usual.

I'm twenty-five years old and new to this town. I've been trying real hard to learn quickly everything about Manhattan and the people who occupy it. It's not easy to grasp "uptown" from "downtown," or the many ways to get off the island.

Figuring that the Poet had it right regarding observing and staying focused, I started to emulate his work habits and lifestyle. As he mentioned early on, "Know the neighborhoods, block by block. Smell the air. Observe the people. Know the exits. Pay attention to the little things. In our business this is important." There are only six ways off Manhattan. After he told me that, I started to count in my head the bridges. Everywhere I went, I walked, observed, and always tried to take a different route. Like some pathologist conducting an autopsy, I also developed the habit of diagnosing people, dead or alive, and city problems.

Today, even in my haste to get to Central Park, what I noticed was First Avenue, which from the Yorkville neighborhood at about Eightieth Street ran straight south for miles. To keep walking would carry you right past the United Nations.

The city's Department of Sanitation street sweepers had been out, but owing to the poor quality of the mechanical sweepers—lumbering expensive machines with unworkable water nozzles, prone to mechanical failures—debris, broken glass, a few condom wrappers, and muck remained at the curb line. A tidy sweep was never evident, and it was no different today. Meanwhile like the wind instruments in a Brahms movement, a fresh breeze picked up, blowing plumes of dust in my face.

In front of me, a green automobile with New Jersey plates stopped at a red light, completely blocking our crosswalk. Although I haven't been here that long, already I'm convinced that in Manhattan cars need to be constrained. Anger sets in, but I back off, doing nothing. Instead, I try to show patience and understanding. Not so, however, for everyone.

A young black man with an afro and horned-rimmed glasses, a student type, carrying books, walking next to me, is irritated because of the vehicle blocking his path, looks over at me, and shakes his head, uttering, "No way." Without hesitating he leaped on to the front hood of the vehicle, walked across the hood, and continued down First Avenue.

I looked around. Everyone was chuckling at this bold move. I focused my gaze at this young black man. I continued to look at him, watching and waiting for the inevitable glance back, that second look and turning of the head. Eventually, it came.

It was like seeing lightning in the distance and then waiting for the inevitable thunder. This time the thunder came with a laugh, the raised finger and bird, and a large smile.

Meanwhile, the driver in the vehicle with New Jersey plates, sensing the foul mood of the pedestrians, kept his window rolled up and remained in the car.

"Welcome to New York," I muttered.

New York City is like a savory meal that's difficult to digest at times, but always stimulating and different. My hometown is Chicago but since I spent much of my time in college outside that city, arriving in New York gave me a feeling of having escaped from some unfruitful territory, where there are farms and fields with pigs and harvest machines, where people spent time at roadhouses and where they would raise a little hell after bowling.

This place was loaded with centers. It was the nation's financial center, business center, cultural center, publishing center, literary center, and fashion center, to name just a few, all of which brought in active creativity, swagger, power struggles, and an artistic lifestyle that transformed the rest of the country. Its 305 square miles are divided into five boroughs: Manhattan, the Bronx, Brooklyn, Queens, and Staten Island (an island that you could reach only by ferry).

Manhattan is a study in contrasts. Some of the richest people in the world live in its townhouses and apartments. But there are also the poorest. Lower Manhattan outside the financial district is filled with Puerto Ricans, Jews, and Asians, many being unemployed but blessed with creativity, able to procure apartments and housing at incredibly cheap rents.

There are over one hundred neighborhoods, such as Chinatown and Harlem. Harlem, which lies north of Central Park, is an area that primarily is composed of poor and struggling residents occupying tenements. Thinking back on everything I've picked up and learned about the city in the six months that I've been here, it's hands down an exciting place to live and work.

It is a city of ambition with people searching for self advancement, a city filled with noise, police and fire sirens, rich with conflict heading for a collision, where people are always in a hurry hustling from one place to the next down filthy stairs to graffiti-walled subway cars, with visible peddlers, subway preachers, evangelists, vendors, and sidewalk merchants along the way selling handbags with fabrics masquerading as something they're not or yesterday's *New York Times* or coniferous balsam and Douglas firs at Christmastime or wilted flowers procured from some undertaker on Seventh Avenue, while others simply hand out pamphlets and manifestos of New Left groups and upcoming sit-ins and social protest meetings, next to people pounding jackhammers; where street art and graffiti, scrawled at times in duplicate on tiles, are created in covert sorties, with colors (red, yellow, and blue) having gangland or homeless connotations, but purposeful because with stoned taggers you need a scheme of aesthetics with all of the right colors to create a burner; where Hare Krishnas in their robes and sandals (and don't confuse them with Pakistani ceremonial drummers covered in embroidered fabric, occasional eccentrics and assorted crazies, nonvisionary types) stand, sing, and dance on street corners near ice cream or garbage trucks, while others, some searching for Bongo (a loose gorilla from a circus) or standing on soapboxes, rage about social injustice with lines from Rap and Stokely, preaching and rumbling revolution; where hordes of panhandlers, despite a city ordinance forbidding begging, work the sidewalks with an attitude, sticking to some kind of grinding daily to sell their wares, always hustling, doing it with people and passersby, who are suspicious toward anyone and with no time to spare; where in Central Park, not like central Staten Island, the wildest place in the city, with its sweet gum and blossoming linden trees, an island within an island, a mecca for hippies, on a New York dog-day stormy morning comes now sounds of polyrhythmic beats of Caribbean drummers, percussionists, tom-toms mimicking heartbeats, some on rock bluffs or gazebos, sounds that pierce windows and shake leaves off Central Park trees, unremitting noise, turbulence, no peace and quiet for visitors craving tranquility; where young rootless, nomadic souls, old enough to kill but not to vote, free-spirited, reckless rich kids, alienated by the repressive mores of war, anarchic flower children, a collection of creatures lost but liberated now with no dress code, the evanescence of youth numbering over a thousand, fill thirteen acres of the great lawn, establishing a venue for mass political action, not to denounce any official infraction of their right to free sex, but protesting the draft, with statements like "white people sending black people to fight yellow people to protect the country they stole from red people" or quoting Ali, "I ain't got no quarrel with them Vietcong"; where this scene is not a gathering of Eagle Scouts or the Ohio Amish but a battlefield where no one has yet fallen, a tribal rock celebration and response to all of the divisiveness in the world, many camouflaged in army-green or nude, not camouflaged at all, running away from something or trying to make a statement, long hair, not Mohawks, pompadours, or shaved heads these but afros and wild manes with a tangled tease, and beads, long chains, with a scent of sweat, flowers, and smoking joints, some with bull horns, standing side by side like a Latin American conga line with arms around one another's shoulders, chanting, "Up against the wall, motherfuckers; up against the wall, motherfuckers," with voices answering, "Preach it," and, "Do away with the pigs," while on the opposite side, a football field away, standing together now, the vile pigs, an army, the uniformed police, New York's finest, forming ranks, in formation like a marching band but under orders to cut these liberated souls some slack on anything, drug laws and misdemeanor laws, stroking and slapping their billy clubs against their thighs to the steady beat and rhythm of "Up against the wall, motherfuckers; up against the wall."

This was the city I was living and working in and the demonstration I encountered at Central Park—and me without a camera.

I found the Poet and stood with him off to the side, observing this chaos, all the while receiving a real education on political life stemming from events in Vietnam. This could've been a political rally for Senator Kennedy; all that was missing was red, white, and blue bunting.

The meadow was loud, like a fiesta or a movie or play, unreal, far removed from rational behavior. With this gathering someone was going to get hurt, needing only a spark or something stupid to bring on a blood bath, shotgun pellets or a police dog to sink his fangs in faded Levi's.

I looked over at the Poet, shouting to make myself heard. "I detect tension and a real lack of Midwest public decorum. It could be a weed overdose."

The Poet paused and with his Death Valley Clemson drawl said, "No, Deuce. We're receiving an education on political life.

It's the fucking war, man. Too much bloodshed. It's a big drag. The place is headed for a colossal nervous breakdown. This group would never pass muster at the Citadel, and they are not going to be treated conscientiously."

"This is the cool pot and pill gang that grew up in the 50's," I said. "They are protesting our leader's hypocrisy. They feel good about themselves. If conscription were abolished, we wouldn't have this."

"True," said the Poet, "but then who would do the fighting? There aren't enough volunteers."

Good point, but I thought to myself, can you blame this group—many being liberated, privileged baby-boomer students—for not wanting to be involved in a war they regarded as criminal? Yet, the opposing argument was that other younger people were being killed for them.

"At least they are not waving Vietcong flags," said the Poet.

"It's beyond anything I've seen. Terrible manners."

The Poet looked at me and smiled. "Yeah, but which of us is perfect?"

"What do you think?" I finally asked.

"What I think is that instead of calling the cops 'motherfuckers,' they ought to be singing 'We Shall Overcome.' The cops aren't going to take away their citizenship. They are here to kick ass. Get ready for some carnage."

It was a time of protests, tear gas, violence, free love, and patriotic parades.

CHAPTER 2

B-BALL IN BED-STUY

Wednesday, June 5, 1968.

My name is Deuce Ballou. Don't call me Ishmael. Call me Deuce. I'm an FBI agent assigned to the New York office in Manhattan. The beauty and fun of working as an agent was that each day was different.

Months after covering the demonstration in Central Park with the Poet, I found myself on another assignment, this time in Brooklyn. That meant a lot of things, although mainly a stressful commute from Manhattan, a place where I lived, worked, and had an incredibly good time.

Here I digress to explain how I arrived in New York. My being an agent and working as an agent in New York came about in a roundabout way. After training school at Quantico, I had to serve time for about a year at the Miami office. When I heard the news that I was heading for Miami, it was like, "Oh, please, please don't throw me in that briar patch!" I knew, however, that Miami was going to be a short stay, and it was a short stay, like nine months.

I was then transferred to New York City, considered by many agents to be a fate worse than death for many reasons, not the least of which being that death was much cheaper. A lot of people hung on by the skin of their teeth. The city with its high cost of living made it extremely difficult to live comfortably on government wages. To avoid an economic apocalypse one had to adapt and know the ins and outs of buying food, where to eat and so forth.

As a single person, with no wheels, no insurance expenses, and living in a cheap New York City apartment, meeting expenses for me was not that arduous. I had worked my way totally through college and knew what was needed to live tight with a budget.

Once I learned the streets and the ins and outs, the money part became of little consequence. I was thrilled and excited about coming to this city. It was the most populated of any city in the United States, international in flavor and scope, bringing with it great federal cases, considered to be high caliber, visible, and tough.

After a successful, albeit stressful, commute, on this the beginning of the work week, I finally arrived in Brooklyn. Not having a homing pigeon's sense of direction, I stood with one hand in my pocket and took out a map, which showed me to be somewhere on Bedford Avenue, a section of the city where there were very few white faces. In Brooklyn it was easy to get lost, and lost was the position I found myself in.

I was told that this area was loaded with ex-cons and felons. I was in the valley of designated wrongdoers, where one could get a crash course in the mores of a former incarcerated state.

The area was like Harlem. It was a risky place to be lost in at any time of the day. Today it was even more risky. There was more turmoil throughout the country. After President Johnson announced that he was not going to run again for president, Martin Luther King was assassinated in Memphis. King's assassination resulted in arson and chaos throughout the country. Things had not yet settled down.

Locally there was conflict. In Brooklyn two diametrically opposed camps had been picketing the board of education regarding their integration plan. Some civil-rights groups had asserted that the plan to integrate youngsters in the most de facto segregated neighborhood schools was a sell-out to tokenism.

The neighborhood had become a combat zone where whites were afraid to go, and if they did venture in, they were told to keep their head down or face the strong probability that they would be mugged.

In this section of Brooklyn there were poor working-class inhabitants, employed in or out of bodegas searching for the American dream. These people were the good guys. On the other side of the coin, or street, were the young tough bad guys, dope peddlers and pot heads selling drugs either next to or out of other bodegas, and if they were not selling drugs, they were serving as drug runners for their parents, who often were heroin addicts. Drugs, gangs, and drive-by shootings made it unsafe for everyone.

My FBI mission today was to meet and interview a high-level Russian KGB intelligence officer. He was a spy. I'd been assigned to this guy since I arrived in New York. I had a file on him a few feet long. I was here because I was advised by my supervisor that this guy wanted to distance himself from the KGB and his home-land and defect, which was serious stuff and could be a real coup for us, if we could get him to join us and come over. Apropos of which, I was enthused and a little excited to see how this was going to play out.

My supervisor picked Brooklyn as the place for us to get together, for several reasons. It was remote. It gave one ample time and space to clean oneself, making sure that you were not being tailed. That applied both to myself and the Russian I was about to meet. A subway system of course, where you can jump in and bail out quickly, is a great aid in accomplishing that.

Our meet was to be at a monastery the size of a medieval castle. The Poet planned to join me and was driving over in a bureau car. I knew the monastery was close, but locating a building the size of a castle was not easy, when in Brooklyn.

Fortunately, I was real early and had a lot of time to kill. When meeting a spy at a designated spot, it was not good to arrive ahead of time and then walk or sit around and wait. Neighborhood residents would get suspicious and call the cops. If that were to happen, my cover would be blown, and I would have a lot of explaining to do.

So I found a bench and sat down next to an elderly gentleman reading a newspaper. In front of me were street and stoop ballplayers playing their games. I was thankful I had a job, any job, that allowed me to enjoy sunshine and daylight. When I'd graduated from law school in Illinois, at no time had I ever envisioned that I would find myself sitting on a park bench in Brooklyn, New York, two years hence.

FBI special-agent work, my first salaried position (other than a short stint working in a law office), was a job that I'd coveted while in law school. I was relieved when my appointment came, for it at least meant that I would emerge from a long period of debt and insolvency. Actually it went beyond that. I was tired of school and not interested in a desk job. The thought of a daily grind of maintaining a law practice, arguing about pots and pans in a divorce case with some woman sitting across my desk, weeping, was anathema to my young thinking process. I would even have to wear a suit.

With the FBI and being in New York, clothing was not a big deal. In fact, I was sitting here casually dressed with tan corduroy slacks, soft-soled brown walking shoes, and a light army fatigue coat. Except for the color of my skin, I was in the mix appearance-wise with the people I saw around me. It was June in New York and one of those beautiful cool days when everyone wanted to be outdoors.

Before me was an ethnic mosaic of mainly blacks and mixed immigrants, who were now out and about clamoring for physical activity. That had a way of alleviating stress.

I was told by my office friends that in this neighborhood everyone was distrustful of anyone connected with the government. This was no surprise.

When Henry Hudson, that English navigator, arrived in 1609, searching for the Northwest Passage to Asia, he got a mixed reception from the natives. I expected no less.

It was now eleven o'clock in the morning. The final advice that came down from the office was to keep a low profile.

Sitting on the bench, I rehashed in my mind the New York City subway system, the trip over, and Brooklyn itself, for Brooklynites as a group are residents that Manhattanites make fun of for their attitude, ignorance, and dialect. It would make for a great doctoral thesis. To understand what it is like to live and work in New York City, there is a definite need to understand the subway system. It is something that I need to wedge in here because there is so much to be said about it that is amusing and interesting. The stress of noise, vibration, and a packed subway car popping sparks on tracks has been known to kill rats. You may be called upon to ride the subway to Brooklyn at some time in the future. The subway system deserves some discussion.

Unless you are going by foot, car, or boat, a journey from Manhattan to Brooklyn to the spot where I am sitting requires a series of uncomfortable, exhausting subway rides, generally a stand-up, lurching, screeching ride, in a densely packed herd, during a one-hour trip, with at least ten stops. The subway is the underground life arteries of New York, the container of the masses for their obligatory commutes. At certain hours it's a Kafkaesque commute. Let me explain. It's a gathering spot for people seeking intimacy, straphangers, seat hoggers, gropers, muggers, derelicts, strangers, and simple honest folk, some even eating fried chicken, trying to save money and earn a living, who daily endure a lot of sweat, noise, anger, and the potential for danger, because in a subway car nobody is hermetically sealed from the elements or the sound or, for that matter, other people. Lest I forget, there were also the door standers who neither enter nor exit, who like to be in position to eventually make a quick escape.

For a city the size of New York, it represented the right concept in moving people from one place to another. Alas it suffered from poor planning and more often than not poor execution. There were constant delays from trains coming down from the Bronx heading to Crown Heights and Utica Avenue in Brooklyn. It was a bummer to travel this way for it brought a mountain of subway stops, starting with the poor and struggling in the Bronx and culminating in Brooklyn.

Track work, unexplained power outages, and the time-consuming habit of making repairs by patching over and making do brought delay, frustration, and amusement. Of course there was also the irritability and sweat that arose from the wall of heat that radiated into the subway station from the sidewalks and pavement overhead that commuters encountered upon entering the subway station itself. A blast of hot air and blowing papers hit you as you walked down the steps past hipsters, squatters, and musicians to the subway, making it feel like the entryway into the gates of hell. Then came entry into the subway car, hell itself, which brought with it the closeness of human bodies and flesh, all sandwiched in a sweaty mob, straphangers being tossed back and forth waiting for the next stop. What could be worse?

The answer was getting stalled in this underground prison and hell hole between stops with no means to escape. All of this discouraged subway users but never subway singers, violin and saxophone players who for a few coins did public gigs and created scenes before captive audiences in rooms that echoed with intense noise. Well, maybe it was more than a few coins. There were some musicians that got their kid through college with money they collected playing and singing songs. Were Brooklyn closer, I would have walked. Had I been dressed by Gucci, I would not have used the subway system.

That said, however, once in Brooklyn, with music that beat hysterically in your head, a visitor was treated to an interesting and confusing suburb, particularly when it came down to locating an address or residence. Street patterns were a puzzle. To make matters worse, no one knew where anything was.

It was probably best said by Thomas Wolfe, in one of his short stories I'd read in college: "Dere's no guy livin' dat knows Brooklyn t'roo an' t'roo, because it'd take a guy a lifetime just to find his way aroun' duh f----- town."

I awoke from all of these thoughts, for in front of me now things were happening. There were serious games going on, street ball, on a paved playground, riddled with excitement, swarming with urban souls, playing games of three-on-three and four-on-four, with a few black youths soaring high and periodically dunking the ball through steel handmade unforgiving rims to score points. The rims were the key. They were stiff and would vibrate.

The kids in Illinois and Indiana did not play basketball with these kinds of rims. Making baskets from the top of the key with these rims required a lot of adjustment, which is why many were taking the ball directly to the hole. These courts groomed stars and legends.

I smelled sweat and detected polyglot utterances of Spanish and English. My heart rate was going up. I felt a need and desire to be out there.

New York City has more parks or playgrounds than any other city in the United States. However, most of them are small and overcrowded, which is why kids play in the streets. Thus came the name *street ball*. In the Midwest, where I grew up, street ball was called *basketball*, and looking at these players I felt a pang of homesickness and restlessness in not being able to simply walk out there and get in a game.

It was a carnival and street fair of sorts with wailing music and people who appeared to be on holiday. Surrounding the players were a crowd of spectators, luminous visitors, onlookers, street vendors hawking hot dogs and ice cream bars, and some card- and dice-playing gamblers on the corners that serve as casinos. The dice game was cee-lo, a popular game that unlike craps requires three dice.

One of the gamblers, the lookout or sentry, was looking up and watching me out of the corner of his eye. To judge the way he was eyeballing me, I figured he was speculating that I was the heat here to bust up their action and play. On the perimeter of this carnival, there were some young girls playing double Dutch with long clothesline-type ropes, the rhythmic clicking of the pavement bringing street-smart, talented Bedford-Stuyvesant jumpers quickly into the fold, dancing on athletic legs to the sound and movement of the ropes like a tap-dancing group on center stage. For young black girls in Bed-Stuy, learning to jump rope quickly follows learning to walk.

About the only New York thing missing from this scene were children running through the spray from an open water hydrant. I thought to myself, why aren't any of these people working? Then I surmised that it was due to the economy, which was not so good. A bad economy brings with it unemployment. In such a state, trying to find work and striving to get ahead was meaningless. This also meant a rising crime rate, because when people have no money and need money, family turmoil results. That brought robberies of people and banks by threat or violence. I'd learned that in training class. Of course it also could cause crime to go down, because when nobody is working, people have no money, and there is no one around to rob.

A basketball rolled by in front of me. I got up and retrieved it and looked down at a young pudgy kid, approximately twelve years old, wearing untied sneakers that squeaked as he walked, his arms hanging limply down. He looked at me with puzzled eyes.

"What is it? You've never seen a white man?" I asked.

He kept giving me an expression of curious inquiry like I didn't belong in the neighborhood. The kid was right.

"Good morning," I said, as I bounced the ball back. "Your shoes sound squishy like there's water in them. What's your name?"

"Ricky."

"Ricky, where am I? I'm looking for the Mount Carmel Monastery?"

Ricky looked up at me. "It's like a church, right?"

"Right."

"That way," he said, pointing in a westerly direction, "about three or four blocks, but you don't have a prayer getting in there."

"No prayer, huh?"

"Yeah."

"Aren't you a little young to be coming up with those kinds of puns?" I asked.

"Nobody is home."

"Someone will let me in."

"Fat chance."

"You mean there are no priests, abbots, lookouts, or sentries?"

"Nobody ever goes in and nobody ever comes out. But sometimes when you stand real close, you can hear voices."

"Good. So somebody is in there."

I walked over to him. I bent over on one knee and reached down, grasping his shoelaces.

"Ricky, before you trip and fall and break your neck, let me give you a little tip about tying these sneakers."

No sooner did I say this when an ear-splitting, hostile greeting came from the playground.

"Hey, white boy!"

I looked up to see a muscular basketball player over six feet tall with heavy shoulders coming toward me with two of his pals. He had stopped his game and was holding a basketball with his right hand and spinning it on top of his index finger. These dudes were very big and very black.

My college roommate, Mouse Jacobs, a bright, five-foot-five accounting major and alcoholic, the son of two physicians, who thought of himself as a physical coward, would describe these guys as "big motherfuckers."

I watched the tall guy coming toward me. I thought to myself that a beating appeared imminent. The guy was a destructive presence and self-proclaimed hot-shot, with an inflated view of himself—loud and vitriolic.

I could only think of him as the reincarnation of Horse Higgins, one of the biggest, meanest bullies I was forced to grow up with through grade school, the kind of demented unpredictable boy with mental issues who enjoyed tormenting everyone and making them miserable, who had the capacity and will to inflict violence, like sitting on your head or rubbing your nose in dirt, without cause and without leaving marks, who would intimidate you and make you run the other way, simply by looking at you. I've known a lot of guys, but I was afraid of only one, and that was Horse.

Even the nuns feared Horse. When Horse wanted something, and in grade school it was always Butterfingers, we kids would run and get it, to quiet down the beast and keep him from hitting somebody. In our eyes it was never a brotherly spat. It was Horse and Horse was a monster, and when you were scrawny and eleven years old, you didn't mess with monsters. The guys I'm now looking at were not going to be content with Butterfingers.

All were wearing basketball shorts and cutoff sweatshirts. Two had silver necklaces, slave chains, hanging from their necks. I figured the guy doing the talking was a weight lifter or worked in a steel mill.

All of the games stopped, as did most of the noise, and a lot of heads turned. All were interested in seeing what was going down.

Thoughts of simply fleeing entered my mind, even though I was never one to pedal away and retreat from a fistfight. The alternative was simply waiting to get the shit kicked out of me, just like Horse used to do.

I've never side-stepped or relished confrontations. I preferred to be cordial and diplomatic, but New York City was not a place that permitted that. In the profession I was in, risk taking and self-preservation were traits I picked up in training class. Being armed here would have been a wise precaution. But I wasn't armed. Simply by mistake that morning, I did not have my revolver with me. Despite its absence I was confident I could hold my own and was determined to make a good account of myself.

"You talking to me?" I asked.

"What have we here? Looks like a full-blooded honky."

"I said, are you talking to me?"

"I don't see any other honkies. I'm going to whip your ass. Why are you messing with Ricky?" He glowered at me and thrust out a forefinger of his raised hand in my direction.

The three of them didn't fan out. I stood up and walked toward the leader doing the talking, deciding in my mind that there was little use to start off with him by shaking hands. They stopped.

"Are your eyes OK?" I asked.

"My eyes are OK."

"I haven't had my ass whipped for over ten years. If you are thinking of doing something, don't."

"Say what!"

I reached into my pocket, pulled out my credentials, and dangled a gold badge a few feet in front of his face.

"I'm a federal officer. I can think of a better person to pick a fight with. Do I look like a knee-jerk racist, showing you no respect?"

Horse looked at me with a blank expression and now pulled back a bit.

"Let me put this in simple terms," I said. "You stop your game like you're on automatic pilot. Nothing blocking your view of what I was doing. You come over to pound on some white guy who is behaving himself. Are you stoned, cuz when I collar your ass and haul you before the man, your singing a tune that you didn't know what you were doing is not going to cut it with the judge. Assaulting a federal officer can bring you five years down the road in the pen. Today, it will bring you only a trip to the hospital, because if you lay one hand on me, I'm going to drop you like a used rubber."

"You are going to do what?"

"You heard me. If I have to, I'm going to do something far more violent than simply breaking your fucking nose. You'll need an ambulance."

In all honesty, I did not know what I was going to do, but blood, guts, and a knee to the nuts was a good place to start. Then I'd go for his knee cap. We stood there glaring at each other, for what seemed like several minutes, until finally Horse grinned, showing white teeth with a gap between the front two. To the side was a gold-capped incisor. He tossed me the ball.

With that the playground and activity returned to its normal self.

"I've been watching you play basketball," I said. "Your stats must be off the charts." I extend my right hand and grinned. "The name is Deuce, and yours?"

"Anthony."

We shook hands.

I looked at Anthony, who was all muscle. He looked like someone who spent several hours a day in the weight room.

The style of basketball played on the grounds of New York, all muscle and brawn, was completely different from what I'd experienced on the courts back home, where we would execute and play with a ton of passing and finesse in getting the ball to the hole. In New York, it was all drive and physical play, almost one-on-one with whoever got the ball, selfish play with no team plan. But there were always a few common things that existed. Everyone was on the court to establish an identity and announce his presence. Today, I felt a need to announce my presence.

Singularly, Anthony and the others were good and stood out, but they were a throwback to games past, with no real future, no plan, no picks, no rolls, no style, no willingness to share the ball, to pass, to execute, to hit the open man, going nowhere, but simply breaking a sweat.

Although team play was out, what they did have—and I'll give them credit for it because it could not be overlooked—was tricky individual ball-handling skills and dunks. This was after all street ball. There was individual prowess and athleticism that allowed many to become legends.

"You're good, Anthony. Bet you could steal Ebbets Field."

"Ebbets Field is gone, man."

"Yeah, but it was good in its time. Like your game. Out of style and a bit anachronistic, but it will get you a sweat," I said.

I thought they might be the only guys in the nation still shooting hoops in the oldest style of play. Anthony and his buddies stared at me with a perplexed look on their faces.

Finally Anthony grinned. "Sheet, man, what the fuck you talking about?"

"Look," I said, "I've got time for only one game of one-on-one to ten, five buckets. I've got five dollars, and it's yours if you beat me. If you lose, you owe me nothing." I removed my coat and placed five dollars on it. "You can't beat that can you? Are you in or out?"

"I'm in," said Anthony. In the back I heard voices, heckling and wisecracks.

"This ought to be good."

"Take it easy on him, Anthony."

"Take that motherfucker, Anthony."

I turned around, grinning and thinking, yeah, right.

One of my passions growing up was the game of basketball. Every shot could be analyzed. Each was different. The team game could be looked at like orchestrating a symphony.

I'd walk a mile and a half to school every day, carrying a backpack filled with books and dribbling a basketball, starting out dribbling and bouncing the ball high and then low, around my back, through my legs, even over ice and snow. Ball handling and dribble penetration to get to the bucket were my strong points. I was good, but good now—after college and law school—only meant being picked early in pickup games. Get me around the free-throw line or near the top of the key, and I was able to hit shots fairly consistently. I figured I could hold my own with Anthony in a game of one-on-one; he was big, a nice player, but a bit slow.

I picked up the basketball.

"Anthony, since it's my money, I wish to mention a few rules. The game is to ten. First one to ten wins. Five buckets. Make it; take it. The first four buckets have to be made from beyond the free-throw line. With the last bucket, you have to take the ball to the hole. Are you OK with that?"

"I'm OK with that. Where are you from Deuce?"

"Hoosier land," I replied.

"Hoosier land?" said Anthony.

"Yeah, Chicago, which is near Indiana, where this game was invented. Here. You can have first outs." I flipped him the basketball.

Anthony was a rugged-looking player, probably best playing inside, rebounding as a forward. He was big and awkward out front dribbling. I stood there with arms extended, guarding him from a position slightly beyond the free-throw line.

"Hey, Anthony, take a shot. Today. Before I die. I've got work to do."

Anthony grinned, moved toward me and arced a jump shot, all net. The crowd roared.

"Great shot, Anthony. You're up. Two zip." I again threw him the ball. Anthony again dribbled around in front, but this time moved to the side, all the while eyeing me, grinning. He again took a jump shot, this time banking it in.

"Another great shot, Anthony. You are just too good. I have to tighten up my defense."

I now moved forward and extended my arms, touching him. I knew I had to start controlling the tempo.

"OK, Anthony. Four zip. Let's go."

Again, Anthony moved around dribbling out in front, but farther back. Quickly, he threw up another jump shot, but this time it struck the rim. Unforgiving rims could be tough. I took the rebound and casually dribbled the ball back court. I looked at Anthony. "You set, Anthony." He nodded.

I dribbled slightly past the free-throw line, moved my right leg wide away from the bucket, and launched a fadeaway jump shot, all net. Anthony responded by closing the space on defense, but again from the top of the key, I launched three more fadeaway jump shots. All net. I looked over at Anthony.

"Anthony, it's a tough shot to defend against. I've been practicing it for years."

"What's the count?" asked Anthony.

"Eight to four. It's crunch time. One more to go. You ready. This one is going to the hole."

I moved back all the way to center court. It was time to crash the boards. Anthony positioned himself slightly above the key. His legs were wide. His arms were extended. I dribbled toward him. I knew I had him. It was all about quickness. As I reached him, I threw in the other ingredient, the crossover dribble. I whipped by Anthony, headed for the hole. To the left of the spectators surrounding the basket stood Ricky. I pointed to him, leaped high with my right arm and banked it in off the board nice and sweet.

I picked up the ball and motioned to Ricky to come over. I picked up my coat, handed the five bucks to Ricky.

"Lunch money. I'm outta here."

I looked back. "Thanks, Anthony," I yelled. "I got lucky. You are a far better player than I'll ever be."

"Deuce," he said, "this Saturday, come back and see us. I want you on my team. We're going to float like a butterfly and sting like a bee."

"We can do that. This Saturday, huh? Maybe," I said, "I'll see what's on the agenda."

CHAPTER 3

LIVING IN YORKVILLE

————◆————

FOR THE PAST YEAR I lived quietly and uneventfully in the valley of the beast. I was in a neighborhood known as the Upper East Side of Manhattan, a stretch from 61st to 110th Streets, where cheap rent-controlled apartments north of 86th could still be found if you were lucky or had some clout or knew a friend with clout, in neighborhoods that one would never guess were part of New York. This particular neighborhood had several delis and restaurants and a sweaty smell and odor, as if horses had just passed through, which if they had would have come as no surprise. It was also the kind of neighborhood where if bulbs burned out, no one replaced them.

It reminded me a lot of the neighborhoods in Chicago where I grew up, with people sitting outside on porches and stoops in the summer because it was hot inside, talking back and forth, and if you passed by, they would say something like, "It's real close, isn't it?" I always wondered to myself what was so close that was coming.

There were other language idiosyncrasies. I had to adapt. *This* was "dis." *Girl* was "goil." And *Thirty-Third Street* was "Thoidy-Thoid Street."

It was a Jewish neighborhood with perhaps a thousand Jews, and that may be too high of an estimate, who lived in a four-block-square area. They were everywhere, with observant women wearing ankle-length black dresses. Because of the distress of the economy and the stress on the citizenry, many men even walked the streets in pajamas or last year's clothes, muttering something unintelligible in Hebrew, undistinguishable at least to my ears from doo-wop groups one could listen to in coffee houses on the Lower East Side.

Although a Jewish neighborhood, it still was a diverse cultural ethnic village. I dropped off my cleaning at a Chinese laundry. One block away there were Greek and Italian restaurants and an Italian deli, where standing once again on a tile floor, as I once did at my grandmother's bakery, I was able to get a huge sandwich on Italian bread, containing mortadella, provolone, prosciutto, tomatoes, and *sopressata* all covered with vinegar and oil.

Jablonski's Bakery was also nearby, specializing in Polish and Lithuanian baked goods and breads, which I often took as gifts for friends at my office at Christmastime. I purchased my *New York Times* from a Muslim at a newsstand around the corner.

I loved all of this diversity. Once implanted in the neighborhood, these people became acquaintances and friends.

My Jewish friends, Moe and his wife, owned and ran Moe's Deli. They were special, probably because I spent so much time there and got to know them like family. I was never mystified or perplexed by Jews.

My best friend growing up was Jewish. I probably spent more time in his house than my own, where I continually ate well, obtained a working knowledge of Yiddish expressions like chutzpah and klutz, attended synagogues for various affairs including weddings, while receiving a lot of advice, both religious and cultural along with encouragement that when I grew up I should be doctor. If I wasn't going to be a doctor, I had to be a lawyer. The conversation with me was always about the future and never the present or what I already had accomplished.

I did everything with my friend except accompany him to Israel. I quickly learned and picked up on the rituals of bar mitzvahs and bat mitzvahs, chanting with my friend, memorizing prayers, and discussing with him his *dvar* Torahs as he blazed his path to manhood. Meanwhile, I remained a Roman Catholic goyim.

In New York City, I wandered around the neighborhood in the Kingdom of the Jews. I was in my element.

Not in my element were the dank, decaying, and gloomy buildings in the neighborhood. In years past these buildings sheltered immigrants, the huddled masses, who came to the United States looking for jobs and new lives. Many of these buildings were hit by foreclosures or simply abandoned, resulting in empty houses with broken windows.

Yet, some houses, as bad as they appeared, were not empty. Squatters and homeless people moved in, leaving after a few nights after stripping out the copper wiring and taking with them the kitchen sink.

Other squatters took a different approach. They refused to leave, contacted pro bono lawyers, or became jailhouse lawyers and in the cantankerous New York way challenged evictions. They considered themselves part of the structure, like human bricks. A court order was needed to evict them and then maybe a few cops to haul them out to the street.

The concrete tenement building I occupied, which cast a shadow on the neighboring vacant lot, wasn't exactly a flophouse or a decrepit building filled with transients, but it was only a cut above. The building was beaten up, but not as bad as others or those found in the Bowery.

Surprisingly, many tenants, nonluminary types, public and private, in these rent-controlled apartments paid bribes for this type of housing, without anyone getting caught. Others were simply illegal tenants and squatters who shouldn't be in the building in the first place and who escaped the city's dragnet, because the city's housing agency was understaffed, weak, and lame. Everyone wanted in, but it was all about pull and money, rolled up in a system up to its neck in illegality, with little or no enforcement.

My three-room flat ended up as a fourth-floor walkup that comprised a living room (where my bed, barbells, and weights existed), an antiquated bath, and a small kitchenette. On the counter was the inevitable ubiquitous Chianti bottle with a candle on it.

There are over 125,000 walkups in New York City. The higher you go, the more stairs you have to climb, and the less rent you pay. My dwelling was not a place to be ushered in by a fanfare of bugles, but yet given the moldings and copper cornices, the building itself was an archeological find, if it ever had occasion to be totally covered by volcanic dust.

The interior of the apartment was surrounded by walls of bookcases from floor to ceiling filled with books and papers, a mildewed lot, which I had not catalogued. I knew not entirely what I owned. Books, collecting books and retaining them, had always been one of my passions. They were scattered all about. Despite my modest income, I purchased them liberally at discounts from booksellers, stocking them on the shelves along with other bric-a-brac. My habit was to never throw anything away. This I learned from my mother, who told me, "Deuce, trash can be cash."

With money saved up, I decided when I moved in to install a new six foot bathtub to replace the antiquated bathtub that existed, which was ringed with rust stains and pumped out water brown as iodine. To accomplish this, however, I had to check with my landlord, Dr. Lipski.

Lipski was happy I moved into his building, seeing me not as a deterrent to crime, because the bad guys didn't know I was there, but rather a heavy who could be called upon to kick some ass if the need arose. To persuade Lipski to pick up some of the expenses for these interior improvements, I started to make noises about finding a place to live in a better neighborhood.

With that, Lipski decided to foot the tab for the tub. He also replaced the carpeting and repainted the limited open walls, which weren't lined with book cases.

As it happened, the luxury tub Lipski installed worked out beautifully. The water unfortunately continued to be iodine in color. That was OK. It seemed to have healing powers. I exercised and worked out a lot, lifted weights and jogged. There was nothing more pleasant following this activity than to relax in a hot tub, which was the highest quality furnishing in the place.

As I relaxed one day in my tub, I looked around the room. I had a desk, a mattress on the floor, a large table, and a sofa for friends and family passing through who needed someplace and something on which to crash. This was all I needed and wanted.

I owed this lifestyle to a law-school friend, a religious Notre Dame aeronautical engineering health nut, who engendered in me the sound-mind-and-body approach to everyday living. Time will tell if it was worth it. A strong work ethic was already ingrained in me. I was taught right from the get-go to produce, work hard, get a good education, and a good job would follow. The downside of this was unremitting toil. Work was all I did and still do. The most that can be said was that I was driven then and driven now. I was intense when I landed in New York, but New York City in time doubled it.

For food, I ate out a lot. There was little food stocked in the cupboards or refrigerator. But there was dirty underwear and shirts piled in a basket waiting to be taken in a pillowcase to a Chinese laundry. For heat and hot water, I made due with a faulty boiler and rusty water heater, located in the dimly lit basement. On the weekends when I needed its services, it had to be kicked to give it sustenance and life. This was home.

The living room of the apartment had a door that opened into an outer hall with apartments down the hallway, occupied by tenants I rarely saw, barely heard, and did not know. The inhabitants of this building number under thirty. They came and went, locked their doors, and viewed each other as strangers.

Life on these streets was peaceful, in contrast to the seventies and eighties, when gentrification brought extensive development, noise, and exceedingly high rents. Crime, if it came along, tended to be petty, with a few car thefts, some joy rides, but no shootings and in some blocks during the spring, there was total peace and tranquility.

Once I moved in, I settled in to some daily routines. Work took me out of the apartment for ten- and twelve-hour days. I went out to eat almost daily having dinner at one of the local restaurants or at Moe's delicatessen, in company with a friend or friends from the office.

We rarely got indigestion at Moe's, unlike some New York spots that could cure you of anything, including life. Moe's Deli was run by Moe and Libby, a husband-and-wife team. It was a place where you could not only load up on provisions, like cheese, beer, and wine, but was a good restaurant as well, manned by trustworthy, hardworking people. The food at Moe's could be mysterious, but not mysterious was Moe's corned beef, which was alive and well, moist and garlicky, sliced thin by hand by Moe and then placed a few inches thick on rye bread covered with spicy mustard, all of which then melted in your mouth. According to Moe, for the corned beef to be moist, there had to be fat. Fat for Moe was good.

So intrigued was I about Moe's delicious corned beef, that once I got to know him well, he took me to his basement where he cured and pickled his own, showing me his barrels, filled with some solution or marinade that Moe, like some witch or chemist, brewed on his own. I was never present when he was making this brew. I figured that it was like making sausage and wanted no part witnessing it.

Beyond the corned beef, at times it was hard to tell what was being eaten, so when I didn't order one of Moe's sandwiches, I settled on something I could visibly decipher, which was chicken in the pot, filled with garlic, noodles, carrots, and matzo balls and whatever else Moe could find for his homemade Jewish penicillin. Moe taught me a lot about food and life. The only thing I taught Moe was to drink olive oil neat. However, I insisted on the best.

Moe's was a place where we could also get cheap rose wine or Rheingold beer, and Schaefer beer, made in Brooklyn— the Milwaukee of the East Coast. Better still, to save money, Moe allowed us to bring in other wine that he didn't stock and drink it with dinner, and once Moe found out who I worked for, Moe would let us do that, because Moe loved to shoot the shit with everyone, loved cops and FBI agents, and everyone loved Moe. For cops and FBI agents, he would double the chicken that went into the pot. At night if I was slurping soup at one of the tables and it wasn't very busy, Moe would sit down and drink wine with me. Moe never quizzed me about work or what I did all day. He was only interested in food and life, particularly life in the Midwest since he had never traveled west of New Jersey.

After dinner I returned home, read, drank more beer, or took more walks. Work during the day brought with it a certain amount of frustrated rage and edginess. Each night I fought a battle with insomnia. To shake off these moods and allow eventual sleep to ensue, I left my dusty library in the evening, joined the living, and took to wandering the streets of Manhattan, always taking a different route.

This brought me into the seamy undercarriage of New York City life. Some of the streets I chose were dark and narrow, and with few people about, often in the silence you could hear the footsteps. The few people who were out were always strange. Walks took me to sections of New York that were a culture shock. These evening prowls invariably would end up at some jammed bar for a closing beer, and jammed they were every night of the week. The nights in Manhattan were sultry with things happening and people, from God knows where, coming and going in spasmodic shifts.

In the early morning, I jogged the reservoir path in Central Park, showing up generally at the reservoir's south gatehouse, in good weather, rain, or snow. The distance around the reservoir is 1.6 miles. When jogging I packed heat.

Other people were jogging with similar daily rituals. Carrying a sidearm was elementary. Think about it in these terms. Unless holed up in a New York City police station, and even in there it was not the safest place, there was no secure spot that existed in Manhattan. Shit could happen at any time, anyplace, and in any fashion, and it often did.

However, it was the week after Thanksgiving, my first year that I received a note from my landlord that he wanted to talk to me. I didn't want my landlord to come into my apartment, so I called him. I told him I'd meet him outside at dinnertime. I'd never received a note from my landlord, so I knew it must be serious.

My landlord, Lipski, was Dr. Lipski, a dermatologist and skin man who saw patients and performed hair transplants on the first floor. He was the cold, remote person who presided over his Taj Mahal.

Lipski was about fifty, short, balding and in need of his own hair transplant. With a compact paunch and the right costume, he could pass for a Macy's Santa, which the store needed that time of year, except that he had never been known to be jolly and as best I knew never gave gifts to orphans.

Lipski believed in homeopathic remedies. I was told this by a fellow tenant. I was also told he was some kind of genius. He had excellent educational credentials, Ivy League and Harvard Medical. He walked, talked, and glowed with self-assurance. Once you got to know him, what could be said about Lipski, as I'll explain, was that his educational achievements had not blunted his genius for ineptitude.

Anything is possible with a genius. He was a restless soul who never found himself, stuck with a building that needed a serious face-lift, which he was unwilling to sell or even maintain.

Unplanned encounters with Lipski generally occurred early in the morning. Lipski was always accompanied by his maintenance man, Sal, who said little around his boss. Sal was a little squirt of a guy, about five feet four, not more than forty years old, and always wore T-shirts and Levis. He never looked you in the eye when he spoke. Sal was handy at fixing everything, except for the boiler.

That evening I went down from my apartment to call on Dr. Lipski, who stood on the sidewalk with Sal. Lipski's face looked haggard, like it had lingered beyond its bloom, maybe ten years past its best moment. I figured the lines were battle scars from New York City regulatory fights, fire code violations and maintenance issues for his Taj Mahal.

Lipski, with his forefinger, knocked off ash from his cigar and began pontificating.

"What I like is living like one of the blue bloods over on Park Avenue, and I shall, just as soon as my investments pay off. Glad to see you, Deuce."

"Well, Dr. Lipski, how are things going? I like your pajamas."

I meant it as a joke. His gaze told me he didn't take it that way. He threw his head back like a horse ready to bolt.

"Things are going no good, or I wouldn't be in these pajamas."

"Got your note, and by the way, thanks again for footing the cost of the bathtub. Let me guess why you want to see me."

"OK. Take a guess."

"I'm sure it is about this building you love, right?" I pointed to the third story of the building.

"We all have noticed the serpentine ornamentation, the terra cotta and copper cornices. You want to designate the building as a landmark, so you can get some federal tax credits to make improvements. You think because I work for the feds that I can help you. Correct?"

Lipski stared up at me with a blank expression, as if I was speaking Swahili. He then looked over his shoulder and back, as if he were about to tell me a secret. This was a habit of Lipski's that at times made me suspicious of him.

Before he could say anything, I continued, "No offense, Dr. Lipski, but preemptive demolition is not a bad alternative either. Maybe you are better off to simply get explosives and a wrecking ball."

Lipski, looking away again and at his watch, gave the impression that he wasn't listening. "Listen, Deuce, you have been cooking fish again, right?"

"Well, my day is so hectic I really don't have the time to cook vichyssoise."

"Take no offense to this please because we like having you in the building. But please don't use your stove to fry any more fish in your apartment, OK. A lot of smoke and the neighbors find the smell very offensive. I'm getting complaints."

I smiled. Lipski was referring to the one time I had friends over after deep sea fishing all day. We ended up panfrying fish and drinking beer in my poorly ventilated apartment. The fish was cooked in a large skillet over high heat in two inches of bacon fat, with smoke rising and grease going all over the place. Lipski had obviously never tried to cook fish in a kitchen without an exhaust vent.

"Dr. Lipski, may I point out to you a few things, please."

"What's that?"

"As I mentioned I appreciate the financial help with the bathtub, although sitting in hot rusty water is not something I contemplated, but the fish incident, of which you speak, was a one-time event with friends, where we had fish, drank some beer, and had a good time. To avoid afflicting you with further stress, I will refrain from such events in the future. Not having a lot of friends over is not important to me—no major setback. But in exchange for this I ask a favor."

Lipski looked up at me with a curious expression and a sigh. "Yes."

"Pretend that you don't know me or that you have me as a tenant in that apartment. Pretend that I am some kind of reclusive writer who wants to be left alone. I'll pay my rent, but treat me like I do not exist. Talk to no one about me. Seal your lips and say nothing. I want to remain incognito. Do you understand?"

"No."

"Just do what I ask, Dr. Lipski. It's a small request. Do all of this for me, and I'll protect the place and give everyone some security, behind the scenes as best I can." I looked at Lipski, and for a while, both of us said nothing.

Lipski then smiled, extended his hand to shake, which we did, and said, "Deuce, you got a deal."

I concluded that I deserved this reprimand. There was never a kind, complimentary word that one would hear from the lips of the aggressive, always tense Lipski. He would generally spout a surfeit of drivel. He had not yet risen to a level where I could call him a "mensch," for all I ever heard from him were complaints. No person could be called a "mensch" if he continued to be a pain in the ass.

This was one of many encounters I had with Lipski, who told me many other curious things, primarily about his investments. Financial investments can give a quick fix on the measure of a man, which measure for Lipski was not good. He worked and wanted to game the system on Wall Street. He was driven by greed and money and appeared surrounded by slow-witted financial advisers.

One day he commented, "Japanese bowling balls—they are beautiful. Bowling is on the upswing." He peered behind himself again like a guy regaining consciousness and then letting me in on a huge secret. "You ought to be investing in this commodity."

"Tell me, Doc. Do they hold together after you pitch them down the alley? You know what. I don't like to bowl. I really don't give a shit about Japanese bowling balls, and I have more important things that are occupying my time right now. Money at this juncture of my life is not that important to me."

With that he said nothing. He then tilted his bald head and drifted up the stairway to his office. He then turned, commenting, "Well, remember that you first heard this from me."

Lipski further accumulated antique cars and watercolor artwork from a Spanish painter who resembled Picasso in appearance only, all stored in his son's warehouse. None of these ventures paid any dividends, and Lipski was reluctant to face reality or even talk about the fact that these investments were stupid and dumb—simple truths. But Lipski didn't want to hear it. That's one of the problems with truth. People don't want to hear it. He was in denial. All of us recognized denial, and it wasn't a river in Egypt.

But for all of his shortcomings and chronic proneness to go into oddball ventures, and my fish cooking episode notwithstanding, I was amused and liked the guy. Lipski was happy with me, which was all that I cared about. He continued to feel that my presence gave the occupants and building some measure of protection, even though I was rarely there, because I was always on the street, hitting the bricks, as they were accustomed to saying at the office.

Life thus in Lipski's apartment took on daily routines. I spent a lot of time cleaning and oiling sidearms. My weapon of choice was a small five-shot air-weight aluminum-frame snub-nose .38 Smith & Wesson, which, unlike a four-inch Smith or .357 Magnum could be casually concealed under a coat or sweater on my waist, ankle, beneath my arm pit, or the side pocket of my army fatigue coat or brown field jacket. The surface and barrel of this sidearm was silverfish and immaculately smooth and was kept well oiled and fully loaded.

I'd carry the Smith & Wesson in my right pocket and a dozen extra shells in my left. A bullet from my snub-nose spins approximately one thousand five hundred revolutions per second, and at a distance of seven yards, the flesh laceration can be severe, particularly since I loaded my revolver with wad cutters, not something recommended, but something I did anyway. The other weapon I carried, strapped above my ankle, was a small 25-caliber Browning automatic.

About the only thing I haven't mentioned is prayer. I prayed a lot. Although I never took a vow of chastity or dispensed spiritual counseling, being alone left a lot of time to think and pray about family, sick friends, and life. My parents were Catholic. I was nominally, at least, also Catholic, albeit a poor, inconsistent church-attending Catholic, who believed in God but wanted him to present himself to prove his existence, wanted something more than stained-glass and incense, had trouble with guilt, the confessional, the sixth Station of the Cross, virginity in women, moral decline, annulments and not divorces, the Franciscan order, and the Catholic magisterium, but whose only problem was reconciling God's existence with the ongoing killings, pain, and suffering that I witnessed on the street. With this state of affairs, it was easy to be a troubled believer. If God existed, why would he permit all of this stuff? If he existed and wasn't able to do anything about it, then he was a weak God with very little power. To get over these contradictions, I convinced myself he had some kind of plan—a plan for I knew not what, but a plan nonetheless—and thus I did not rule him out. I couldn't.

There were signs of God. When I was nine years old, I concluded from some Chip Hilton all-American books that I wanted to grow up and be six feet two, 180 pounds, just like Chip. My mother was five feet two, and my father was five feet seven. I knew, even at age nine, that I had a snowball's chance in hell to reach six feet two, so I turned to God. Every night for well over three years, I got on my knees and prayed and prayed to be six feet two and 180. I prayed so hard, at what now seems like such a selfish motive, that tears would roll down my cheeks.

But God—it had to be him—delivered. It was enough for me to keep me with him. Someone else said, after seeing all that has been done in the world, that it's hard to deny that there is a captain on the bridge. I believe there is a captain, some kind of counterbalance to the decadence witnessed on the street. For me there were only three certainties in life—evil, suffering, and death. I could do nothing about suffering, death, poverty, and hopelessness. But in the occupation I found myself, I could do something about evil. There were always going to be crooks, crime, and gangland disputes. There will always be low-hanging fruit that needs to be picked. It's the nature of the beast and human life itself.

CHAPTER 4

POKER WITH THE CREW

FRIDAY, MAY 17, 1968.

IT WAS ONE OF THOSE gloomy May days in New York. While walking home from the office, it was raining. To make matters worse after a tiring week, the world was still going to hell. A year ago we had draft card burnings and riots in Newark and Detroit. "Black Power", a racial slogan coined by Stokely Carmichael, had resulted in a movement to counter American white supremacy and we had continued chaos in Vietnam and war demonstrations on the street.

The war was becoming the most difficult and important issue facing the nation, due, many thought, to the fabrication of a Gulf of Tonkin resolution, which enabled Johnson to dispatch a large number of troops to South Vietnam. To the New York liberal crowd the war appeared to be aimless and destructive with no compelling reason to hang in there. There was no end to the conflict in sight. At the office there was a serious debate about what to do. On one side were the vets and patriots, coming to the aid and support of their country, talking about freedoms and ideals. On the other side were the questioners, called "dumb heads," who thought the war was a mistake and didn't want their kids and grandkids ending up in the jungle getting hurt fighting for a dubious, worthless cause. I fell into this category. There was no consensus on a solution to the conflict.

As I walked home, I felt a definite need to get away from all of this and start the weekend with entertainment. I was several blocks from my office when I realized that I had better pick up two cases of beer. Tonight was poker night at my place with office friends, the gravel crunchers, streetwalkers, surveillance guys, a patriot and dumb head or two, and thin guys, some of whom resembled marathon runners. Typically we picked end-of-the-week nights when it was nasty out, a time when no one wanted to be walking around visiting bars on the streets off duty.

There was a modus operandi of the crew coming to my pad. They would all traipse into the building without wiping their feet on the welcome mat, sometimes even using the floor as an ash-tray, producing further complaints by Lipski, who like a Sherlock Holmes would follow wet muddy footprints or a cigarette butt or two to my apartment door.

These were evenings that we drank a lot of beer, to a point that many a night we all felt we were on our way to becoming Bowery inebriates.

Poker was played around the clock, with a break only for TH, who after five hours, if he was winning, had to lie down and take a rest in a planned effort, we thought, to run out the clock, even though his winnings were never over a hundred dollars because the stakes were never that high. No one in this crew had the wherewithal to toss around C notes.

When the money ran out, as it often did, then cuff links, pocketknives, and as a last resort Mardi Gras beads might be thrown into the pot simply to stay in the game, because nobody wanted to accept anyone else's IOUs, which were quickly forgotten and never paid once the evening ended.

Around the table, this rogues' gallery of characters were all sworn to celibacy on poker days and came from all walks of life and all parts of the country, but mainly Southern guys, including Shenandoah, also known as the Poet, Pat the Knife, Big D, Old Yeller, TH, and Big Al. Big D could devour a whole platter of chicken and a few six packs of beer at one sitting, but he always remained thin and was as tall as a stalk of September corn.

With few exceptions, as I'll explain, all were government guys and, except for the Poet and Old Yeller, were all law-school grads, who worked with me at the office, who like me came from a humble background, and who managed to arrive as agents in the New York office swimming against the current. This meant it wasn't that easy getting here.

New York City was the most active office in the country with the hottest significant criminal and internal-security federal cases. It was viewed by agents everywhere as the most aggressive office in the country. That meant that during the course of doing criminal investigations an agent would stretch to the limit what was permissible, in making searches and arrests. It also meant things would be done that were technically illegal, like entering a residence and making a search without a warrant. Skirting the law and breaking the rules did not happen often. There were occasions when we were in a pinch for time, working on a case that was a slam dunk. By that I mean that, if in the unlikely event certain evidence was thrown out because of the Fourth Amendment, the evidence that remained was strong enough for the prosecution to proceed with and win. On other occasions we simply wanted information on targets considered violent and a threat to national security. Skirting the law was the only way to get it. This epitomized the thought process of the crew around the poker table.

Needless to say, in this environment we viewed ourselves as the best, the cream of the FBI crop, and developed an attitude, haughty, arrogant, and insolent but one we felt we deserved, not prevalent in other field offices outside New York City. On the other side of the coin, due to the high cost of New York–style living and the necessity of a long commute to the office for the married guys living outside Manhattan, not all the agents in New York were happy to be there, but collectively, we, the poker group, were happy and we immensely enjoyed each other's company.

When I finally arrived at my apartment, I put the two cases of beer away on ice. It was the end of a long day. I needed a slug of whiskey. I needed a vacation, but all I had was a hot tub, so I jumped in and commenced soaking my body, absorbing myself in reading one of Earl Biggers's novels, a Charlie Chan mystery. After about thirty minutes, I heard the door open. The voice of Big D yelled out the usual sophisticated witticism.

"Hey, Deuce. You have to start cleaning up this place if we're going to play cards here."

"I've not yet improved my slovenly habits. If you play poker here, you'll have to endure a slob," I yelled back.

"Yeah, but I thought you were going to get some carpeting," said D.

"Something wrong with using old newspapers?" I said. "What do you expect on a government salary?"

"Cleanliness. According to Mr. Hoover, cleanliness is next to godliness."

"Yeah, well, Hoover never had to live in New York."

Profanity came from the other room. The rest of the troops had shown up. When I walked in, the Poet was sitting at the table shuffling cards. He lit a cigarette.

"Sit down, Deuce. We're ready to start taking your money."

"It won't take much. Even if I cheat, I rarely win."

"That's the only reason you have us as friends, right?" said TH.

So began a night of poker.

"What have you been reading in that hot tub of yours?" asked TH.

"Biggers. Charlie Chan."

"Oriental wisdom will get you nowhere."

"I remember Charlie," said Big D. "It's good you are taking him out of mothballs. My instructor in training class enjoyed reading Biggers. He thought detective stories and mysteries would help with investigative techniques and solutions to crimes."

"It beats searching through garbage or dumpsters," said TH.

I picked up copies and spent a lot of time reading Earl Biggers. I enjoyed the honorable, humble detective, Charlie Chan, who in addition to the novels appeared in countless Hollywood movies during the forties and fifties. There was never a lot of blood or violence in Chan's movies. As an agent I would fanaticize and imagine myself examining a crime scene just as Chan would do. I would lean over the dead body and say, "Killer is both clever and cunning. No one leave room please." Hmm. A garrote mark existed around the neck of the corpse, and the butler was standing there holding a cord. A tough case all right, but like Chan, I was on it.

"Is there any food in the kitchen?" asked the Poet. "Even bagpipe will not speak when stomach is empty."

If someone around the poker table wasn't spouting off a Charlie Chan or fortune-cookie aphorism, it was something else like poetry, for when the Poet was around, it had to rhyme. The verse disbursed around the table was often of such poor quality that it was disparaged by the Poet as lacking creativity. Most of it was focused in my direction, like,

Call the doctor; call the EMT.

But first call the lawyer who's gonna keep you free.

Had some vodka? Had some gin?

On your face is a shit-eatin' grin?

Lawyer Ballou is only a phone call away.

With his help, you'll drive another day.

And there was more.

You have a problem; it couldn't be worse.

You won't find the answer in his alligator purse.

Deuce's suit is Armani; his tie is real class.

He won't let the FBI kick your ass.

He doesn't come cheap; you'll pay for his time.

But you won't get locked up with low-life slime.

Or call one of his pals; they are all savvy.

And Deuce is in line for some of the gravy.

All we needed for more legal chatter around the table was another lawyer, and we got it with a law-school pal of Big Al's, Lone Louie, who was a quiet and amusing addition. We called him *Lone* for a lot of reasons. Lone was introverted; he always showed up alone, lived alone, traveled alone, ate alone, and according to Big Al even talked to himself when alone.

When I first met Lone, he showed up at our poker party all disheveled and wrinkled, unshaven, with long hair and worn shoes. He looked like he had no home to return to or visible means to support himself. I wondered if he was living on a park bench in Central Park. He cut a sympathetic figure. I learned later that his father was a very successful and prominent mortician in Oxford, Mississippi, which explained his deadpan manner and personality.

At his first visit to one of our poker parties, Louie stated, "You guys want to know something?"

"Yeah," said D, "please spit it out."

"I haven't had anything to eat for two days."

"Jesus. Other than the cost of living in New York City, is there a reason for that?" I asked.

"No money, not even from home."

"Would five bucks help you? Why don't you come around here more often for sustenance?"

We grew to like him, although for a while we wondered if Lone was wandering the streets of New York in the throes of the delirium tremens. There was always space for him at the table, even though everyone knew that they were not going to get anything off a guy like Lone since he didn't have anything. He was another recent law grad out of Ole Miss and was now working in a New York City publishing house that lacked literary éclat, humped over a dusty desk in some cubbyhole updating legal publications and textbooks, documenting citations of cases of yore that would never see the light of day. We figured he was the lowest drudge in the office. This was one of the dullest, lowest-paying jobs in the city, which meant he was making even less money than we government guys were.

Playing poker often resulted in a loser asking to be staked or given a loan during the course of the game to continue play, but when Lone was losing, which, like me, was always the case, no one wanted to loan Lone money for several reasons. The likelihood of being repaid was remote. Further, in the incredibly leveraged circumstances in which Lone found himself, any new debt of even $250 would have sent him over the cliff.

All of us were sympathetic with Louie's plight. No one wanted to hurt him. He had no positive cash flow, and in fact he told us he was bleeding out to the tune of a hundred dollars a month and survived only because he got loans from his parents.

Some of us thought that New York was making Lone paranoid and desperate.

Even with little money, Lone still liked the action at the table and regretted not being an agent for the government instead of getting bored doing research alone like some monk. Lone was like a civilian playing poker with a lot of hard-driving, hard-drinking marines. Socially no one understood Lone.

He was not discordant, but he had the annoying habit to talk about one thing and then move to a different subject with no discernable connection. He would spit out anything that bubbled up in his head. One night over cards, the conversation went something like this.

"You in, Lone? The bet's a half," said Big D.

"Looks like you have a flush. In? No, I'm not in. I think I left my coffeepot on."

"Say what?" said TH.

"My coffeepot—I think I left it on in my apartment. I may have to run back."

Add to this the fact that Lone could be inflexible, headstrong, and unyielding. If Lone told you he was not going to take a piss for three days, then we knew he would not take a piss for three days. He was also the shortest guy in the group but a guy who did not want to be short. He displayed extremely erect posture.

Still he looked like someone who had been pounded into the ground with a mallet. Standing next to Big D, who was six feet seven in his stocking feet, we would kid him that he came up to Big D's navel.

Although Lone had no badge and had no gun while breaking bread and playing poker with armed agents, he was in fact the runner, and enjoyed being it, running for this and running for that during the course of the evening, down to Moe's Deli for more beer, corned beef (sliced ultrathin with spicy mustard) sandwiches, chips and dip for much-needed sustenance and lubrication. Heartburn for the troops around the poker table became prevalent during the long evening.

Louie would say, "I'm the go-getter. You tell me what to go get."

A run by Lone would generally start by a comment from Big D, a Shakespearean nut, who would look over at me and say, "Any more beer?"

"We're out, man."

"Is prohibition back, or is it simply bottle fatigue?" asked the Poet.

"Whoa," I said, "I detect in your eyes a slight flame of hostility. Quench it, please."

"I would like to quench it, with some beer. Where's the midget?"

Lone looked over and said nothing. *cue*

"My lord," said Big D, "the Russians are advancing up First Avenue. Shall we circle the wagons?" This was a queue that it was time to send Louie down to Moe's to check it out, restock provisions, and reconnoiter, because we were out of beer.

"Hmm. Are they in hired carriages? Perhaps they are coming north for a woodcock hunt."

"No, my lord, they are raw recruits, young lads with bundles. The procession includes donkeys wading through the grime along the street."

"It's the cold winds that bring them," said Big Al.

"Are there beautiful Russian women, bimbos, among them?" I asked.

"Why do you ask, my lord?" added D.

"Because if there are, I must leave these drab chambers, repel the intruders, and capture the women myself."

"No, my lord."

Meanwhile, the Poet was sitting calmly taking this all in. He finally looked up and said, "If I were you all, I would go very light on the vices in this town. According to Satchel Paige, the social ramble ain't restful."

"Look," said D, "all I want to know is, do they all appear to be heterosexual? We don't want them hitting on Louie if we send him down."

"He's so short they will never find him," piped in TH.

"Oh, you know how the Russians are, silly," replied Big D.

I would then look over at Lone and say, "Louie, did you hear that? See what's up, please, and when you are down at Moe's, bring back the usual, with some chips."

"And, Louie," said TH, "bring up some seltzer. Get the strongest Moe's got. The kind that causes pain." TH was a nut for seltzer and said it always helped his digestive tract.

Off Louie would go.

Since Lone was always nervous and played light, not having a lot of money to lose but not spending a lot of money either because always being alone didn't cost him anything, it was the Poet who finally proposed, outside of Lone's presence, that at the end of the evening if Lone was close to being busted, we would let him win several hands so that he could at least break even.

"The guy is like a mushroom," said the Poet, "quiet, in the dark, and miserable."

"Yeah," said D, "but it's not like we're covering him with horse manure."

"We may as well be," said TH, laughing. "The guy is broke and does less than a grand a month. Probably lives in a hovel like this place and eats on a table like this one, something that you can pick up as a discard off the street."

I looked at TH. "Can I help it if burglars break in here when I'm not around and leave things?"

"All right," said D, "I move we let him win several hands." The motion carried.

This unanimous decision didn't come down primarily because we all felt sorry for Lone, who lived in a low-rent flea-bag apartment and was always a step or two away from insolvency, but rather because we were scared that if his losses continued, we might lose our runner. Anything that cut into card-playing time was a no-no, and none of the troops wanted to lose one invaluable moment of poker time having to go down to buy grub and shoot the shit with Moe, who after eight o'clock was always lonesome and loved to talk.

So we started cheating a little, allowing Lone Louie to win and cover his losses. Lone was very happy and none the wiser. We simply threw our money in with a smile, folded after a few cards, complimented Lone on his good luck, and then sent him back to Moe's for more refreshments.

CHAPTER 5

WE GOTTA GET OUTTA OF THIS PLACE

———————

THE POET WAS ONE OF the elders in the office and arguably the leader of this motley crew, not counting the likes of Lone Louie, who as best we knew had no leader, not even a girlfriend. The Poet was a former Jesuit priest applicant. He'd somehow meandered into the FBI as an agent, after meeting an attractive gal and then making a decision that marriage was for him, instead of a life of celibacy.

"Women cause many a man to change careers," the Poet said.

According to the Poet, he went into the Jesuit order because of a religious calling, which is always difficult to define but was more, according to the Poet, like a summons—something you felt you had to do. However, he found kissing and the attraction of the female touch, not to mention their flesh, more to his liking, a not altogether uncommon experience that happened frequently in New York City. The Poet, thus, discerned that calling before making a commitment and taking his final vows.

We became the Poet's disciples both at work and off duty and did everything together except praying the *Liturgy of the Hours* and attending mass, which I regret to say we all felt we didn't have time for. At the office and while on the job with the Poet, it was a bunker type of mentality. When it came to matching wits with the Russians or criminals, it was us against them.

The Poet was the most literate of the group and could finish the *New York Times* crossword puzzle every day using black ink in under one hour. This by itself was a feat that elevated him to special status. The Poet approached each day trying to extract the maximum humor and witticism from the curious and bizarre events that were witnessed on the street by agents daily at the office. He would then record the episode in a poem or his journal.

When I first came into the office, the Poet remarked, "We have a great bunch of guys here. There are a few dingbats who think statutory rape is doing it standing up. Overall, however, it's probably one of the best groups of agents ever assembled in the New York office, unsurpassed with unconventional and varied personalities."

"Really?" I asked. "Does this mean we are all a group of oddballs? Where do I fit in?"

"Deuce, if we can make penicillin from mold, we can make something out of you. You have animal cunning. The women love you."

"Animal cunning? I like that. I'm finally being recognized."

Most of the agents, except for the Poet, were single or wishing they were single, for once married, it was curtains. Living in Manhattan, walking the streets of Manhattan, and visiting the bars in Manhattan, where all of the sexually precocious visible nymphs and nymphets looking for a good time hung out, aroused too much excitement and intensity to want to return home.

When new agents and new blood came into the office, the Poet sat with his feet and legs propped on his desk. He'd light a

Camel and then settle back on his swivel chair, dispensing nick-names to the new recruits.

"Over there, he'll be 'Bugs.' Just look at those eyes. And did you see how he reacted to that cockroach in the corner?" I didn't see any cockroach. That had to be a figment of the Poet's extraordinary imagination.

"We will call that bald guy over there the 'Bald Eagle' and that guy 'Dullard.'"

I looked over at Dullard, who without question had a face no one would remember. Dullard was a very tall, gaunt, sorrow-ful, sad-sack-looking guy wearing a rumpled suit. He appeared exhausted and resigned to another day of toil busting his buns for America. He had a melancholy hangdog face that expressed both kindness and trust, which was a great face to have for a guy who was supposed to obtain facts and information by going around and interviewing Russian émigrés and commie sympa-thizers for the government. He reminded me of Satch, one of the Dead End Kids who used to hang around with Jimmy and Leo Gorsey near the Queensboro Bridge in Queens.

The Poet was on the money with Dullard, who turned out to be one of the most reticent, dullest, saddest human beings who ever showed up at the office, a decent, hardworking human being so quiet you would never even know he was around, and if he was around, he could be disguised as a maintenance man or hidden in the closet. Being around Dullard was like watching paint dry.

What was peculiar about Dullard was that no one knew what he did all day or what he was working on at any given moment. Some joked that he took off each day in a hot air balloon. Even worse he was accepted as part of the crew although no one knew much about him. He had drifted here and there from one office to another and finally landed as a single person in New York City, intent on finding a rich female to marry so that he could retire early. Amid all of the naked lust roaming around in Manhattan, he was successful and moved into a plush condominium on Seventy-Second Street.

Then there was the recruit, who had a strange disappearing act.

"You know," said the Poet, "I was talking to this guy. I turned my head to light a cigarette, and when I turned back to speak to him—poof—he was gone. He vanished like Houdini into thin air." Thus arose the nickname: "Puff."

The Poet, Old Yeller, Big D, and Big Al were all Deep South guys, but with no exaggerated Southern accents or family backgrounds connected with stock-car racers, rednecks, or moonshiners. They had no fondness for New York City, its ruthlessness, its incivility, and its lack of decent gentlemanly behavior and public manners. This of course was in direct contrast to the genteel and mannerly behavior that was expressed by all of us around the poker table.

Big D called it right when I first arrived in New York. "In this town it's dog eat dog. Occasionally you must respond in kind like a thirsty plant to rain, or people will walk all over you."

"Why is that, D?" I asked.

"Deuce, when you are thrown into a climate and mix of such coarseness and acrimony, some of it is bound to rub off on you. You become so disagreeable your own shadow won't stay with you. You find that out when you go back home. You are more aggressive and intense to a point that even your own mama doesn't recognize you as her boy. Even worse you start to look at your own mom as a type of stranger, a person with a problem, because she is just too polite and not aggressive and profane enough."

Deuce

"Jesus, I thought I just had indigestion."

As a midwesterner I found much of what Big D said to be true, for there seemed to be little visible kindness and thought for others in New York, almost as if being polite was anathema to everyone's thinking process. Everyone was pugnacious and appeared to be spoiling for a fight. On the streets or in the subways, New Yorkers were always involved within themselves, locked up with intensity, without any room for courtesy or politeness. It had to be expressed. Once it boiled over, it came out, at any time or any place, either with words that hurt or physically.

It carried over to the FBI troops. I became a New Yorker and noticed it in myself particularly when I went home to my neck of the woods. To the chagrin of my mom I showed up as an intense combative warrior with a raised voice and lack of composure. At times when home, I thought I was going to have a nervous breakdown because things were simply too calm and quiet.

When I took her to lunch she would ask me, "What's happened to you, boy?"

"Mom, it's my nerves. The city and its lifestyle is intense. But I love the job and the crew I work with. They think I have animal cunning."

"Animal cunning? Boy, I didn't raise you to become some sly fox. You need to get out of that place."

In New York, where anger and rage could be found daily on the street among the city folk, the temptation to respond in kind to harsh rude behavior was powerful. Certainly, it's best to resist it.

"Confront the problem," said the Poet, "but treat it with nonchalance, with no emotion, anger, or bitter taste in your mouth thereafter, because these events are ongoing and commonplace. Simply move on, or it will create a lot of stress."

57

Unfortunately, it took me a while to realize that and develop that type of appearance and style that eliminated anxiety from my otherwise tense and nervous makeup. After arriving in New York City, I often found myself hit with visible pugnacity, particularly when I was in a bureau car on the streets of Manhattan.

It happened for the first time on Madison Avenue in broad daylight. I was riding shotgun in a bureau car with the Knife. A yellow cab, after stopping at a red light in front of us, started moving forward and ran over a motorcyclist's foot, causing the motorcyclist to squeal in pain and shout obscenities. The cab ignored the incident and moved on. As we continued down Madison, the same taxi driver began to bob and weave, cutting us off in our lane of travel and nearly sideswiping our vehicle.

So I flashed my badge, and we pulled him over. I rolled down my window and looked over at a driver of foreign descent, with a stocking cap, who kept his hands on the wheel and stared straight ahead. A female passenger sat nervously in the backseat.

In a very calm voice, I said, "Hey, pal, can I ask you something?"

The Knife immediately cut in, chuckling and whispering. "Deuce, for Christ sake, you are a federal agent in New York City. You don't have to ask for permission."

"Good point," I said.

I looked back at the driver, who was still staring straight ahead.

"Hey, numb nuts!" I yelled in a loud, angry voice. "Look at me. Judging by the profanity directed at you with your window down, you are aware, of course, that you drove over a motorcyclist's foot a few blocks back, right?"

The taxi driver turned his head in my direction, raised his arms and hands upward in a gesture that suggested he either did not understand or was feigning an ability to speak or understand English.

I continued. "Your driving reveals a shocking lack of taste and good judgment. What part of New York are you from?"

The driver refused to acknowledge me and said nothing.

"You are some kind of stupid cocksucker driving that cab, you know that? You are a menace to traffic and pedestrians on this street. You're driving a Yellow in America. You can't drive over people's feet."

He responded finally quietly by saying, "Please. I have a lady in the backseat."

"Yes, but what about the motorcyclist? You are driving on one of the major roads of commerce and have what appears to be a blighted, retarded, undisciplined worldview."

"Atta boy," whispered the Knife. "Give it to him."

Urged on by the Knife, I hit him with the best snarling, raised voice I could muster, saying, "I don't give a shit who you have in that cab. If you persist with this type driving in the future, I shall, the next time I run into you, drop you like a used rubber. I will make sure that your taxi medallion is taken from you. Then what are you going to do for a living?"

"Now you're talking," said the Knife. "Drop him like a used rubber. I like that."

It was rude conduct on my part. No doubt about it. But this was life in the city.

As Walter Lippman once said, "Men have been barbarians much longer than they have been civilized. They are only precariously civilized, and within us there is the propensity, persistent as the force of gravity, to revert under stress and strain, under neglect or temptation, to our first natures."

CHAPTER 6

BORN TO LOSE

———◆———

AFTER ARRIVING IN NEW YORK, it took me a month to get into the Poet's favored circle. It was a gorilla poem that accomplished it.

I concocted a few lines about Dullard: "Beneath the starlike gleam of prolonged indulgence lives Dullard, man of a thousand disguises. No less a child of the universe than the trees and the stars, he too has a right to be here."

They were not original, but I took those lines and placed them beneath the photo of the face of the gorilla in the movie *King Kong*. We then placed this on Dullard's desk. It was lightheaded, farcical gibberish like this that brought a lot of laughter from the Poet.

In this group you had to drink, play poker, and remain on your toes. The alternative was getting riddled unmercifully with cutting remarks. Going to the john during a poker game was perilous. Those remaining at the table would be talking about you or, worse, trying to come up with some prank.

Early on, the Poet came to me and said, "Deuce, you're a bright guy: law degree, a person who could easily be making big bucks on Wall Street in some hollow money-grabbing profession. Yet here you are, on a measly government salary, having to put up with a lot of bureaucratic crap. Is this simply a bump in the road in your career?"

"Well, you got a few of those remarks right."

The Poet chuckled, "Let me guess."

"Don't bother," I said. "The answer is it is all about choices. Do you seriously think I would prostitute myself working on Wall Street for something as crass and soul robbing as...listen now, money? I'd become rich. Weekend home in Long Island. Country club, champagne, girls, a yacht. Do I look like somebody who would enjoy that?"

"I'll have to think about that," said the Poet, "but it won't take me long."

"Well," I said, "don't answer that question. The work here, and life itself, is not about money. It's about justice and fighting evil."

The Poet grinned and nodded. "I knew we could count on you to protect America."

I finally got my colors. I was in.

I became a close friend and ally of the Poet, who was twelve years my senior. He was the wind under my wings to stay calm and approach work on the streets with a sense of humor. We worked on cases together, ate breakfast and lunch together, and generally consulted one another on tactics and issues that came up with the Russians.

Although I was in with the Poet's group, as to poker, like Lone Louie, I was clearly out, eventually out of cuff links, pocketknives, and Mardi Gras beads, out of luck, outgunned, outclassed, and outsmarted when pitted against wry Southern boy card sharks, who grew up in smoke-filled rooms sitting around poker tables, and the Poet, who could read the opposition and know what other players would do with a hand, was always up plenty, with poker winnings up to his armpits and enough beads around his head to bring his head down.

If he wasn't winning money in cards, then it was golf, because the Poet was a scratch golfer, and nothing would stop the Poet from gambling or making bets on any sporting proposition, whether it was football, golf, or hockey. If money was changing hands, it was always flowing in his direction because his focus and mind game always gave him an edge. In poker, you either won with the best hand or you bluffed and made the better hand bail out. To win the game required strategy, math, memory, knowing the odds, and manipulation of your opponents into making bad calls, matters that I didn't have time for or interest in when playing poker but I did have interest in when it came to the Russians.

I was a sacrifice on the poker table, and the execution of each game proceeded rather quickly. Lyrics from Phil Harris would often pop into my mind. "My money would go like it had wings, if I had jacks someone else would have queens. Each night I would deliver all my coin."

I would get up to go to the bathroom, and when I came back, the Poet would light another cigarette and remark, "Deuce, you ought to go take a piss more often. I just won the last two hands." Raising his glass, he said, "Here's to wealth, women, and all card-playing spooks. Pour me another bourbon and ginger while you are up, will you, please."

In these games the Rheingold and Budweiser also flowed immensely and freely, which explained many of my losses. Fortunately, Moe's Deli remained open to provide needed supplies.

Invariably the conversation around the table always turned to women. As my losses mounted and depression set in, even though it was not realistic to think I could win all of the time or even any of the time, I generally felt an urge to be somewhere else, and toward the end of the evening, when Lone ran down to Moe's for more beer, and in our relentless search for eligible brides, he was asked to check out the nearby pubs and fleshpots along First Avenue, the street of dreams, for chorus girls, college girls, and females of every type; provided they were worth several peeks, he reported back if they were by themselves or with somebody. These local pubs were found on the East Side along almost every block, and inside the bars on a weekend night, there was always a spirit of liberation. On the street of dreams, one could find anything, including actors, both male and female, pretty waitresses and bartenders dreaming about becoming actors, nightclub entertainers, musicians, and pickpockets hanging out in front of restaurants.

As Louie left, TH would yell, "And by the way, Lone, to get us out of our chairs, tell us if you see some café dancer who is forty percent inside her dress and sixty percent exposed."

Big D played Hamlet, the doomed prince of Denmark, in the theater at the University of North Carolina and was always quoting Hamlet, to the amusement of his troupe of poker pals, who half the time never understood him. D shot his arm straight up from the long-sleeved undershirt he wore and yelled to Lone, "O what a rogue and peasant slave am I. Louie, give thy thoughts no tongue, nor any unproportioned female a glance."

"Listen, D, the nominations for the Academy Awards are closed," I remarked.

"Yeah," said TH, "don't give Louie Shakespeare this time of night."

Louie, oblivious to the Danish prince, looked back, blinked several times, and stared in puzzlement. He'd never read Shakespeare and felt Big D was filled with bullshit and wasn't all there.

Louie exited to find us an Ophelia, and being a graduate of the University of Mississippi, the habitat of many a Miss America, Lone, despite his quirks, had a good eye for beauty and quality and, being somewhat of a lone wolf anyway, enjoyed this sort of intrigue and surveillance of potential prey, which was not to say that such targets were easy pickings, because it never turned out that way.

Finally, to the distress of Hamlet and his friends, who never liked a loser to leave the table, I got up and said, "I'm fixin' to go."

"That's real good Southern talk," said the Poet. "Why you goin'?"

"Because carousing and hopelessness in the streets of dreams below beckon."

"There you go."

"I can dream about and get tips on how to be a champion poker player."

"That's better."

My losses were of such a magnitude that they inspired the Poet to pitch this poem.

Born to Lose

It looked extremely rocky for Deuce Ballou that day.
Bleary-eyed and hungover, he'd dropped most of his pay
to Pat the Knife and TH in a friendly little game.
"We'll hold the limit to a dime." Deuce had believed their
    claim.
But with the clock approaching ten, it was "no limit" stud,
and Deuce Ballou, though playing tight, was losing his life's
    blood.
He'd checked his holdings earlier; his stock had gone to pot.

On Rails he'd dropped a half of yard; Utilities were shot.
But like the true-blue gambler, he'd dreamed of future fame
and heeded not the caliber of players in the game.
He opened with a loser, tried to hit a bob-tailed flush,
and TH raked the marbles in with just a modest blush.
"Good hand, big Deuce. A shame to lose," they'd whisper in
    his ear.
"I'll get them yet," thought Deuce Ballou while gulping his
    ninth beer.
But Lady Luck smiled not on Deuce; his roll diminished fast.
"I'll cash in my insurance. I'll show them who laughs last."
He'd get two pair, but Pat the Knife would take him with
    trip' threes.
With straights he'd lose and flushes till they beat him to his
    knees.
He hocked his watch and ring for one last stack of reds and
    blues.
(He even asked how much they'd give for his eight-dollar
    shoes.)
Cowboys and nines came to him; he was betting for his life—
but cruel fate! The dead man's hand was spread by Pat the
    Knife.
And Deuce Ballou, since playing light, said, "I'll give you my
    note."
The Knife retorted, "Uh-uh, boy, just leave your overcoat."
Oh, somewhere in that Game of Life, a winner plays his hand
and hits each last card draw as if each card's at his command.
There's sunshine there and laughter; players never count the
    cost,
but there's no joy for Deuce Ballou: he played 'em well but
    lost.

CHAPTER 7

SUMMER IN THE CITY

———

ON THE NEW YORK CITY streets, there was always something happening, something different, with added antiwar turbulence and mania, no matter what time of day, and always, since my existence on a government salary was close to the poverty level, finding it involved walking, which kept me in shape and was extremely pleasurable. A conservative estimate of the number of miles walked daily was ten, for at the office surveillances of Russian agents were 90 percent on foot. The only sour note was that the Russian meanderings, as I will explain, were 95 percent without purpose, without being dirty, and took them into Madison Avenue stores only to look and shop. This produced very little excitement.

Weekends involved trips and visits to museums or walking up and down Madison Avenue or in the Village. I spent time on Long Island, a change of pace, which meant traveling over the Queensboro Bridge, a 3,724-foot span of stone and steel, which was a beautiful sight but even a better sight once you crossed it, in that one could look back at Manhattan and the city.

My companion on these weekend outings, not retreats, was my girlfriend, Cathy, otherwise known as "C," a Pan Am stewardess, of which Manhattan had many. C was easy and a paradise on the eyes. Since there were no legal or labor restrictions on refusing to hire or discharging overweight girls, pregnant girls, and not-much-to-look-at girls of every variety, the airlines had freedom to sell sex appeal, which they did, choosing stewardesses in large part for their looks to tend to the comfort of their passengers on their planes. Did they need to do this to fill their planes?

For whatever reason, C was one of those glamorous stewardesses who could help fill planes, with both beauty and a sensitive personality that would break your heart.

I met C in Central Park at the zoo. I spent a lot of time at the zoo. I enjoyed watching the seals. The admission prices were reasonable, and it was in the middle of Manhattan on a six-acre tract of land.

I met her on a day I have full recollection of. There were hints of sunshine reflecting off of apartment dwellings on the west side of the park. It was about fifty degrees. I noticed her right away because of her dark, shiny hair, striking good looks, slim, trim body with breasts that appeared at a distance large enough to nurse triplets, and black boots that extended up her beautiful legs slightly below her knees to a blue dress. Above the boots were buns that called out for seizing and squeezing. She was, I guessed, in her early twenties. She was carrying a camera and taking photos of seals.

I was not a paragon of urbaneness, but she did look over at me, saw me coming, and smiled, which was sufficient to cause some tingling in my flesh. Trusting my animal instincts and feral characteristics, which on some occasions got me in trouble, and since it was getting reasonably close to Christmastime and everyone was in the holiday spirit, I moved next to this brightest of ornaments and, although a bit tongue-tied because she was so pretty, asked her very lamely, "Hi. Are these Christmas Seals?"

She laughed and looked me up and down. "No, they are not Christmas Seals, but Good Housekeeping."

"Really. They look a bit dirty for good housekeeping. My name is Deuce."

"Deuce? As in deuce of clubs?"

"No, Deuce as in Deuce Ballou."

"Not a very aristocratic name." She bit her lip and turned to me.

"Well, on Park Avenue it strikes fear in burglars, thieves, and gangster types."

"What do you do, Deuce Ballou?"

"Very little. Read, run, walk, go to lunch, read…"

"So you are one of those rich Park Avenue types?"

"Well, I once was. My entire fortune went down the tubes when someone pickpocketed my wallet on the subway."

With that we both started laughing. I knew we connected and were on our way, which as it turned out, ended up with dinner that night and a visit to her apartment later, where she said she was staying with other stewardesses, who were not around.

We sat down in the living room in an apartment house on East Fifty-First Street. We drank rum and fruit juice. Her skin was smooth and clean. She had the glow of good health. We discussed her job with the airlines quite a bit, but then she began inquiring about my job as an agent working on Russians.

She smiled. "I'm based in Washington, DC. I want to transfer up here to be with my friends. But you are a spook?"

"Sort of. Our job is to make their blood run cold and scare them away."

"I met a Russian on one of my flights once. Ever since I started flying international, my mother has been afraid I'd fall in love with someone foreign."

"I don't think your mom has anything to worry about with Russians."

"Why is that?"

"They are different. It's a culture shock when they arrive here. They don't blend in. It takes them a year or two to become Americanized."

The evening ended, but after that we saw each other frequently. The more I saw C, the more I came to view her as full of secrets. Her pretty face concealed something, but I knew not what. From my questions and conversation with her that first night and other nights, I was left with the impression that she was holding back some things from me, hiding something regarding her background, playing a part of something she wasn't. I interviewed a lot of criminal suspects. I thought I was able to tell if someone was being evasive or concealing something. It was never easy. C raised some suspicions but not enough to deter me from seeing her.

Although it was not love at first sight, the relationship blossomed and continued rather vigorously, even though she was based with the airlines in Washington, DC, and we were apart a lot and entrenched as workaholics with our own separate jobs. When she came to New York City, she would say that she stayed with other stewardesses, all female, whom I never met.

As the relationship progressed, she told me that she didn't want to become emotionally involved with someone who might be dead in a week. Not a bad point.

I reasoned that until I could convince her that I was a real tough guy who could take care of himself, it was understandable that my determined assaults on her virtue, which were many, would bear no fruit. Finally, whether it arose from long walks, shared trips to a health club, or mutual animal magnetism with body charges and sparks, we finally developed a loving and close relationship resulting in hours of serious coupling, even in Central Park—incredibly hot.

In Central Park, Manhattan's 843-acre green oasis, there were always numerous soirees visible, normally at dusk, at a time when I did not wish to be excluded. Copulation in Central Park was one of the summer rites of thousands, although I cannot point to any statistical study by a New York City governmental agency. It didn't require much beyond a blanket, wine, and a patch of grass adjacent to an obscure flower bed on the great lawn. Gazing to the west, one could see the iconic and luxurious walls of the San Remo Towers. This helped in maintaining some semblance of control for it was difficult to escape the thought that someone was in the towers with a telescope watching.

The national pastime in New York City during summer months was never about visiting Yankee Stadium. Under the stars, even though the stars were not as vivid and clear as they could have been if one were lying in the desert or even in Brooklyn, such activity, thought by only a small segment of the populace to be unspeakably offensive, had a great appeal for girls living in New York who were smothered and confined in New York apartments for much too long.

Weekends with C in New York followed the usual pattern, with lunch somewhere and a lot of walking. From the Upper East Side, it was generally a visit over to the Museum of the City of New York and then down Fifth Avenue to the Metropolitan Museum of Art. We'd then skip over to Madison Avenue and back to the apartment; then we'd head out to dinner with more walking and then to a concert or bar. I recall with some pleasure taking her for a boat ride around Manhattan and on other occasions sitting on a blanket or park bench in Central Park drinking wine from paper cups.

Our shtick was to do fun, kinky, invisible things, wearing old clothes, eccentric-looking hand-me-downs and knockoffs with disguises. From my end, whether I was with C, on duty or off duty, to accomplish a disappearance and succeed in vanishing and assuming a different identity, certain things had to be addressed. My wallet contained whatever documents I needed that day along with my credentials. My pockets included cash, a razor-sharp pocketknife, a small Leica camera, and my five-shot Smith & Wesson.

My wardrobe consisted of denims, khakis, windbreakers, army and nautical fatigues, which I picked up at an army surplus store and which probably needed to be deloused, hand-me-downs of all sorts, forage caps, pea coats, nautical sweaters, great coats with mantles, an ankle-length green overcoat and London Fog trench coat, faded khaki shirts, numerous disguises, combat boots, walking shoes, one dark blue suit (not a Seville Row, but nonetheless a suit that did not wrinkle), clothing guaranteed by John Paul Lee, a Chinese tailor, just in case I had to go to a funeral—and of course the weapons.

To go around off duty in Manhattan unrecognized required hair, long hair, to cover up your own. Hair too long was taboo at the federal office. With hair or a wig, what was important was not style but length. This coupled with worn threads, polyester or cotton, made it all come together, providing a spirited, energetic weekend thump.

Think about it in these terms. A fugitive who wants to remain undetected has to do certain things and be somewhere. New York City was a great place for anonymity and invisibility and was a super camouflage for fugitives, spies, and counterspies. It offered the perfect environment for deception, con artists, dissimulation, and smoke-screen skills.

Truth be told, it was best and more fun to be a fly on the wall and observer in camouflaged garb. C and I, as young eccentrics or hippies, were invisible, playing roles of someone else. It fit in with office work. Bullshit of course was also needed.

Armed with a detailed map, a plotted course, and good pairs of walking shoes, we walked, walked, and walked, combing and observing the streets and people of New York, down Broadway, through the Village, visiting delis, stepping over the vagrants lying near their sidewalk boxes and watching the well-dressed men and women hailing cabs in the middle of the street, because with the streets of New York, it was like taking the three-mile journey through the Louvre. Each block had its own piece of art, and as we walked down the street, it was like moving room to room within the Louvre, but without the noise of the coal-filter humidifiers that at the Louvre ran round the clock.

With walking nothing was an impediment. Fog and rain were things to be welcomed. The city still surged. With added weather elements, everything took on a mystical quality, with human shapes barely visible at times but still shuffling from one place to the next. Bizarre events often happened but would be dismissed as nothing out of the ordinary.

On one occasion a half of a block in front of us, pieces of concrete from a projecting cornice of a four-story building tumbled down to the sidewalk, creating a lot of noise and dust. Incidents like this were of the type that happened quite frequently.

In law school we often referred erroneously to such incidents as "acts of God," things that simply happened like a lightning strike without a will of its own, pleasing to insurance agents.

Sorry, they would say, no coverage. In fact, falling cornices had more to do with negligent maintenance.

Generally, C and I walked and laughed about these happenings. It was such a natural, commonplace occurrence in New York that there was no reason to stop and sound an alarm. It was on the order of a scene from the movie *Midnight Cowboy*, where a person lay flat on a Fifth Avenue sidewalk. People simply stepped over him and continued on their way.

C told me she was from Arkansas, near Little Rock. I never checked. Hog heaven. The Razorbacks. Seemed like a great country address. Occasionally, she would rattle off big Arkansas power names like Morse, Williamson, Ledbetter, and Simpson, as if she knew their families. Later I learned that she didn't know any of them.

She was quiet and reserved, five feet seven, beautiful, the right curves, and always wearing tight jeans, which accentuated a pair of buns on her behind that would knock your socks off. The shape of her bottom excited me, along with her sweet womanly scent that enticed me like a honey bee. For a while I thought she sprayed herself with vanilla, that extract from a podlike fruit that my mother often threw in to her apple pie.

We were not a permanent couple. This was after all New York City, a place of desire and delights, and we were both dating other people. At least this is what she told me. But C was special, and we became more than just considerate friends. I enjoyed her company and was slowly imbibing and assimilating into myself everything she had to offer.

Regrettably, there was always the subject of time. We both were extremely busy with work. I was embedded and totally involved and interested in my work. She was the same. Thus, it was hard to define our relationship or where it was going.

During the time we were together, I worked on communication. I never knew what she was thinking and at one point suggested she needed an analyst. To be incorrigibly inquisitive can be a failing. Some people get upset with this. C, fortunately, did not view it that way.

She mentioned that this aspect of my personality, the curiosity on my part, was charming. Not many females tell you that you are a "blend of contradictions and contrast." That was amusing.

After months of being together, she began to respond and become more open, independent, communicative, and questioning, particularly about my office work and Russians, which remained puzzling but did not seem out of the ordinary, for much of the detail discussed was nothing beyond that which could be gleaned from *The New York Times*. Ordinary conversation at times got interrupted and slid into vociferous and heated debates on demonstrations, the Vietnam War, and world affairs.

"You are just not listening," she would say, at which point I would say, "OK, you just enlightened me, so what's the big deal?"

In truth, her independence and willingness to communicate and speak openly what was on her mind became very attractive. When C wasn't away on a trip, she would spend a great amount of time in my apartment, where together we would read, talk, cook, and drink, until darkness came, when we would venture out on the street in some disguise to some distant bar where a band or music group was playing, where we would drink more and dance and then return home. The island of Manhattan has a lot of bars and taverns, and to understand city life, a brief reflection on the bar scene might now be in order, to give a glimpse of how fun evenings were spent.

New York evenings were sultry. When that happened, C and I walked down to have drinks at Bachelors III, a small sports bar at Sixty-Second and Lexington, which was owned by Joe Namath and a few of his friends. When Joe became one of the owners, the joint quickly became a popular hot spot. We were attracted there not to gab but to look and listen to conversation about football, gambling, and betting. The beer was good and relatively cheap.

We went there fully disguised like someone out of a Russian novel and hung out, with the journalists, jocks, and pretty girls who would saunter in and out looking for jocks, friends of jocks, gamblers, and other seedy-looking types (many with rap sheets), clusters of guys drinking beer and talking football (many being present to pick up tidbits of information about a sick tight end or hobbled split end of the Jets or some other NFL team that might give them an edge to make a bet, beat the spread, and make some money). These were not neighborhood drunks, but money guys from all around the city. For a time I wondered if a legitimate guy could be found in the place. All of them took a real interest in C, who was a looker in every sense of the word. C would seldom say anything except maybe to ask a question. Their willingness to reveal a lot of criminal tips and shit to C led me to make a suggestion at the office that we needed to cultivate more attractive female informants. When asked by one or more of these honchos what we do, we explained we were not working but were prodigal children of families on Park Avenue.

Without cavernous dimensions, the place had everything going for it by way of atmosphere, except a dance floor. Acoustics were good. We watched and listened to the talk of characters one could find in stories by Damon Runyon. We went in there enough that the bartenders and pretty mixologists finally looked at us as regulars, even though they were never the same, and when one or more did show up, it was never a conversationalist who would build up a following. I was convinced that there was no way they could tell what I did for a living with the garb that C and I wore.

It was late evening on one occasion when we walked in, again looking like ailing itinerants. There were a large number of customers in the place. I nodded at the bartender. C and I took our usual two seats at the end of the bar and ordered two glasses of draft beer.

During the fall, ongoing shop talk was mainly about weekend college and pro football games. Since it was late, it was a time that the unemployed gamblers and lost souls showed up, of which there were many, mob guys, who liked to kibitz about not just football but horses, basketball games, and anything else that was capable of carrying a wager in Vegas, producing at least for some of them winnings to get them through the next day.

It was in the midst of this noisy group, near closing time, when a guy walked in who resembled Peter Lorre, looking as Lorre did in the movie *Casablanca*, all pallid, nervous, and jumpy. He was carrying a stack of cardboard cards as if he were in there to make a quick delivery from a car or van illegally parked outside the tavern, loaded with newspapers. Peter surveyed the crowd and immediately commenced handing out cards to those of us sitting at the bar.

"What do I do with this?" C asked as she lifted the card to her eyes to see what it was about.

Nervous Lorre yelled at her, "Keep it down below the bar!"

I looked over at C, took another sip of my beer, laughed, and said, "Gee, you better do what he says."

We both peered down at this card, which we held below the bar. It was a football bet card, with a list of games coming up Sunday and points representing the spread.

"Who is this guy?" C whispered.

I looked at her and winked. "He's connected. Not a capo but one of the lower-rung hoods."

She looked at me inquisitively. "What do you mean: 'not a capo but one of the lower-rung hoods'?"

"He's a street-level guy. A runner. Collector. Mafia type. Works for one of the Cosa Nostra families."

"But he's by himself. Where are the brawny henchmen?"

"Good point. Probably in the car."

"So isn't this enough to arrest the head honcho?"

"You mean the guy on top?" I asked and chuckled.

"Yeah."

"C, this guy works for someone, who works for someone, who works for someone. He is five or six levels from the top of the chain. We could never connect him to the guy on top."

The truth was that his presence represented an incident of mob gambling activity, which wasn't much but something, a single and isolated event, but yet, I thought, it could provide some connecting link in a chain, which could produce some prosecutorial fruit. I decided to do something with it. Connecting dots could lead to something big or somebody bigger beyond busting a grain of sand, a little guy like Nervous Lorre. It would be hard for a defense lawyer to convince a jury that his client Nervous Lorre had no clue as to what he was delivering. Possession of a stack of bet cards was like possession of a large amount of marijuana, as opposed to an ounce.

I looked over at C, smiled, and said, "Well, you are now a witness to something that—who knows—could end up with some prosecutorial action."

I whispered, "Turn around slowly and take a good long peek at Nervous, but don't give him the kind of look that would show you are interested in him, OK?"

C looked at me wide-eyed and then slowly turned around on her barstool. I sat there with my elbows on the bar, cupping the beer with both hands in front of me. In the mirror I could see Nervous walking around the bar, greeting the customers like goombahs. I looked toward C and laughed. "Hmm. Is Nervous giving a Runyon big hello to any one?"

C turned her head and smiled. "Not yet."

"Well, if he does or hugs someone, take a picture of that someone in your mind, OK, so we can pick out that someone in a photo later."

In passing out these bet cards, Nervous, like a pirate at sea, had effectively raised his colors as some underling or connect to organized crime, which was not to say that Broadway Joe or the other owners who I had never seen in there knew the pennant that Nervous flew.

I finally looked around and closely scrutinized the crowd to see what Nervous was doing and how he was handling himself, hoping that maybe he would adjourn to the basement and use the pay phone. It was common knowledge at my office that Bachelors III was being investigated by the NYPD for gambling activity. The basement pay phone was bugged.

Nervous, being now a visible, identifiable guy with no insulation, stayed on the first floor and, being nervous and fidgety, decided that he should not spend much time there or even take the time to make a phone call after handing out bet cards and left in a hurry.

After this incident C and I began to go in Bachelors more often, simply to document in our minds what was going on. C loved the excitement and felt she was contributing to the cause of justice. I discussed all of this with the top hood agents on the sixth floor, asking them what they made of this. Their answer to that was "very little." It was virtually impossible for any NFL star or owner of a bar to screen all the hounds and foxes that they daily came into contact with. Few understood or even comprehended the vast amount of money that changed hands over the outcome of a football game.

The dollars wagered each year exceeded one billion dollars. Although supplying the public with what they wanted was not per se insidious, the vast amount of money involved promoted corruption, extortion, and sports bribery. Maybe the mob had obtained a foothold with the game. Viewing the spread, the scores, and the outcomes of some games, there were times that I often scratched my head with amazement and wonder: had this game really happened this way, or was there some sinister force that motivated or didn't motivate the players?

CHAPTER 8

MEETING THE SPYCATCHER

Monday, June 19, 1967.

THE FBI OFFICE WAS LOCATED at 201 East Sixty-Ninth Street. It resembled an apartment building and was within walking distance from my apartment.

When I entered it for the first time, I was greeted by an FBI agent sitting behind a counter. He examined my creds.

"Go upstairs to the seventh floor. It appears you are assigned to Russian counterespionage matters. You'll need to go see and check in with your supervisor, Charley O."

"What's he like?" I asked.

"Some call him the Spycatcher. Good guy, originally from New York City. Aggressive. He is the kind of an investigator that turns over stones to examine the undergrowth. You'll like him. Prepare to work hard."

Here I fast-forward to give you a bird's-eye view and summary of the work and what it was like to be on Charley's squad.

Charley was a desk-jockey supervisor in charge of about ten agents covering Russians. The Soviet Union had legal bases within the United States that included their embassy in Washington, DC, and their mission to the United Nations in New York City, from which over three hundred Russians or Soviet nationals; many being diplomatic and consular officers with diplomatic immunity came and went as they saw fit. They did not necessarily live in the embassy or mission. In New York City, those assigned to the mission could live somewhere else in Manhattan and even have a summer abode out in the Rockaways or Long Island. These Russians were ostensibly here to work at the United Nations as economic attaches and officers. In fact they were well-trained KGB intelligence officers. We knew that and they knew we knew that.

Their principal aim was to locate and assess persons within the United States for recruitment to serve in rolls that would advance Russian interests. They befriended American targets. They then played on their weaknesses to turn them into spies. Regrettably, many Americans did not have to be recruited. They volunteered to help, in exchange for money. We viewed these individuals as the walk-in trade to their business.

In contrast to covering the Czechs, Romanians, or Poles, Russian counterintelligence was of the highest priority. The United States was the principal target for Russia's intelligence gathering. Conversely, Russia was our main threat, with active spies coming and going from their mission in New York and other Manhattan buildings they occupied. These were people intent on obtaining secrets, which would harm the security of the United States.

Charley O was in his fifties. We called him "Charley" or simply "Boss." As the supervisor of a squad of agents, Charlie's world meant spending most of his time at his desk, reading their reports and case files, going over strategy with agents, handling and assigning new work and cases that came in, and of course deciding who got what case. Several times a day, he ventured outside his office to discuss a major or high-stakes case, and when he did, it was never a modest piece of theater.

He was a nervous, intense, overweight man with coronary problems but intelligent and good-humored. He came up from the ranks like a species out of Darwin, wanted to stay out of trouble with the bureau by not calling attention to himself, and wanted to keep his nose clean, all the while contemplating early retirement. Yet, he was unequivocally aggressive toward the Russians with unquenchable curiosity about what they were doing all day. After I got to know him, he told me that his aim in life was to be as happy as possible and make other people happy, except the Russians.

One vice that he had was that he smoked a lot. He was told by his doctor to quit smoking, but this advice he ignored. He had unusual ways of expressing leadership. He would do it with encouragement and stimulus, which often was exaggerated. During the day he often exited his cell to visit with and bark out brainstorms and occasional hyperbole to the street agents. He did this as a motivational pitch more than anything. I'll give you an example.

One day he came out and advised, "Guys, now hear this. The seat of government has advised that the Russians have a new listening device."

Someone then yelled out, "Be careful what you say, Charley."

Charley then paused. "They have something that can overhear conversations without a bug at a distance of a hundred yards. I want you guys to be careful."

Many of us thought this was a fabrication. Charley was constantly concerned with eavesdropping and agents conversing and perhaps giving away secrets in open public places. We viewed this particular tidbit as preposterous with no semblance of truth, designed to keep us on our toes, keep us thinking and avoiding discussion of office information and tactics while on the street or in a coffee shop. From that standpoint this was a harmless, good managerial approach. It also allowed Charley to disburse frustrated steam from the daily stress he encountered.

To understand Charley meant distinguishing fact from fiction. He wanted facts.

He was a tough, no-nonsense kind of guy, often with a bewildering look at times, who wasn't aloof or remote. Once he met me, he appeared dismayed but tolerant and amused at my often disheveled, rumpled appearance and casual, wrinkled clothing, but, since I was one of the new kids on the block, he thought this was the bureau's new look. He rarely commented on it, for it blended in with the characters in the office and everything present on the New York streets.

Unlike many New York City guys, I never observed him seriously outraged or angry. He had the intensity. Yet he was able to maintain a happy demeanor and consequently was extremely popular among squad members. We looked at it as our job to help him ride out his career without getting into internal bureaucratic trouble, which meant taking the blame for miscues.

Another little quirk of Charley's was to call all the agents, no matter how well he knew them, by their last name: Smith, Jones, and so forth. He did that with everyone, except me and the Poet. Why was that? I never asked him. Right from the get-go, however, the Boss and I seemed to hit it off, perhaps from our mutual hardworking roots.

But there was always that other side of Charley as well. If you did something that was not by the book, like searching an apartment without a warrant or pursuant to an arrest and without first getting approval to do it, he didn't want to know about it. He would then say, "I didn't hear that." Or he would say, "I don't want to know about it. If I'm ever tortured by the KGB, I won't be able to give them anything," all of which provided food for thought among the troops.

It was taken for granted by field agents that after a certain number of years or at a certain age it did not bode well to go out and risk your neck if you wanted to move up. Think rubber gloves and fingerprints. As a supervisor and desk man wishing to advance, the idea was not to leave fingerprints on potentially harmful decisions that could kick you in the ass.

So Charley would often don rubber gloves in dealing with cases and issues that came up. The upshot of all of this left the street agent the ability to do his own thing. That, by the way, was fine with me and others because it resulted in freedom, freedom to act and make your own decisions. In handling files, the last thing anyone wanted was someone constantly looking over his shoulder.

To Charley's credit, he never took the fun or enthusiasm out of covering the Russians. It had to be done aggressively, nonstop, thoroughly, and completely. Charlie divided the Russians into two groups.

One group was the "regs," short for *regular guys*, or nonproductive do-nothing stiffs and downtrodden commie drifters, who were here physically in the United States and mostly shopped, doing very little spying. With these types there was nothing to worry about, so we were told. There was no need to pay a great amount of attention to them.

But then there was the other group, the "pros." Ah, the pros—these were the guys we had to unload resources on and pay attention to. They were the smooth English-talking and walking James Bond types wearing Johnson and Murphy shoes. These were the badasses. With these types Charley would say, "Whatever it takes. Cover that son of a bitch like a blanket. Follow him like the tail on a kite. You have to think about what they do in this light. They have to deliver intelligence to their homeland. These spies have to produce, or they are sent home."

I often wondered what happened to them when they were sent home, perhaps consigned to some moldy shack in the slums of Moscow. I gradually learned that these spies, because of homeland fears and ambitionless living in Moscow, loved it here and wanted to stay.

The essence of counterintelligence work was penetration. Ideally, this meant penetrating the Soviet mission and KGB apparatus by having a defector or agent in place or some other Russian source who would provide information on US citizens or US government or military personnel who were on the Russian payroll or providing information to the Russians. Penetrating the Russian establishment to procure an agent or defector in place was no easy task.

To find or turn a Russian KGB agent into a mole, it was necessary to focus on persons we felt were receptive to a pitch to come over to our side and work for us and with us, which meant studying and knowing their characters, lives, and human frailties, thus having something to exploit and hold over their heads. It took hard work, luck, or the fickle finger of fate, like a Russian walk-in or something else.

Nothing succeeded like persistence. Nothing succeeded like false documents and identities, the principal weapons of subterfuge and deception. One common thing that existed with the guys around the poker table was never sleeping, never wearying, and never tiring in trying to beat the Russians.

CHAPTER 9

PARANOIA IS GOOD

———◆———

AFTER EXITING THE ELEVATOR ON the seventh floor my first day, I walked over to meet Charley O and knocked politely on the door to his work area.

Charley came out, removed a cigarette from his mouth, and welcomed me warmly, shaking my hand. "Come on back," he said, motioning me to his office.

I entered a large cubical of an office, containing the usual governmental issue, a steel desk, a few uncomfortable metal chairs, bookcases, and several metal cabinets. Two of the walls were glass. From this position Charley was visible to the rest of the agents, who occupied desks surrounding it, like in a large newsroom for *The New York Times*. Within his office was a generation of bureau-like clutter, filled as it were with paper, memos, and files.

Charley sat down at this desk and motioned me to a chair, propped his feet on the desk (exposing brown worn boots), raised his arms, and placed his hands behind his head. He needed a haircut. His uncombed hair on the side protruded out, giving him a disheveled look, like Albert Einstein. Unlike Einstein he did wear socks.

On one hand was a screaming eagle, drawn it appeared as a doodle with a ballpoint pen. In front of him was a brown accordion case file that I assumed held my personnel documents.

"What brings you to New York, Deuce? Shopping? A decent meal from greasy burgers you've been eating in a rural roadhouse?"

"None of those," I said, laughing.

"I see you are here from Miami."

Something from Joseph Conrad entered my mind. "Yup, I'm like Kurtz in *Heart of Darkness*, coming up the river to New York City. I'm expecting to encounter the ultimate horror."

"Well," said Charley, "you may not find that, but it's guaranteed that New York City will make you hard. Working in Miami will make anyone soft."

Charley put on his reading glasses and glanced down at the brown file.

"I see you were known for your integrity, sobriety, and honesty."

"You have two of those right." Charley was obviously unaware of the amount of time I spent drinking beer with the class crew of agents.

Charley continued to read from notes in the file. "Good athlete. Decent with a handgun within the seven-yard kill range. Says you are street smart and observant. You are the only one in your bureau class, who correctly knew the number of steps leading up to the training center and the number of windows facing the street. That's very impressive."

"Thanks."

"You counted every step you took to get into the building. Why would you do that?"

"Habit. I've often had the habit of gathering useless information."

"Maybe it's a quirk in your personality."

"Not really. In college I worked during the summer for a contractor. My work included building staircases in houses. A total rise of about 102 inches necessitated about 13 stairs or steps. After doing that kind of work I became interested in the number of steps I had to climb from one floor to the next."

"Actually, that will help you with intelligence work," said Charley.

"What? Useless information?"

"Ah. Useless information in this trade can become priceless. Observation and perception of small, insignificant details can be the key to breaking cases."

"Thanks."

"Also enjoyed your definition of *probable cause* on the exam."

Charley was referring to the closing examination of the bureau class. Agents were asked to discuss and define *probable cause* in making an arrest. My response was to give them an example. Assume that you are driving along and you observe a man standing in front of a restaurant. He has a toothpick in his mouth, mustard on his tie, and a napkin dangling down from his waist. He is also carrying a small bag like a carryout. *Probable cause* is simply a fact or set of facts that give you cause to conclude that this gentleman was probably in that restaurant.

"I didn't look at the definition as too extraordinary."

"You're not a language guy. No Russian?"

"No."

"That's OK. You'll be working mostly with the Poet, who speaks Russian. So how do you like New York?"

"We are on an island. The waters clear my head."

"Mine too. By Christmastime you will like it even more."

"Why is that?"

"The townies mellow."

"I haven't yet noticed that. We'll see. I don't plan that far ahead."

"You know what we do here, don't you?" Charley asked, as he sat back and again put both arms and hands behind his head.

"Russians."

"Yeah, but this squad deals with espionage. What do you think that involves?"

"In training class they told us it's the development of agents."

"Correct," said Charley. "Our job on this squad is Russian counter intelligence to counter Russian spying. Clandestine stuff, and we do that with the help of agents."

"Business has been good?"

"Very good. The United States allows the Russians to have an embassy and a mission to the United Nations in our country, and all they do is send over bad guys to spy on us while they live here."

"The nerve," I say with a grin. "These bad guys come and go from the mission to the United Nations daily. Correct?"

"True, and other places than the mission. Some live in New York apartments. Generally they are duly accredited diplomatic or consular officers with diplomatic immunity."

"We're dealing here solely with their intelligence operation—no sabotage, propaganda, stuff of that sort?"

"Wrong. Everything is on the table."

"Like what?"

"Anything goes. On both sides. We both have kidnappers, bag jobbers, bug installers. Probably the only thing we are missing that the Russians have are executioners."

"Maybe that should change. There should be a side here in the office with a criminal bent."

"Not a good word—*criminal*. Use *internal security*. Anything goes because it's needed."

"So what are the Russians looking for?" I ask.

"Top-secret stuff. Information on weapons, atomic submarines, military installations, communications, electronics. The list is endless."

"Their economic and political intelligence gathering is not something that concerns us, correct?"

"Right. They have readers that sift through *The New York Times* and magazines for much of that stuff. What is published and what they extract is out of our control. It's incredible, really, what you can occasionally find published. Even the location of all of our Minuteman missiles."

"Who are they primarily contacting and working on?" I asked.

"Government officials and those in private industry, mainly engineers. They operate out of the embassy or mission and try to recruit these people to gather and feed them information."

"For free?"

"Depends. Some people they recruit do it for reasons other than money."

"These persons then become their agents for clandestine activity."

Charley smiled. "You are catching on. Your job is to identify, locate, arrest, or double up these Americans and if you are lucky maybe even turn a Russian into a mole."

"I shall march off resolutely and do my best," I said. "What about the KGB guys? Short of killing them, how do we put an end to all of this?"

"We don't. The most we can hope for is control. Unless our government prohibits embassies and missions, we will always have spies that murder, blackmail, and kidnap. We have to live with it and fight our own little war, which is where you and the other agents come in."

I look over at Charley. "I take that to mean that I am one of the grunts fighting this war on the New York City streets."

"You're one of the field hands. There is one thing I wish to make clear." Charlie paused.

"OK," I said.

"We operate on the theory that if you do something clandestinely, you do not get caught."

"I'll be careful."

"If you succeed, you get no recognition, and if you fail or need assistance, you'll get no help. You may get tired of the mission because some of the work can be drab."

Charley apparently had not totally looked at my personnel file. In it there were multifarious and variegated drab jobs I'd had prior to arriving at the FBI, which were not altogether stimulating. Working with one small-town lawyer during the summer college months, I'd even been asked to help an elderly mom get her forty-seven-year-old son out of her house because he wouldn't leave to find a job.

I looked at Charley and asked, "Drab? As in monotonous or irksome? I have a suggestion."

"What's that?"

"Garbage. Maybe we can collect some intelligence on what the Russians are up to by going through all of the waste they throw out."

"We've done that and still do that. They use incinerators. We don't gain much doing this."

"So what's the drab work?

"Surveillance," said Charley, "as in when you are out, waiting and waiting for something to happen. At some point when you are tired, see nothing happening, and grow impatient, you may regret being here."

"Doubt it," I said. "I'm here out of fear of a missed opportunity."

"What does that mean?"

"As soon as the offer to work here came in, I was sold. I never wanted to be in a position where I would look back and have some profound regret that I missed something important. Same way with a surveillance: wouldn't want to miss something."

Charley shook his head slowly. "Well, I've seen a lot of new guys come into this office. Working for the government doesn't pay much. Sometimes I wonder why they don't make a career in a law firm."

I thought to myself that Charley obviously had never worked in a law office because the law can be a dreary business, and the public can make you out to be bad guys. My epiphany in pursuing a government career came during a bout of back pain when I was on some strong meds. I was sitting at my desk and realized that lawyers were becoming a persecuted lot. The thrill was gone, and I even pondered moving to DC to become a lobbyist. The ones I knew, referred to by friends as shitheads, seemed to have a lot of fun and partied a lot. Yet, I knew what Charley meant. Working in a law office is looked at as big bucks, but when you are actually doing it, it's so easy to get caught up in enrichment, to a point that your home or apartment runneth over with luxurious items. Leaving the law office for a job with the government was a big step down in pay and blowing a chance at a partnership, which paid even more.

"Charley, let me say first of all that humility is not my strong suit. When I dabbled in the practice of law, I honestly felt I was doing some good helping people, but in many respects the world demonizes the legal profession, making us out to be crooks. I was not in the profession for money, and I'm not working for the government for money. It may sound strange, coming as it does from a lawyer, but money is not important to me."

Charley now leaned forward with his elbows on his desk. "Jesus, money is not the root of all evil."

I chuckled at this comment. "Are you suggesting Charley that St. Paul had it wrong?"

"Not at all. But we all strive to get ahead, prosper, and get rich. *Capiche?*"

I started laughing. "Capiche? Count me as a person that feels that decadence and consumerism is damaging America. To me we should be a lot less so, and when we die, we should leave the earth as we found it, putting back into it everything that we took out. Anyway, that is definitely not the Russian way or the Wall Street way, right?"

"Right. Great philosophy. I'm going to have you over for dinner so that you can discuss this with my wife. Question?"

"Fire away," I said.

"What characteristic more than any other can make you real successful with a law firm?"

"Understanding people might be a good place to start."

"What else?"

"Probably the ability to always picture the worst out of any set of facts, and then coming up with a plan to avoid it."

Charley paused and gazed at me in a dumbfounded fashion. "Well, that wasn't what I was thinking about."

"Keep in mind Charley that there comes a point that a lawyer has heard every conceivable problem and symptom. You want to dispense good advice. You want a satisfied client, but try this. How about imagination?"

"Why do you say that?"

"Because there are times when a person walks into a law office with a problem. He or she spills out a set of facts, perhaps like making a bad investment that appears fraudulent. Something then pops into one's mind from a seminar, law-school lecture, or something you've read, and this peanut of a case mushrooms into a large, profitable antitrust suit."

"Deuce," said Charley O, "I think we will get along fine, because resourcefulness and inventiveness is what I preach here. This squad deals with Russian espionage matters and clandestine operations, and it's imagination and creativity that can get results. We also try to keep the Russians off balance, by being clever, aggressive, and crafty. The Russians are the enemy. They have a job to do. They are out hustling US secrets, cultivating relationships with Americans who occupy sensitive positions, and intimidating Russian émigrés. Our job is to counteract all of that, and we can best do that by being creative."

"I'll go along with that."

"In New York you are going to find that we do things differently. Look behind me. What is that?"

I took that as a rhetorical question. I didn't reply. But I concentrated on this puzzle. I looked at the wall behind his desk. On it was a chalk board. An oblong circle was present inside a larger oval shaped like Lake Michigan. I might have replied that it was an island surrounded by water, but I was sure that this was not what Charley had in mind. Finally I looked at Charley, grinned, and started laughing.

"Charley, I'm a Neanderthal when it comes to maps and finding places. I have no idea what that crude drawing depicts. Whatever it is, is it in friendly hands? I give," I said.

Charley turned his head and looked up. "The borough of Richmond and the island, Staten Island, are no good for spy activities. Communications can be tough. But the other boroughs—Manhattan, the Bronx, Brooklyn, and Queens—are OK for spying, and these boroughs are what we focus our attention on. Behind me is Manhattan, and the inner oval is Central Park. Inside the park is another oval, the reservoir. Last week an agent was murdered."

"I thought this is the type of job that no one is supposed to get hurt."

"It doesn't always work out that way. They tried to make it look like a suicide. His body was found near the reservoir, and we don't understand—why the hit? Why? We know the Russians are ruthless, like the Mafia. They would just as soon hang one of us from a meat hook over a meat grinder in Jersey. We did an autopsy. Do you know what killed him? Poison. We think it's saxitoxin, made apparently by clams, but we don't know. It causes respiratory failure. And just in case someone hits you with that, there is no antidote. We think one of our Russians had something to do with it, which by itself is rather strange. Our intelligence services have always had a modus operandi of not hurting or injuring someone on the other side. The Russians are aware of this. If they were to hurt one of our guys, we hurt one of their guys. This agent was alone on surveillance. The killing of an agent, even in a large office like we have here in New York, is a rare occurrence. But it happens and the case is our number one priority."

"Looks like with that case all you have is a lot of circumstantial evidence," I said.

"That's right," said Charley. "You know what that means."

"Yeah. It means," I said, "that unless you catch the culprit at the murder scene, success at solving the case and winning a conviction is just a matter of luck."

Charley stood up, walking around nervously, pacing. "Luck—that's right. Ask any defense lawyer. I'm going to give you a few basic rules. Rule number one: never go anywhere around town without your gun even when you are off duty. And if you have to pull it, point it at the person's least vulnerable spot—their heart."

"Least vulnerable, huh?" I said. "I'll remember that, Charley."

"Rule number two: pay attention to details. Our business involves spies and espionage. You live in the shadows. When you are on the street, it's the details that count. They can break a case and even save your life. Where are the shadows? Is there an open area or avenue of escape if you get in trouble? You are supposed to be street smart, which is why they put you on my squad."

"Rule number three: when you report on things, don't exaggerate or invent things to make the facts look better. Be totally honest."

"May I interject something? The Russians will also be writing their reports."

"Yes. But there's a difference between what we do or write and what they do or write. Their stuff is shaded."

"Rule number four: you cannot be afraid of taking risks or bending the rules, but if things go wrong, we—I—disclaim any responsibility for it."

"Finally, rule number five: don't trust anybody, and don't accept people at face value. The information that emanates from this office can lead to the injury or death of a valuable agent or source. The bureau, to my knowledge, has never had a mole, but—who knows—maybe one can exist even now, passing information to the KGB. Pay attention to patterns of behavior of everyone, including your own companions. It's all very telling."

"Moles?" I asked, smiling. "Does this include the guys that take money at the poker table? That wouldn't happen if one of them was a mole, would it?"

Charley grinned. "Look. Moles are too busy. They don't have time for poker."

In thinking about what Charley said about not trusting anybody, it sounded like the standard agency paranoia and the type of mentality that emanated from the KGB. Enemies everywhere. Limit access of information to those who need to know. Otherwise, there will be leaks. Charley had dealt so long with the Russians that he was starting to think and behave like them. I stood up to stretch my legs and began to pace around like Charley.

"You know, Charley, if I start looking at all my fellow agents as potential traitors and not trustworthy, or all my sources and informants as potential plants, everyone will feel I'm paranoid."

"Precisely," said Charley. "Being paranoid is good. Spies are paranoid. That's why most of them do not get caught."

"Yeah, but Freud linked paranoia to homosexual tendencies."

"Fuck Freud. He was consumed with sex. Being paranoid is the price of liberty. In this business you have to be paranoid. It will not only keep you on your toes, but it will give you an edge. Now, come with me." He stood up and took me by the arm and ushered me to a desk, perhaps twenty feet away from his, upon which sat several files with a large number of papers and documents.

"You can work here and can begin by familiarizing yourself with current Russian cases contained in these files. It will give you a bird's-eye view of what is happening and how we do things.

But before you get started, do you see Alex over there?" he said, pointing to a large man standing next to a conference room twenty feet away.

"Wow. I thought the bureau had weight restrictions."

"Not if you are born heavy. He needs you to sit in with him while he interviews one of our informants. Take a break and give him a hand."

CHAPTER 10

STREET SMARTS

———◆———

I WALKED OVER ACROSS THE room. Twenty feet away was a small office, and standing outside the door gesturing me to come over was Alex Santoya, a large, brawny fiftyish agent, with unkempt dark hair, wearing a bright blue shirt and tie that emphasized what I surmised was a Florida tan.

Large and brawny may not be enough to describe Alex. He was huge, perhaps three hundred pounds, and one of the most intimidating, frightening men I had ever encountered. For some reason I wondered to myself where he bought his clothes. They were rumpled and not color coordinated. Up until this point in my life, I'd never seen any man wearing a suit with red socks.

Alex had enough ample flesh that when he sat down, he could easily break a government chair. He radiated power and had the physical demeanor of someone you didn't want to mess with. On his side was a holstered .357 Magnum.

I walked over and held out my hand. "Hello, Alex. Charley sent me over to sit in on this."

"You look too clean and nice," he said pleasantly.

"Just got here. Trying to make a decent impression."

"Excellent. Come on in and meet Tony." We shook hands, and I stepped into the room, where I observed our informant standing and looking around.

The room Alex picked had the smell of a dentist's office, something unique and recognizable. When I was small and entered such an office, the odor, perhaps from the drilling and grinding, always terrified me. I thought to myself that maybe this was the interview room's purpose. I entered this one trying to keep smiling.

The place was cluttered with the usual stone-gray government filing cabinets, a desk, several uncomfortable-looking wooden chairs, and a hat rack. This brought to mind contradictions from what we learned about interview rooms in our FBI training class, which at the time seemed a bit bizarre, studying and thinking about what furniture should exist or where it should be placed in an interview room, or where you should sit, but then I thought to myself, "Hey! Maybe there is a method or some useful purpose to their madness, like calculating the number of stairs or steps needed to build a staircase."

A good interview room, according to our government bible, had two chairs, one table, and a lamp with something brighter than a 50-watt bulb. That was it. If someone had to look into the light from a window, let the interviewee be the one. Don't sit him near the window. You sit between him and the window, with one caveat. When doing the interview, if not in the room that the government owns or is renting, always sit facing the door, because you don't want someone popping in before you see them first. Doc Holiday had it right. There are many people you want to see first before they see you.

I was thinking about all of this when Alex motioned for me to close the door, which I did. Our informant, a thirtyish guy, stood in front of me. He reached over to an ashtray to stub out his cigarette.

"Deuce, this is Tony Brazzale. Tony this is Deuce," Alex said. "Why don't you guys sit down."

I shook hands with Tony and took a chair near the door. Tony sat down next to the desk, peered straight ahead, ignoring me, and looked like a morose inmate about to be interrogated about a murder or rape charge by the cops. He was wearing cotton trousers, a sleeveless sweatshirt, and soiled dusty boots. He was muscular, with callused hands. Brazzale had to be some outdoor construction or dock worker. He didn't belong in a building like this unless he was constructing it. Later I learned that Brazzale worked on the New York waterfront, tending to the ships that came into the harbor. The docks were a place where violence and corruption ran rampant, where workers lived under a state of suspicion and it was always for more than the theft of a few bananas. Brazzale supplied information on union activities.

The government reasoned that since there was money around the docks, a lot of money, you would always find someone in the union who was going to pig out. It was never a case of the government looking through dirty glasses and always finding something dirty. With unions there was always something, something that you could find to pin a felony rap on someone. Brazzale was simply another means of getting access to it, an alternative to wiretapping to find the something.

One of my favorite books in my American lit class in college was Robert Penn Warren's book *All the Kings Men*. There was a passage in it I memorized. Willy was speaking to Jack Burden and said: "There is always something. Man is conceived in sin and born in corruption and he passeth from the stink of the didie to the stench of the shroud. There is always something." Yes, there was indeed always something dirty you could find on just about everyone.

It didn't help the unions that they had been a major thorn in the government's side. When that happened, there was always a reluctance to cut them slack and give them the benefit of the doubt that everyone was going straight and everything, copasetic.

I had to give Brazzale credit. Here he was in a small room talking to two government agents, one being an intimidating monster of a man, and he didn't look scared. He had the eyes and fearless stare of a coyote. He also looked tough, like someone who would snuff you out, just for recognition. His arms offered a plethora of tattooed emblems, one being an uncoiled serpent. It always seemed like the common denominator of every informant that was interviewed was some kind of tattoo.

Informants are not altar boys. Brazzale had served two years in the slammer for grand theft. Back on the street, Brazzale did not become an honest man, which was probably good for us. He became useful, providing information on criminal activity because he was involved with criminal activity, or at least around criminal activity, which was what made him a great stool pigeon. I suspected that he assumed this status because Alex leaned on him, threatening to revoke his probation and send him back to the slammer if he didn't cooperate.

To be an informant, to become a made man with us, Brazzale had to have given information leading to two or more separate federal cases. Brazzale was a criminal informant, and if he was good, if the information he supplied was decent, which could prevent or resolve criminal activity and lead to the prosecution of some bad guys, he would receive on a regular monthly basis considerable bucks in exchange—money that he never need reported on his tax return, if he even filed one.

As it turned out from what I learned from Alex, Brazzale was extremely good and was the source of many useful tips, providing accurate advance information on criminal activity that led to several felony convictions.

Alex was now standing in front of Brazzale. He looked down at Tony for about a minute without saying anything. He had a puzzled expression as if he were trying to read something on the face of Tony, who sat there motionless, looking up. Finally, he asked, "How old are you Brazzale?"

"Thirty-one."

"Tony," Alex said, speaking in a calm voice, "the trouble with you is that you haven't grown up yet. I like you. I've enjoyed working with you, and we appreciate the information you have provided from time to time. You know that. It may seem like a nothing to you, but how many times have I asked you in a nice way not to fuck around or harass the young female clerks when you call or come into this office? Huh? How many times?"

Brazzale looked up with a smile and smirk on his face, simply shrugged, and said nothing. He was now sitting hunched in his chair, hands folded in front, staring at the floor, shivering.

"I think you know," Alex said. "Don'tcha? These girls are impressionable, Brazzale, real young, right out of high school, and when some meathead like you jolts them with profanity and hits on them, they run home and tell their mamas. Their mamas find that offensive. They get very upset, and do you know who they call, Brazzale?"

Brazzale didn't answer. He looked away from Alex like a young kid being scolded.

"Me—that's who. It creates personnel issues in this office, and I get blamed because you are my guy. I don't like that. My ass gets chewed out. Do you understand, Brazzale?"

The blood was now up in Alex's face, and he was pacing in front of Tony, shaking his head.

I looked over at Brazzale, who now had a smile and smirk on his face, and I thought to myself, Jesus, all of this because Tony got a little fresh with one or two of the young girls in the office. For a long moment, I thought that this was going to be the end of it, a reprimand and admonishment of sorts, something that would now stick with Brazzale, but it wasn't the end of it. I knew something was coming, so I just sat there and waited for it. I looked over at Alex. He caught my glance and winked at me. It was theater. It was like something I was viewing and worked on in one of my college drama classes, from the writings of Konstantin Stanislavski, the Russian theater guy and daddy of method acting, which was what spying and counterespionage were all about.

Alex momentarily looked away, peering outside the window. I watched Alex pace back and forth in front of Tony, and finally he stopped. Then with one swoop, he sprung around and, with his right fist, swung and coldcocked Brazzale on the left side of his jaw. The blow sent Brazzale spinning wildly backward over the chair, landing on the floor with a bloodied face and head against the hat rack.

"Goddamn it," Alex said. "No more harassment, Brazzale, do you understand? Give me some kind of sign, Brazzale, that you know what I'm telling you. Are you going to do it again?"

I sat there motionless, saying nothing, doing nothing, looking at the sprawled body of Brazzale, who for a few minutes lay prone without moving. It was a hell of a punch. For a moment I thought we might have to summon an in-house doc, if there was one, to bring Brazzale back to life or keep him alive. Finally, however, Brazzale leaned up on his right elbow and, with his left hand, covered the blood that was streaming from his mouth.

"I understand," said Brazzale.

"No, you don't understand. Speak up louder, and tell me you understand," said Alex.

"I'm telling you I understand!" yelled Brazzale.

"You do this one more time," said Alex, "and you and I are going to part company. There will be no more money going to you to help you with your rent."

I looked at Brazzale and thought to myself that his face looked worse than anything Horse Higgins had ever inflicted. Brazzale's eyes looked numb, probably like his jaw, and he had considerable blood coming from his mouth. Alex looked back at me and said, "Do you have any tissues? If not, look for some Kleenex on my desk outside the door, would you please?"

After the interview was over and Brazzale left, with a few hundred bucks in his pocket, Alex called me over to his desk.

"Look," he said, "we don't write this up. OK?"

"OK," I said.

"I'll put something in the file that he was here. Security logged him in. We don't lie."

"OK," I said. "We don't lie. We just omit certain things."

"Right. I know you are relatively new here. I suppose you think I should not have done what I did in there?"

"I think I'm beginning to understand why we have an ACLU. Frankly, it's a little late to be asking me that question, isn't it? Even if you had asked my opinion before we got started, you knew damn well what you were going to do anyway."

"Perhaps. After you've been around a long time, experience will tell you to always go with your instincts. My instincts told me that this was the best way to remedy the situation."

Alex paused, leaned back, and extended his arms and hands behind his head. "Besides, the blow to his jaw will wear off, and the laceration will heal. If I wanted to, I could have broken his nose or his jaw as well as other body parts."

"Yeah, or killed him, but aren't you concerned about what it does to his heart and his impression of us?"

"Heart? This guy is like most lawyers. He has no heart or even a conscience."

"But what if he was to haul off and die and the ACLU gets involved? Striking his head could cause internal bleeding in his brain. How would you explain it if you are now a defendant in a civil-rights suit?"

"Deuce," Alex said very calmly, "as a defendant I might start out by saying this guy's brain needed some fixin'. A blow to the jaw is not torture. We're not using a cattle prod. We deal with liars, rogues, psychos, prostitutes, pimps, drug dealers, and hustlers. Brazzale is a tough, corrupt, street-savvy dockworker and not an industrious honest man. The problems in this world are generally caused by people twenty to forty. Hitler, Napoleon, Lenin, Brazzale—the list is endless."

"I'll buy that."

"OK, then listen to me. In this job you have to care about people, protecting them, not just the young girls in this building, but everyone walking the street. When you fight to win, you have to be ruthless. Even brutal. All else is secondary."

I sat back and thought about that, for if that was the case, it was not going to be tough to avoid excitement in this town. Maybe, I thought, Alex had a problem with his blood pressure, but refused to live quietly. I said nothing. Alex was behaving like a teacher, talking to a pupil who wasn't yet familiar with New York City streets. And I wasn't.

Alex then propped his elbow on the desk and pointed his index finger at me. "Answer this question. How do we change man so that he doesn't do this sort of thing? A guy like Brazzale doesn't understand certain language like 'please' or 'we would appreciate that you don't do this.' What he does understand, however, is violence. Sometimes hitting someone is the only way to get the message across. Today he got the message. This is New York City. You have to be aggressive and tough."

"Alex," I replied, "yes, this is New York and I intend to be aggressive and tough. Frankly, I think I am at times too impatient, aggressive, and tough. But the likelihood of my ever agreeing to sit in with you on another informant interview is remote, because what you did in there is simply not right. Have you read any of Dostoyevsky's stuff?"

"Some," replied Alex.

"Good and evil is the yin and the yang of the human condition, and evil is the exercise of power, which is what you had going in there. We are interviewing the guy in the FBI office, aren't we? What is Brazzale supposed to do? Fight back. The line of good and evil cuts through the heart of every individual. You can be on one side or the other. We are supposed to be in here fighting evil, right?"

"Deuce. Yes, evils exist that can't be justified, but life is not totally immersed in good and evil. Look at Don Quixote. He was mad. When he entered reality, he had to live. It's living and being alive that gets you in trouble."

"Yeah, but if we start to become evil ourselves, then we've lost it."

"We haven't lost anything, and we're not being evil. Look, you're wallowing in false spirituality and flawed logic. Empty rhetoric. Like you, I grew up in the Midwest, went to college, became a cop working in the Bronx, and then joined the FBI. I arrived here, like you, very idealistic. That was fifteen years ago. When you have been here long enough, you will start to see things differently. Every day we are up to our neck with shit. When you fight crime in this city, the very best you can hope for is control. Crime can never be totally eliminated or defeated.

What little we are able to do, we do as best we can. That includes sending a message to guys like Brazzale in ways that you may now believe to be unorthodox."

"So what is it you are trying to tell me?"

"What I'm trying to tell you is fuck Dostoyevsky. Dostoyevsky never lived or worked as a cop in New York City. If our purpose is to do what we can to stomp out wickedness as a whole, virtuousness, goodness, and righteousness in saying 'please don't do this' to guys like Brazzale is not going to cut it and is booked for defeat in New York. Always has been. Always will be."

"Really."

Alex paused and looked at me. "You got it. Revenge, reprisal, and violence—it's all there for you to read about, even in the Bible. Check out Hebrews 11."

I sat there, and for a long time, we just looked at each other and said nothing. I finally shook hands with Alex, got up, and left.

That was my introduction to New York.

For days and weeks thereafter, I pondered the future, what I would do with guys like Brazzale and New York City, where the woes of America were visible and present. Create a better life for the people. I thought about what Alex had said and did, and in time after the work load grew, after I became dug in, in the city, and saw what was happening on the street, I concluded that Alex had found the right reason for violence. The place had to be saved. You had to administer justice through faith that you were doing the right thing. I knew that even the nuns in grade school would hit you in the kisser occasionally. There was no doubt a "give 'em hell" streak existed in everybody, and under certain circumstances, it was necessary to do what needed to be done, including following street rules, reprisals, and things that are unorthodox. Part of it comes down to losing patience and becoming tired of dealing with nonsense. Certain individuals are so inherently evil and bad that no amount of rehab or psychiatric counseling will help or cure them. Trying to talk sense and reason with these types of personalities is not going to happen. Working in New York, who had time for this? In a world rife with social injustice and corruption, we were here to fight crime and protect the security of the crime capital of the world. With the Russians it wasn't just about crime but internal security, and it wasn't just about New York City. Protection had to be extended to the Pacific. That meant we had to do what we needed to do to win. I was pumped and ready to get on with it.

CHAPTER 11

PAYBACK WITH THE MOB

———◆———

FOR WEEKS FOLLOWING THE BRAZZALE incident, due to lack of sleep (not from the Brazzale incident but simply trying to get dug in and used to the city), I arrived early at the office. The words of Alex had curiously given me some intense motivation. Although initially I felt I would have trouble working around a lunatic like Alex, my impression changed. I began to view him as simply a tough, eccentric cop whose heart was in the right place and who was calling out the best in me, calling me to take risky steps if necessary. His gung-ho commitment to fighting crime was becoming contagious. Run with perseverance to help people. It wasn't important what Dostoyevsky felt. The question to be asked is, what does God think of what I am doing? Am I on God's side? For lack of a better word, I was hungry and anxious to start producing in some fashion. I spent several hours of each day at my desk, reading and going through voluminous files, FD 302s and Russian investigative reports and memos, piecing together the MO of Russian spying in the city and Russian espionage in general.

After hours I even immersed myself in all the reading material I could find about A. R. (Kim) Philby, probably the most important Soviet agent to have penetrated Western intelligence.

Kim contended that he, Donald Maclean, and Guy Burgess were not detected mainly because of the British government's reluctance to investigate anyone with their upper-class and university backgrounds.

Charley was right. Trust nobody. Kim was a charming, likable guy with a lot of friends. If he could betray his country, he could easily betray a friend and even his wife.

The more I read, the more I became interested in unorthodox approaches and ideas that had been done in the past to combat this Russian menace, the likes of which included bag jobs, wiretaps, and even kidnappings of illegals. This should not be perplexing, for I am describing a solitary period of my life, reading and absorbing material, as an agent in New York, where I was growing and starting to think more and more like Alex. I started to view Alex as a guy who was really cool but who, as it turned out, according to Charley, did have blood-pressure problems. Charley's thoughts on this were simple: "Hey, there's not much you can do about high blood pressure except lose weight or leave the bureau. Around here, it's tough to avoid excitement."

One of the things we didn't do in the United States was behave like the British and avoid excitement. The British have a Department of Dirty Tricks. We didn't need a department to do bag jobs or swipe cars. We just did it.

Like any job there was always the initial learning process. However, this being internal security for the United States, I approached all of this with considerable thought, unbridled enthusiasm, and lofty purpose, spending even more time conversing with experienced older agents, picking their brains, and perusing manuals and journals of others who had come before me, taking notes, all the while inside planning on doing whatever needed to be done to eviscerate these foreign, unfunny, perverted Russian souls, who came out of a country whose economy was smaller than California. I gloated about this because the more I read, the more I was convinced that they were schmucks, drags, and comic characters from the word go whom we should easily be able to take advantage of and defeat, physically destroy, and wipe out.

Apart from this, though, there were other aspects of Russian concerns that needed to be addressed, which were becoming visible on the street, like war protests. We knew dissent of any kind within the United States was of interest to the Russians. Thus several of us, including Big D and the Poet, gathered at a coffee shop to round table procedures and a plan of attack to counter what was then a growing concern about Russian activities vis-à-vis these war protests, including New Left groups like the Black Panthers.

For me these coffee-shop discussions turned out to be one of the best parts of the day, with friends from the poker table, bullshitting about Russians and their routines. We were coming up with imaginative scenarios on how best to turn them to come over to our side.

Most of the discussions centered on antiwar protests. Much was happening on the streets. The anti-Vietnam protestors were out there, and the bureau learned through information procured from informants and foreign sources that these New Left groups—like the SNCC, SDS, Black Panthers, and others—were being funded by the Russians to foment unrest, burn cities, and create national havoc.

Charley mentioned that plans were being considered by the bureau to have agents and informants operate covertly within these groups to disrupt the antiwar movement. From the information obtained, we would then go on to make arrests, conduct bag jobs, the works. We were further considerably interested in the sources of revenue for these groups.

Back at the office, all of these Russian concerns were suddenly broken up when Charley walking hurriedly out of his cubbyhole motioned for me, Alex, the Poet, and several others to join him in a conference room.

He was looking serious and pale and beckoned us to sit down. I knew that something was up, perhaps a shooting, bank robbery, or some other emergency, which generally produced immediate attention and activity. We would drop everything we were doing and rush off to lend assistance to other agents doing criminal work in the city.

Charley came directly to the point.

"The Top Hood squad on the sixth floor has a problem. Several of their agents were in Brooklyn this morning on a surveillance covering a Guinea funeral at a Catholic church, taking photos and gathering license numbers. One of our guys was accosted outside his car. They took his gun. They beat him up bad. He's in the hospital. As I speak it's now a standoff. We need more agents out there. They are at the church. Get the details and location on the car radios. Go."

Alex looked over at me and the Poet and asked us to go with him by bureau car, with the red, blinking emergency light on the hood. We needed to make it over to Brooklyn in record time. As we gunned it through Manhattan, the hum of chatter and traffic on the car radio made it appear that the problem was not resolved.

Instead of trailing around mobsters taking down license numbers of cars parked at wakes to identify the owners, I wondered why we simply didn't get more informants. One or more could be wired, and the information and intelligence would improve. Then I thought that was easier said than done.

I turned to Alex and asked, "So who are these guys? I assume they all have nicknames: Jack the Whack, Little Lou Lollipops…"

Alex looked over at me incredulously, smiling. For him it was elementary.

"Dat's for real. Of course they all have nicknames. We, the pizza squad, gave them the names. They are under surveillance. We get to know them as well as you knew your college roommate. The nickname usually reflects their idiosyncrasy."

"Like sucking on lollipops," I said.

"Yeah, like sucking on lollipops or eating noodles. If one of their leaders felt it was time for Noodles to sleep with the fishes, he might call upon Frankie Lead Boots to handle things."

"I bet they even have a fallback guy," said the Poet, "like Fat Tony the Wood Chipper."

Alex then turned serious. "These guys are Catholic gangsters. Brutal Italian thugs and I do mean brutal. Cross them and they will hang you on a meat hook. They want loyalty and respect. They are one of the Cosa Nostra families. They make their money on illegal gambling, drugs, and narcotics. They have a monopoly on legitimate enterprises, like vending machines and trucking companies."

"Sounds like they are far beyond simple sloth and licentiousness. Point out the boss to me when we get there, OK?" I answered. "Will he be wearing a panama hat with a black band?"

"Look, I've spent a lot of time covering these guys. You do need to check out their clothes. They wear clothes that blend in to the crimes they are involved in, whether its marijuana, extortion, numbers, or rackets. When on the street, they dress like gamblers, drug addicts, alcoholics, and hippies. Anyway, the boss probably won't be around. We'll see. They are going to pay for this, the sons of bitches. Bastards."

Alex was up and looking forward to this trip. Looking at what he'd done with Brazzale, I started to imagine what he might do with these guys. Given the opportunity, this was the type of event he relished being a part of every day. He grew up in the Bronx, north of 161st Street and Yankee Stadium, went to college, came back, and as a cop worked some of the toughest streets in New York. He was more attuned and suited to dealing with the Mafia and fugitives than anyone in the federal building. He was often called to the sixth floor when they needed a heavy and somebody ruthlessly persuasive to obtain needed information. His demeanor and presence alone, along with occasional force, produced intimidation in the Mafia ranks during interviews with family members. Like Brazzale, that was the language they understood. Alex was a natural for this type of work.

Outside the Catholic church in Brooklyn, we saw Agent Harold Jensen, and upon seeing Alex he motioned for us to come over for a powwow.

"We think we can identify the two that worked our guy over, but it's not important now. It's the weapon we want back. Then we'll leave this place," said Jensen, motioning for Alex to take point and go inside the church to shake it up and give it much-needed tone. I looked at Alex, who said nothing but nodded at the Poet and me to follow him in.

Inside the church was the congregation, and what a congregation. The place was filled with hoods and families of hoods, men and women all crowded in rows from the front of the church to the back, serving God, incredulous, really, mercifully seeking redemption. It reminded me frankly of Catholic churches in Chicago at Christmastime, when everyone who had not been to church all year seemed to come out of the woodwork to attend mass. It was standing room only.

In the back of the church stood Sam Battaglia, a known Mafia chieftain with several body guards, who saw us coming and were waiting for us.

Alex nudged me. "See the guy there with the black suit and tie—that's Sam. He's the sotto capo, the underboss. We deal with him."

Sam looked every bit a gangster out of a 1940s movie. It was always amusing viewing Mafia guys. It was like they were trained to use their bodies to express toughness. Sam was standing there, chest out, ramrod-straight posture, erect and tall, with an unblinking gaze, as if he had had intense dramatic coaching.

As was customary with most Mafia chieftains, we had a lengthy file on Sam and his activities back at the office. He had a reputation of being a philanderer, which had him in half of the beds in Little Italy. To his credit, all of our investigative efforts identified his partners as females.

The congregation remained seated. No one appeared to be praying. No one was talking. It was total silence, except for occasional coughing, perhaps from smoke from a censer, I thought. No ringing of bells up front. If a priest had been conducting a mass, he apparently had run for cover.

Alex looked at Battaglia. Given the circumstances, I thought that Alex was controlling his rage quite well and, somewhat out of character, becoming amiable and tolerant.

"You know," he said to Battaglia, in a soft-spoken voice, "what you have done is very disrespectful and very stupid. The power of prayer here is not going to save you. We want the gun."

Battaglia stood upright. "We have no beef with you. We are here to honor the dead. I don't know what happened outside. Perhaps some of the neighbors acted foolishly."

Alex stared at Battaglia for a minute, and now his face wore a look of agitation and impatience. "Fuhgeddaboutit. That's not good enough. Did you think you were just taking from our agent a bottle of olive oil or vinegar?"

"Wait here," said Battaglia as he walked down the aisle to the front of the church. When he reached the front pew, he leaned over and whispered something to someone sitting in the front row. This man then raised his arm. In the center of the church, a sound of something moving under the pews could be heard. The sound was moving from the front of the church to the back. Finally the bureau Smith & Wesson revolver became visible under the last pew in the back of the church. Alex looked down and then looked over at me and nodded. I reached down and retrieved it.

Alex looked at Battaglia. "We know who did this. You've got uncontrolled roving wolf packs. We want you to give those chicken heads a message."

"I'm listening," said Battaglia.

"Tell them that today we are on your street. But tomorrow, tomorrow, you will be on our street."

We left the church with the revolver. I knew this was not the end of it. When dealing with the Mafia, being polite G-men was never in the cards. The issue was respect, reprisal, an eye for an eye, and making things right in a way like the Brazzale incident. Something would have to go down in a fashion they would understand. The agent who got beaten up could not identify the Mafia hoods, but we had a pretty good idea who was responsible. In Alex's world and the world of every New York agent, you couldn't let this incident stand. Letting the mob beat up one of our own was not something that we could let them get away with.

In the bureau car on the way back to the office, I turned to Alex and asked, "OK, what's the plan?"

"The plan? Something from your boy Dostoyevsky. Never let an enemy go unpunished."

A week later, I again arrived early at the office to be at my desk to go through Russian and KGB investigation files. I looked up to see Alex coming over with a copy of the *Daily News.* He smiled at me, winked, dropped the open paper on my desk, said nothing, turned around, and walked away.

In the middle of the paper was an article and photos of two white males, with Italian names lying prone in the middle of a street outside of a Lower East Side restaurant. They had been involved in a street fight or altercation of some kind. Although they looked dead, they weren't dead but had been taken to a hospital for serious fractured ribs and head injuries. The police reported that they refused to talk and were unable to identify their assailants.

CHAPTER 12

TRUE OR FALSE DEFECTORS

Thursday, May 23, 1968

ONCE A MONTH, ON THURSDAYS, the agents on our squad had a meeting reviewing cases with the Boss. We gathered in a large room and went over contacts made, new informants, and new material that came in from Washington, DC. There was a general discussion on what the KGB was doing and what they were interested in. These meetings were very informal, with no agenda.

Occasionally a CIA rep showed up. Today one did.

As usual he spoke in general terms, with no specifics or details. This was not unexpected. They knew a lot more but fed us generalities without disclosing a lot of details. It was like giving us placebos for psychological benefit to calm us and create an impression that they were in fact sharing.

We viewed the CIA guys as wimps, as in weak, timid chickens. They were bright, capable, Ivy League–type analytical guys who could read and dissect reports and then debate theories and solutions to problems. Get them on the street, however, and they were devoid of street savvy and toughness. Caught up with an inflated view of themselves and not wanting to get their clothes dirty, they didn't know how to throw a punch or when.

The most that could be said was that the two services got along, politely and civilly, but if they passed each other on the sidewalk, they behaved like two dogs with their fur going up. They were like parties to a pending divorce, each not entirely trusting the other and one or both complaining that the other side was concealing assets and valuable information. As with any divorce case, in truth they wished that the other side was dead and not around.

Initially at these gatherings, I felt very ill informed compared to the battle-tested FBI veterans, who had been around the block doing counterintelligence business for years. In dealing with the Russians and understanding their MO, many were savvy street fighters. I consequently was curious and excited to simply sit there and listen, contributing very little to any discussion.

The discussion centered on spies, a defector in place, wiretaps, installation of bugs, and the tools and strategy best needed to fight the Russians. But today was special. The Boss had resurrected and called into this gathering retreads and retired spooks to contribute and give their thoughts on Yuri Nosenko, a former KGB intelligence officer who'd defected to our side.

These spooks were in mothballs, old-school types and dead wood. They had studied Marxist dialectical materialism. They were retired now with some serving as bailiffs with the federal or state courts, double dippers, with the opportunity to draw yet another pension. They weren't begging for reinstatement.

Yuri Nosenko grew up in the Soviet Union, the son of an engineer, was educated by private tutors, and went on to graduate from the State Institute of International Relations in Moscow, before becoming employed with the KGB. The CIA recruited him in Geneva. He was a walk-in, which meant essentially just what it says. He initiated the contact and came in out of the blue to the surprise of those at the US embassy.

He was not the first Russian to voluntarily walk in. In 1961 a KGB major by the name of Anatoly Golitsyn walked into the CIA in Helsinki and thereafter provided extremely valuable information on KGB spies in several countries. It was Golitsyn who launched during the sixties the great mole scare within the CIA, claiming that the KGB had a spy or mole working within the Soviet division of the CIA. This ultimately caused a lot of investigation and soul searching by top management within the CIA, leading to much discontent and paralysis within the agency.

Nosenko and Golitsyn were at the core of this in-house discussion, the reason being that the two defectors took conflicting views. Golitsyn claimed there was a KGB mole within the CIA. Nosenko disagreed. These two opposing views led to elaborate case studies of the two defectors to try to determine who was telling the truth. What were the reasons for the contradictions? One faction within the CIA felt that Nosenko was a Soviet plant sent to deceive us.

We sat around debating this issue. One agent, George, now in mothballs, blamed the CIA for withholding and refusing to share with its sister agency a lot of facts to assist agents to make an informed judgment on the subject. He had a decent argument.

Golitsyn and Nosenko were both CIA assets. We had no transcripts of their debriefing and interview sessions. We thus had limited data to examine to help in understanding our adversary. Some defectors are extremely valuable. In terms of their credibility, much depends on what their position was in the KGB, what their duties were, and what they had access to within their organization.

Golitsyn analyzed data that came in from spies in many countries who were reporting on NATO. Nosenko was different, not simply in the type of job he held but also as to motivation.

Golitsyn without advance notice walked in and immediately defected. Nosenko, on the other hand, stayed in place and worked from within the KGB for a period of time passing secrets to the United States, which was much more dangerous and daring. In 1964 he finally defected.

According to the CIA rep, Nosenko's motivation in doing this was money. He needed money to pay debts.

I looked over at the Knife and smiled. "It sounds like Lone Louie," I whispered. "Maybe his job at the publishing house is a cover."

Nosenko did not wish to defect because his family was still in Russia. In terms of the type of work he performed, Nosenko was assigned to security in the Second Chief Directorate of the KGB, which meant simply that his duties were to watch over other Russians who at the time were also present in Geneva. After his walk-in and following his defection, the process of debriefing Nosenko by the CIA began in earnest, which meant lengthy sessions or interviews by CIA agents with Nosenko at some secure spot. He was bright, curious, and seemingly cooperative. He supplied a lot of information, including material on hidden microphones that the Russians planted in the American embassy in Moscow, but more importantly, he supplied information on Lee Harvey Oswald. He explained that the Russians looked at Oswald as a screwball and that the Russians had nothing to do with Kennedy's assassination.

Oswald did have a sojourn for a period of time in Russia. But was Nosenko being truthful? Was he a KGB plant?

According to the CIA rep, "In the CIA the jury is still out," meaning the issue was still being debated. After Nosenko testified before the House of Representatives Select Committee on Assassinations, the committee concluded he was lying regarding many of the facts supplied about Oswald. His bona fides, his sincerity, and his credibility were questioned and never accepted.

Further his debriefing brought up a lot of inconsistencies in his background, career, and work with the KGB, and thus for many in the CIA, his defection was some kind of ruse, something clever thought up by the Russians to provide disinformation, causing our government to proceed on some military or scientific project in a different direction, or maybe even to lead us away from finding a mole within the FBI or CIA.

Although having a defector was a reason to gloat with success, ultimately it could end up as a calamity if the guy was not for real. Tying up resources and sending us on a wild goose chase were things we did not want and had no time for.

Thus, what motivated Nosenko in coming over? According to our CIA rep, Nosenko needed money to repay some debt owed to the KGB, as a result of a one-night stand with a Swiss prostitute. Must have been an expensive prostitute, I thought. Why would he defect and abandon a wife and two young daughters, knowing that he would probably never see them again?

The conclusion came down to a whiff that something was not really right about his defection, and if his defection was not felt to be right, if there was a slight doubt, then it was wrong. Assuming that to be true, what should be done about the information he provided? Should we accept it as true? Should we spend tons of man hours going through all the facts to see if it was fiction? Who had time for this?

There were other problems. Now that he had defected and was in the United States, should we let him roam around freely to do whatever amused him, or should we lock him up, until we determined that he was in fact sincere and bona fide? Interestingly and not necessarily puzzling to me, the FBI agents in the room were clearly divided with responses to these questions.

The discussion went on and on for hours.

I got tired of it. Nothing was going to be resolved. I looked over at the Poet and motioned him to join me outside.

"What say we go visit Big D?" I asked.

"Let's do it," said the Poet. "I'll call him and give him a heads-up."

CHAPTER 13

WATCHING THE WATCHER

———

D WAS IN A SAFE house working as a watcher. D was dark haired, lanky, and lean and about twenty-eight. He was a beanpole who could eat and drink enough for two men but would never gain weight. It was always fun and amusing to be around him. With work, however, everything with D took on a serious bent.

Covering Russians and keeping tabs on their comings and goings to Big D was a game of chess, and Big D loved this game. The safe house was located near the Soviet mission to the United Nations on East Sixty-Seventh Street. The Soviet mission was located on a prime piece of Manhattan real estate. It was an eight-story building, brick, dark windows, a foreboding gloomy apartment-looking complex surrounded with a black metal fence. It could have served nicely as a mortuary. It sat across the street from a building that housed an organization concerned about the Jewish community in the Soviet Union.

Outside the Soviet mission, nothing was visible to tell you what it was, except a New York City cop, who stood in front to provide some level of protection and security to those inside. From prior defectors and foreign sources who had been guests in the complex, we knew quite a bit about the building.

The place was filled with offices and apartments where Russian families resided. The interior of these apartments was not typical of ordinary Russian homes in that it was much more modern and stylish. It was filled with Oriental carpeting, chairs, settees, and so forth. The windows in all the rooms could not be opened and were hung with velvet curtains.

The kitchens were beautifully equipped with appliances and built-in cabinets. The apartments were spacious with high ceilings.

On the roof of the Soviet mission, antennae and assorted electronic equipment protruded like so many flowers and weeds. They didn't exist to broadcast nighttime news.

The job of Big D was to monitor the movements of the diplomats and known KGB agents attached to the mission. Big D was good. Houdini could not get by him. The mission had to be watched for good reasons.

As the Boss pointed out, "Conclude that every individual in there is working in intelligence. They are spies, pure and simple."

People would come and go from the mission. Big D knew everybody—well, just about everybody, as I'll explain. He knew their habits, their style of dress, their gait, and their manner of walking. He estimated and knew their shoe size and could tell whether their fingernails were chewed upon, giving some clue to the stress they were enduring.

On the rare occasions that D came across people he didn't know, it was our job to identify them and find out why they were in the mission or associating with the Russians. This was not always easy. The Russians had cars with tinted windows. These were not black Zils, Chaikas, or Volgas that could easily be spotted on the street, but rather American vehicles.

The Russians had an escape hatch from the mission. To depart unnoticed, Russian chauffeur-driven vehicles drove in and out of their subterranean garage. When that happened, we had no idea who was inside the vehicle, up to a point. With the aid of a bloodhound attached or secreted in the vehicle, we could often say, "Gotcha." In a federal courtroom, with the walk-in or collaborator looking thoroughly perplexed, thinking, "I bet you can't answer the question of whether I was inside the vehicle," the judge would rule for the assistant US attorney, stating that they have met their burden of proof. The dude was dirty.

The cars also had telltale UN license plates, which helped in identifying a vehicle on the street.

When out and about driving around, Russians disregarded no-parking signs. They charged through intersections, not worried about traffic tickets or the police. They felt they were back home in the Kremlin, where as part of the privileged class they behaved like czarist nobility and got away with everything. They were of course the upper crust.

Other than the diplomats, there were other Russian individuals assigned to the Soviet mission, such as chauffeurs, secretaries, and maids. We gave these individuals a free pass with no coverage. The task of monitoring was overwhelming. We had to prioritize.

The Russians and their families left the mission in large numbers every day. They loved to shop for American goods, focusing on beautiful, expensive stuff: imported chocolates, French perfumes, name-brand clothing. They brought back to the mission Russian delicacies, such as caviar, smoked salmon, and various imported brands of vodka. After a day of shopping, they came back to the mission lugging bulging bags of clothing, edible goods, and merchandise.

Shopping was a hot endeavor of Soviet society, because a black market in Russia fed on goods from the Western world, to a degree that a diplomat could double his income simply by carrying home Levi's from the United States.

While present in the United States, Russians had no allowance. When KGB officers returned to Moscow to go back to spy school for more in-house training, they could be seen at JFK Airport loaded down with luggage and packages that could fill a small van. When they arrived home in Moscow, nothing was confiscated. They were waved through customs. They were the privileged class.

In Moscow these Russians received the very best medical care. If they needed medical attention in the United States, they visited US hospitals, but they avoided doctors who were Jews, even though the Jewish doctors in New York were arguably the best professionally. They did not trust Jews.

Of course there was the other side of the coin, which concerns itself in part with emigration of the Soviet Jews from the Soviet Union. Jews were not treated well in Russia. Their mobility in moving up the ladder in jobs both within and without the government was limited. Because they were suppressed, Jews started to emigrate from the Soviet Union in large numbers, causing a serious scientific brain drain. Protests and demonstrations by young Jews objecting to the treatment they received were worldwide. This explained the location of the Jewish building across the street from the mission.

After a short walk, the Poet and I entered D's building through the rear entrance. We climbed the stairs to his apartment, where a security guard let us in. Big D was at his desk with earphones on. In front of him was a large ledger to record information, a microphone, and extensive state-of-the-art camera equipment to assist him in his dual role of earnest paparazzi. It was D's place. When you think of mess, he was a Tar Heel all right. There were coffee cups, ashtrays, and mounds of papers scattered about, along with binoculars, zoom lenses, and a slew of technical equipment.

Back in North Carolina, the distillation process for tar and pitch was always messy, but it was a small price to pay for getting the Tar Heels on your side. They were a tough, noble class and caused a lot of trouble for the North in the Civil War. One hundred years later, Big D in his messy compound was now causing a lot of trouble for the Russians.

From this location, it was like being on top of a hill overlooking a valley. It was a piece of cake to see what was going on and a great position for a sniper. D had a great memory for faces. As soon as he identified a Russian leaving the mission, he gave us a call. As foot soldiers, we took over the surveillance.

Big D stood up, all six foot seven inches of him, and moved closer to the venetian blinds covering the window. He stood with his back to me, his forehead pressed against the blinds, peering through a crack between the blinds like a sex-craving satyr. He finally turned around. He was laughing and with eyes glittering motioned the Poet and me to come over.

"Hey! Come look at this, guys. Something is rotten in the state of Denmark."

I walked over, put my arm around D's shoulder, and peered through the blinds. The windowpane was trembling from traffic and noise coming from the street. Below me a large demonstration was going on across the street from the Soviet mission. There were newsmen with cameras walking around the edge of the crowd, along with the blue coats of mounted cops on horses. The crowd was yelling and chanting something unintelligible.

It was the Jewish Defense League (JDL), a volatile, controversial, aggressive Jewish organization, street fighters all, who would go into the streets to make a point, in this case to highlight the plight of millions of oppressed Jews, suffering behind the Iron Curtain. A few of the demonstrators were throwing eggs at the Soviet mission. It was like Halloween in a small town revisited, where kids with eggs or soap would pummel the homes of residents they did not like and use BB guns to pop out street lights.

I stood at the window, looking down at the crowd. I felt like a historian brooding on history. "These guys are unconventional, aren't they? What's going on?"

D turned around and had a shit-eating grin on his face.

"Every time something happens in the Middle East or if there is a problem with Jews behind the Iron Curtain, the Soviet mission gets hit with a demonstration. I don't mind it. There is less traffic in and out. The Russians stay inside, and it keeps them occupied. Who wants to walk to work with egg on their face?"

"I suppose the demonstration accomplishes something," I said.

"Yeah, it calls attention to certain issues, but it costs the city of New York plenty. They pull more police and place them in front of the mission. Ties up Midtown traffic. People get upset. We are never consulted. We never know when these demonstrations are going to take place."

I looked at D and glanced at the Poet. "So what are you saying? They should not demonstrate?"

"They are wasting energy," said Big D.

I was not an authority on anguish and suffering. I thought to myself that the demonstration out there was because Asian Jews were being oppressed. "Maybe we have to look under the surface of things," I said.

"Under the surface of what?"

"D, the Jews and the JDL need money. Up in my neighborhood, they are so hard-pressed they walk the streets in pajamas. It's fund-raising time. They make a splash, throw a few eggs, get some publicity and a few people thrown in jail, and then the money from donors flows in. There is a method to their madness. It calls public attention to the problem."

"Hey!" said D. "That girl Cathy you have been dating. It's about her roommate. From her fair and unpolluted flesh may violets spring."

"So, you change the subject with more Shakespeare and give up on this debate already? I'll work on C to find a date for you. What would you like? Male or female? How about a sweet, black guy, airline steward, nice body, fun?"

"Hey, that'll work."

"What else is new?" I asked. "What's Yuri doing?"

"I forgot, Deuce. You're the guy that Yuri Popov is assigned to. Yeah, I've got some news for you. Mrs. Yuri spends a lot of time with Vladimir. She may even be in his room as we speak. Yuri went off to the UN early this morning. After he leaves, Mrs. Yuri and Vladimir generally have a rendezvous."

I looked at D. I was perturbed and a little angry.

"Rendezvous, as in a tête-à-tête or tryst. Like one today?"

"Yeah," said D, "like one today. They smooch and talk about things like a large necklace or pendant the gal wears."

"Jesus, D, you have to keep me informed."

"Except, it's not a big deal."

"What do you think the KGB is going to do if they find out Yuri's wife is fucking somebody else?" asked the Poet.

"The KGB would probably do very little," I said. "But Yuri might. They could clash, just like we do. How do you know this is happening?"

D grinned. "We have had Vladi's room bugged for over six months."

"Who is Vladi, and how can he get away with this?" I asked.

"Vladi outranks Yuri," said Big D, smiling and winking. "He gets special privileges, professional courtesy, that sort of thing."

I looked at the Poet, smiled, and said nothing for about a minute. Finally, the Poet said, "I know what I would do if he were my guy."

"D," I said, "let me make sure I understand this. We are not snooping with a camera in the interior of the room, but rather a small bug?"

"Right."

"Like how secure is this bug? The Russians sweep those rooms regularly, don't they?"

D shrugged his shoulders. "As far as we know, they are regularly swept. It's not a camera but a small listening apparatus, and it's different. It's more secure, sophisticated, and sensitive. It's outside the building. They will never find this one."

In point of fact, a few things must be wedged in here. Inside the mission, the Soviets had specially designed secure rooms, where they could meet and talk securely. From contractors we knew, they were double walled. What they lacked was ventilation. Outside the building, however, we had bugs and cameras.

Placement of concealed cameras outside buildings directed toward a target like the Soviet mission or something else was interesting and amusing. The choice of a location for a device was often debated. With buildings over a certain height, New York City had fire codes, which required that a water reservoir be maintained to provide water service, for use in the building and for fire protection. The roof tanks were designed to deliver clean water. Many people felt the water was contaminated with E. coli. However, the city's Health Department insisted that the water posed no risk to public health.

Some large office buildings used over twenty thousand gallons of water in an hour. Thus these water tanks, composed of cedar wood that resembled large grain silos, were built. What was convenient was that the tanks operated and provided an available tripod to steady a camera, which looked down on and focused on another building.

Climbing these wooden monsters to plant the camera could be amusing and required an agent with both physical prowess and grappling hooks, but the end result was effective.

"D," I said, "I need to use your secure phone."

"Be my guest," replied D.

I walked over to the telephone, lifted the receiver, and dialed Yuri's office number at the UN building. A woman with a strong Slavic accent answered.

"Miss," I said, "may I speak with Yuri? There is a family emergency, and I need to speak to him immediately."

"Certainly," she replied.

I waited for several minutes. Finally, a strong male voice came on the line, answering, "Yes."

"Is this Yuri Popov?" I asked.

"Yes," came the response.

"Hello, Yuri. This is a friend. It's about your wife. Is she a bit depressed? Your wife's cure-all for everything appears to be sex. She has been having an affair with your associate Vladimir, who himself appears to be undergoing a psychosexual crisis. Things transpire after you go to work in the morning. She was with him earlier, having sexual intercourse. Beautiful necklace. Did you get that for her as an anniversary gift? Do you need more details?"

There was total silence for over a minute. Finally, a response came.

"That won't be necessary. Thank you."

He hung up. I looked over at the Poet and Big D, and for a while everyone was quiet. Then D started laughing.

"Deuce, you are so bad," he said. "Poor Yuri. When sorrows come, they come not as single spies, but in battalions."

"Yeah, right," I said, "if Yuri knew nothing about what was going on, it's certainly sad that it should come to this."

"Were you some sort of tattletale in high school?" D asked. "You know what General MacArthur thought of tattletales, don't you?"

"D, fuck MacArthur," I said as I got up and walked over to the window. "MacArthur was too caught up in his own image."

"Yeah," said D, "but he was good."

"Come on. With the Russians, it's a tough game. Our job is to become a master manipulator, isn't it? I'm trying to manipulate Yuri's mind. We have to sow dissension, don't we? That's how we win, right?"

"Actually," said the Poet, "it's not how we win. It's not like poker. No one wins this game. We never even know if we are winning. Maybe Yuri doesn't give a shit about his wife shacking up. Twenty years from now, if the three of us are sitting in this room, nothing will have changed. In the scheme of things, we are playing a role with a large machine or game. Call it pachinko. This game will outlive us."

"Good point," said D. "We play the game. We try to win. We keep the machine or game running. We're just mechanics, looking in, making a diagnosis, trying to keep all the parts running properly and greased."

"And," I chimed in, "the Russians are like pinballs. We have to bang them around and manipulate them with our flippers to rack up points."

The Poet grinned. "With that information concerning his wife, your flipper might have just struck Yuri in the ass."

"Maybe he'll become disenchanted," I said and looked out again at the Soviet mission across the street.

"Do you ever get the feeling there is a lot going on over there that we don't know about?"

"All the time. That is because there is," said D. "Though this be madness, yet there is method in it. The visible things are not what we have to worry about."

"Yeah, it's the clandestine things we have to worry about," I said as I raised my right hand, separating a portion of the blinds with my fingers. The building across the street was filled with several hundred Russian men and a handful of beautiful Russian women. They ate together, drank vodka neat together, went to The Russian Tea Room together, spooned up borscht together, went to their holiday hideaway at the Rockaways together, went to see *Doctor Zhivago* together, and did a ton of shopping together.

I looked over at the Poet.

"With all of that togetherness across the street, it boggles the mind to think that there would be dalliances, infidelity, and hanky-panky going on in the house that Stalin built."

"What happened to all of their discipline?" said the Poet.

"I'm flat-out shocked. Aren't you?" I said.

The Poet grinned. "I'm shocked. It's like being shocked to find gambling going on in a casino."

"There is so much hanky-panky you can hear hot breathing in the walls," said D.

"Hot breathing?" I say. "How about heavy panting? There is a difference."

"Their boss in there knows what is going on. The interior walls are encrusted with Russian concealed cameras and wires," said D.

"So where do you think they gossip and talk about fornication or overthrowing the government?" I asked.

"Probably in the john," said Big D, "where you can flush the toilet."

"Fornication and adultery are not illegal in Russia," said the Poet. "Shit, you can even get an erection in public in Moscow without going to jail."

Big D started laughing once again. "Hey. It's OK to get an erection on the street in the USA too, so long as you keep it in your pants. And speaking of erections," D hollered, as the Poet and I were walking toward the door, "don't forget to ask C to find me a date."

The Poet and I returned to the office. The conversation there was still on Yuri Nosenko. We hadn't missed much. But like a Jeremiah, Charley O, who was getting a lot of heat from the seat of government, finally stood up. He was still pontificating about Nosenko and called down verbal thunder to reemphasize his plan or focus on how best to meet the Soviet threat, given our limited resources. The thunder was filled with doom and gloom. In his words it was all about priority.

"The Russians are aggressive. Focus and cover the individuals that are critical to national security. Don't let them ever get the advantage. Let them know we are on their asses and that we are the alpha dog."

With that the room erupted with shouts as if it was a Notre Dame halftime locker room. "We're going to take it to them, Charley!" we shouted.

CHAPTER 14

THE SPY WHO WANTED IN

———————◆———————

Monday, May 27, 1968

IT WAS WHEN I ARRIVED at the New York office that I commenced covering and being responsible for the KGB intelligence officer assigned to the Soviet mission named Yuri Popov.

After assigning me to Yuri, the Boss handed me several large files pertaining to his history and background. They contained detailed memos and government reports from the Immigration and Naturalization Service, US embassies abroad, and the CIA.

When Yuri arrived in the United States, photos showed a stout, heavyset, middle-aged male clad in a dark baggy suit, wearing heavy black shoes. Memos from sources in the CIA, defectors, and the State Department revealed the branch of the Soviet intelligence Yuri occupied. He was a high-level intelligence officer. Only the best and the brightest were picked by the KGB to go to America.

We knew that during the first year he was in New York, he would do very little spying. He had to become acclimated to the ways and customs of the people here. He didn't know the subway system, didn't know Uptown from Downtown and was a mere babe in the woods about New York City life. He walked the streets of Manhattan, rode the subway, and would sightsee and shop. He did not seem like a real oddball, but behaved like a tourist. He went out drinking a lot. During the day at the United Nations, he'd ease out the side entrance. He'd then visit a bar for vodka or brandy. On those occasions I was always looking and watching for a connect or drop area.

About six months later, he was called back to the Russian spy school for retraining and for a review of all he had learned. He returned to Moscow loaded down with enough American goods and merchandise of one kind or another to stock a department store.

I was sitting at my desk when I received word from the Boss that Yuri was returning to the United States. I walked over to where the Poet was sitting.

"Do you have some time to accompany me to JFK? My man is coming home."

"Sure," said the Poet. Together we drove out to the airport.

When Yuri stepped off the plane, he was wearing a brown woolen British tweed suit. He looked totally Westernized.

"Did you see him laughing with the stewardess? He's got a smile on his face?" said the Poet.

"He must be happy to be back." Compared to the hard life in the Soviet Union, I thought, he was now living in Midtown Manhattan, with all the modern conveniences, plenty of money, and a summer retreat on the beach on Long Island. The only difference now with Yuri, from his initial tour, was that he had to produce.

Like a sales guy with corporate America, he had to get results, obtain information, preferably secret or top-secret information, data on defense facilities, aircraft, spy satellites, and to do that he had to make contacts, attend conventions, trade shows, meet engineers, contact families of Russian and

Eastern European émigrés and try to reach and befriend military personnel.

Back at the office, I again began rummaging through in earnest Yuri's rather large file. It was so extensive that it took me several days at my desk to go through it. This was Yuri's second tour, and he had to be up to no good. The file was loaded with photographs, notes from the State Department and CIA concerning his background, and comments from agents and contacts abroad about Yuri.

Even after doing this, I wasn't convinced that this was everything that was known about the guy, not down to the bone anyway. We weren't close to his bone. Then I thought to myself that we weren't close to any Russian's bone in knowing absolutely everything about an individual. I wanted truth. We must attack, I thought, and keep digging to learn everything possible about the enemy. I delved further and worked harder, requesting more files from the home office in DC. I also examined other files of Yuri's close associates in New York.

I harbored the distinct feeling and suspicion that the CIA knew something more about him and was holding it back. As I've mentioned, the CIA was not always fully transparent and forthcoming, even to a sister agency like the FBI.

During the weeks I spent at my desk, sifting and verifying what data I could find, constructing what I felt would be a useful helpful profile of Yuri, I was able to compose and peck out a very brief memo to Charley for the file, which I quote here verbatim:

MEMO TO FILE

RE: Popov, Yuri: Code Name Firefly

Yuri is a KGB intelligence officer. On second tour. Unclear which directorate or department, but foreign sources appear to make him high level. Born July 2, 1930. Grew up in Moscow: father, a schoolteacher, married to a woman (Marikova) much younger than himself; from her photograph a beautiful gal, with one daughter and one son.

Believed to have served in the Soviet military during the period of the Korean War. With army intelligence, GRU. Posted to Germany 1955–1962; KGB intelligence office, attended Foreign Languages Institute and the Moscow Institute of International Relations in Moscow.

Observations: Walks to UN. Carries briefcase. Always by himself. Talks to no one. Will stop occasionally to peer in glass windows. Keeps a regular route pattern. Hours irregular. Appears late both at UN and visits to Mission. Drinks a lot after hours. Observed several times in an intoxicated state in company with beautiful wife, who too appears to drink heavily; maintains a calm, stable exterior.

Then something jumped out at me. It was an a-ha moment. In reviewing one of Yuri's files, I came across a small note, probably placed in the file from another agent who had reviewed the file in the past. His wife had given birth to their son at Mt. Sinai Hospital in Manhattan. No one paid any attention to this apparently, and it was treated with some nonchalance. But I was puzzled. If the Russians didn't trust Jews and preferred to avoid doctors who were Jews, why would they have gone to Mt. Sinai Hospital?

I decided to act upon this information and paid a visit to the hospital, where I reviewed the hospital chart and then spoke to the young Jewish doctor who'd delivered Yuri's baby, which is when I struck pay dirt. The doctor informed me that the woman came in with the usual request that the baby be circumcised.

This may have been a usual request to the doctor, but it was an extremely unusual request for a Russian family and KGB spy. This was a remarkable revelation.

When I got back to the office, I reviewed this with Agent Andy Wilson, an agent who had worked on Russian matters for twenty-five years, but who was now bailing out in sixty days and going into retirement. Andy and I pieced together the following scenario. Yuri and his Russian family were trying to conceal their Jewish past, probably for no other reason than that it was impossible to reach a position of trust within the KGB hierarchy if you were a Jew.

Popov had to be a cover name, chosen perhaps so they could claim a relationship and allegiance to the motherland, but yet remain disguised. Without interviewing Popov it would be next to impossible to piece together a family tree and his bloodlines. Andy and I concluded that this circumstance alone meant that more attention should be focused on Yuri as a target for possible defection.

I gave the aforementioned memo to Charley and also inserted it in the file. What followed my review of the file was a discussion with Big D, who as a watcher observed the comings and goings of Yuri from the Soviet mission to the United Nations.

It was on a Monday morning, when sitting at my desk, I noticed the Boss up and about from his chair, wearing his usual drab, rumpled gray suit, motioning me to come into his office, which I quickly did. I took a seat.

Charley looked over at me.

"So how are you making out with Yuri? Are you enjoying yourself?"

"I'm just jumping up every day and clicking my heels."

"The city will do that to you. Good job by the way on that Mt. Sinai Hospital issue. What does Yuri do all day?"

"He walks to the UN with an occasional stop at Bernstein's Deli for a Danish."

Charley's head nodded, and his eyes now opened a bit more.

"I know what you are thinking, Boss," I said. "I've got Bernstein's covered. Bernstein and I are like this." I held up my index finger crossed by my forefinger. "Bernstein may even invite me to his son's bar mitzvah."

"What else? What's Yuri like?" Charley asked.

"Interesting guy. Drinks a lot. Has had two wives but now seems to be a devoted family man. Not much indication yet that he's doing anything dirty."

"Know anything about his first wife."

"Nothing other than CIA reports that she was Swiss and a little fanatical, obnoxious and difficult to be around."

"Hmm. Booze and two wives will do any man in."

"Or may even finish him," I added.

"Maybe this is now happening."

"What do you mean?" I asked.

Charley looked down at a document on his desk and then looked at me. "We've received a top-secret report from the CIA that your man Firefly is interested in defecting with his wife. He wants to come over. Don't ask me how the CIA knows this. It's not important. Maybe we have another Nosenko on our hands. Maybe it has something to do with his Jewish past."

"A defection? You mean he's going rogue. Things are picking up."

When information flowed in from the CIA, and it often did, the source of the information was never identified. How had they acquired it, and what did the CIA know? This was never revealed because they did not want their source compromised.

Thus there was no need for us to know. We accepted the information as reliable and credible.

"To some extent, this does not surprise me," said Charley, "and it shouldn't surprise you. The Russians come in here. They see the beautiful city, the freedoms, the money, and it represents life on a different planet, compared to their own life in Russia, which is crude. Are some ready to come over and help us? You bet."

"It could be a nothing. Maybe even a plot," I said.

"True. But we've got to deal with it. We've arranged to meet Firefly at the monastery in Brooklyn at noon next week. You greet him in the monastery. The Poet will be out there in a bureau car, and there will be a second car in the area with two agents for backup. Interview him with the Poet. Find out why. What does he want? What can he give us?"

I knew what that meant. What's in it for us? What can he supply us? Does he have access to any secrets? We could then decide if we wanted to go ahead with the actual defection or, better still, leave him in place. I was often puzzled by CIA information, or the lack thereof, because in Firefly's file and all of the memos and reports, there was nothing to indicate that he was a candidate for recruitment, but why should it? If a Russian was going to defect, he or she would try to do it and prepare for it in a fashion that no one within the KGB would have a clue that it was going to happen. But still, from our side of the table, pinpointing motivation was important, because it had a definite impact on the issue that would be raised later as to whether he (or she) was bona fide.

Charley looked at me, obviously expecting some kind of plausible explanation for Yuri's motivation even though I hadn't yet talked to the guy.

"When something like this happens—and believe me, these are rare occasions—you have to get into their head and figure out who the hell they are and how they think. Where are their loyalties?"

I thought about this for a moment and didn't say anything.

"Well," said Charley. "You are handling him. Why would he be doing this? Get the Poet in here and let's discuss this."

I got up, walked outside Charley's cubical, and motioned to the Poet to come and join us. The Poet entered Charley's chamber, clutching a cigarette; he sat down and said, "Have I been summoned for something taxing and big?"

"You have," said Charley. "Deuce's man Yuri apparently wants to defect."

"You mean Yuri has finally come to his senses?"

"I suppose you could say that," said Charley.

"Hmm. You don't trust him," said the Poet, "that he's doing the right thing?"

"Hell no, I don't trust him. I wouldn't trust any information we receive at all. Whether it is in Moscow or the USA, getting to know a Russian and becoming friendly with him is a formidable task. Controls are tight."

"Well," I said, "maybe after we talk to Yuri, I'll be able to come up with a few things that will tell us he's the real deal."

"Like what?" asked Charley.

"Like his being a Jew or his wife being a Jew. He may not want to be posted back in Russia. Is he a Bolshevik or a true communist? Maybe he has Hasidic loyalties. Also Russians do have a human side that can be emotional and unpredictable."

"Possibly. I like that."

I rattled on. "He also may have a private agenda, divorce, debt problems, needs money. They are no different from the rest of us."

"Of course money may enter into it," said Charley. "It always does. But when events like this happen, I guarantee that after we know what he wants, there will be multiple interpretations regarding deception. It's always difficult to understand defections. It's a big deal to start a new life. You are giving up so much."

"Probably so," said the Poet, "but he could be a nut or screwball. Also keep in mind that maybe there is something going on that if he returned home, he could be executed."

"When a spy returns home, you generally don't execute him," said Charley.

"Unless he is corrupt and screwed up big time," I added.

Charley was now perusing Yuri's file. He finally looked up. "There has to be something in his daily activity we are missing."

"When he is not at the UN, he shops. I can account for several of his hours. But he's not under twenty-four/seven surveillance."

"I understand that," Charley quickly replied. "Is he GRU or KGB?"

"KGB. His wife is having an affair with Vladimir. We passed this information along to him. Maybe that stirred up some dust. Started something."

"Women problems, divorce? Not likely. Most Russians are bonded to Mother Russia. It takes quite a bit to break the bond. Think about it."

"I am thinking about it," I said. "The Russians lust for things all mankind lust for—money, food, clothes, comfort."

Charley chuckled. "Those are things you don't lust for. The fact that he may like it here is generally not enough to start playing ball with us."

Charley of course was right. This was a KGB officer. Many of them preferred death, or something even worse, to defection. If this were a murder case, the prosecutor always had to find a motive. When people make significant decisions—to murder or defect—there has to be some explanation. Yet I found this kind of guessing disquieting in the sense that it leads generally to long memos and paperwork trying to pinpoint reasons for every Russian move, particularly a Russian defection, and generally reaching a dead end, like the Nosenko case, where you just couldn't be sure. My thinking was, what difference did it make, assuming that he wanted out? But it was important to Charley, so I carried on trying to flush out possible reasons.

"Well," I said, "we may not know the answer until we talk to him, but I still feel there can be a lot of reasons to make such a move, including money, corruption, or crime. Moscow would not trust a Soviet intelligence officer to come under the control of the US. Therefore, he had to be legit."

"On that you may have something," said Charley. "But keep in mind that Golitsyn warned that any defection after his would be false and designed to mislead the West about his information."

He may want to simply pile up dough in a Swiss bank account, I thought. Maybe he has a mistress stowed away in Europe. Perhaps for some reason his head is on the chopping block. Maybe he feels his career is going nowhere, or maybe there are health issues, perhaps even some kind of mental breakdown. That sort of thing.

In the course of reviewing a lot of medical records for a law firm that I worked for after law school, I had acquired some medical knowledge and developed a habit of diagnosing illnesses. At times simply by observing the appearance of someone, it was possible to come away with an accurate reading of the particular ailment.

"There is something else. What about health care? Several weeks ago Yuri looked as if he had lost a lot of weight. He looked pale as if he had some kind of deficiency...anemia? Came out of the mission one day in a wheelchair." I grinned. "Maybe he wants access to American medical treatment?"

"Maybe this and maybe that. Wheelchair? His legs could be gnarled with arthritis," Charlie shouted. "But it's more likely, if he had a rug over his knees, he could be hiding something. Nobody defects because of health issues unless he has just come in from the gulag or the KGB's Lubyanka dungeon, and I've never known a Russian to go crazy, although I suppose a wife or mother-in-law could drive you nuts. Remember what I mentioned to you right up front. Use your imagination. If Yuri came out in a wheelchair, he could be like a parent bird trying to lure a predator away from his nest by feigning a broken wing."

"When you have a KGB mole in the West, under our supervision, it has always puzzled me as to how this was going to pay dividends to the Russians?" said the Poet.

"It may not pay dividends," replied Charlie. "But disinformation, sending us on a wild goose chase, with leads that bear no fruit, tying us up creating tons of memos and paper—that pays dividends for them. Your man Yuri, if his wife is having an affair, may eventually want to fall on a sword. Maybe he wants to make a name for himself to impress his wife. Get his name up on some marquee. Then again he may be like a judge, with an inflated view of himself. They put on a black robe, and all of a sudden they think they are God."

"So how do we smuggle Yuri out, if he wants to come over," I asked.

"We don't," said Charley. "Here's the deal. Think of him as an investment. Our goal is to leave him in place for a while, so we can extract information. We enter into a relationship with him. That requires total manipulation of him from our end. We feed him placebos. Every now and then, we give him something a cut above to improve his standing with his bosses. It's small stuff, but it keeps him active and keeps him going. It's like giving a gambler a small payout on a slot machine in Las Vegas."

"Will that work on a Russian?" I asked.

"I don't know," said Charley, "but it keeps gamblers on slot machines and works in Las Vegas.

"Deuce, when you interview Yuri, make sure you convey to him that we are running the show. Any defection has to be on our terms. Don't make any commitments and instruct him on who to call to make future contacts. And one more thing: we have to be careful. This could be a trap. When you interview him, he could be wired. We don't want them crying provocation. You guys work out the details."

This was going to be an important assignment. It could pull the curtain back, giving us a road map into the internal workings of the New York KGB.

CHAPTER 15

OPERATIONS SMILE AND BLOODHOUND

———◆———

I REMEMBER EARLY ON WHEN I was working on Firefly's case that we started a smile campaign, smiling at the Russians at every opportunity. The purpose was to try to promote defections by showing that we were nice friendly guys. Someone in Washington had done some research, probably with a government grant, that a smile was powerful and could make a friend out of an enemy.

Initially I felt this was a cunning device and that the Russians perhaps would respond like friendly dogs or sheep. However, after debating it with Big D and the Poet over coffee, the conclusion was that whoever thought this up probably needed his head examined. Unless two thieves are working as a team, with one smiling and chatting with a stranger while the other is picking his pocket, it won't be a success. Further, it is by no means common to have New York City residents walking around Manhattan with smiles on their faces. It thus exposed the identities of the good guys who manned the streets. We got very few smiles back.

It was raining in Manhattan when I left the office smiling. As I was about to embark on trying out this smile campaign for the first time, the Poet yelled out, "Hey, let the rain be your umbrella on this smiley, smiley day."

He was right about that, all right. I trailed Yuri down Madison Avenue, trying to maintain a smiling face. Yuri was out on another shopping binge. At various points he stopped, turned around, and came toward me. We had a lot of eye contact, and I smiled. I said to myself, "Come on; smile, Yuri. You can do it. No wrinkles." Getting eye contact back was a good sign, but a smile rarely came. Life and work were too serious for a Russian, and a smile did not come naturally.

Smiling required staring, and in New York, people did not stare. There are celebrities all over the place, and the idea is to pretend not to notice them. The smile campaign was a bust, and about all that it produced was a lot of jokes and laughter at our poker parties.

Beyond smiling there was always the business of surveillance, which involved the monitoring of the behavior and activities of the Russians. There is an art to shadowing people. Unlike playing basketball it was never one-on-one or man-to-man. We needed two or three agents per spy. The Russians adapted. They learned lessons from increased surveillance. They were surveillance conscious and not clueless. When walking on the street in their heavy shoes, they rarely spoke to one another. They avoided conventional phone lines for fear that they were tapped. On this they were correct. It did not take much to tap a phone line. They knew that, and they knew we knew that. All that was needed was an alligator clip attached to one wire.

With any surveillance the idea was for them not to know that you were trailing them, which meant that you had to stay back a bit and avoid behavior that stood out. It was necessary to look, behave, and blend in with individuals on the street and not call attention to yourself. Assistance was helpful. A few other agents were needed, with at least one on a motorbike.

The exception was the smile campaign, when it was necessary to become visible. Then I exposed myself, both literally and figuratively, as the agent covering his ass. I made eye contact with him if he was sitting across from me in a subway. When he left the subway, I followed him. When he stopped and looked in a window, I did the same. Finally, if he entered a deli and ordered a Coke and sandwich, I followed him in, smiling, and picked up the tab. All of this was done without speaking.

On a surveillance, where it was necessary to remain invisible, greater thought and a sophisticated plan was necessary. At some point the Russian, if he was up to no good, had to be convinced that no tails existed. Otherwise, he would not proceed with his spying activity.

When up to no good, the Russian spent hours cleaning himself, which included jumping in and out of subway cars. It became a real feat to hang in there with him, even with the help of several agents. Coverage could be stated in simple terms. Keeping tabs on spies was problematic. Always there were issues. It was never an easy assignment.

From the moment I was assigned to Yuri, I kept a close watch on him, for his fate was linked to my own. I was determined that he was not going to succeed at anything on my watch. So I was aggressive. In fact I pictured myself at times as a pursuing assassin, often ducking in and out of stores and alleys as I trailed him, trying to get into his mind and instilling fear and anxiety that some loose cannon was always on his tail.

In time I felt I was becoming extremely proficient and productive in watching him. I was obtaining informants and started gathering a lot of evidence as to his interests and motives, which supplied clues to exploit his human frailties. There was always something, some weakness, an Achilles' heel, that could be exploited, and New York City and its streets became my laboratory.

As soon as he left the mission, I was behind him on foot, often with TH, a Columbus, Ohio, recruit, a Buckeye who loved to walk or sprint. TH would take the opposite side of the street while I covered Yuri from behind at a distance of about fifty yards. Occasionally we occupied a bureau car; TH manned the field glasses.

When walking from the mission to the United Nations, I rarely observed Yuri speak with anyone. Upon reaching the United Nations, I walked over to TH and said, "It looks like another dry run."

Ever the optimist, TH responded, "Patience. Have patience. Something will eventually pop."

I wanted Yuri to get on with his spying, to do something so that we could catch him in the act. I wanted to score a coup and present Yuri's head to Charley on a platter. For days and months on end, nothing was forthcoming. Yuri took his time going to work. He changed routes and seemed to be enjoying himself. His excursions into stores on weekends, when he would browse around and shop, were brief.

Finally, I decided that I needed something sophisticated to keep track of him, particularly when he was out and about in his automobile. We had lost him on several occasions. That wasn't good. I was convinced that we were not doing enough. I was becoming what Charley wanted me to become—paranoid.

I paid a visit to Charley. "Boss, in covering Yuri, I have a suggestion."

"Yeah. Let's hear it."

"In wearing out my shoes on city streets, a daring scheme occurred to me."

"If it's too magnificent, I may not want to hear it. What is it?"

"I'd like to hook up an electronic bloodhound system to Yuri's automobile to keep better track of him."

"Deuce," he said, "not a bad idea. We have devices that can handle that. But please don't screw up. Don't cause a major incident, or you will be on your own taking the rap for the bureau."

"Yes, sir." This of course was the typical response from Charley, who, being a desk guy, never wanted to risk the bureau being embarrassed or upset his own promotion goals. The street agents on the other hand did not share such concerns and preferred to be aggressive.

The risk that planting a tracking device on a vehicle would get fucked up and cause some kind of snafu or bureau embarrassment didn't give me the least bit of nervousness. Obviously, there was a need to avoid making a mistake, which was another rule of Charley's. There were to be no mistakes planting a bug, shaking a tail, using miniature or concealed cameras, visiting a safe house, or doing something else.

In Charley's world, every assignment had risks. In his words: "Be circumspect and make sure you don't do things that expose that you weren't on top of things."

At college my tennis coach once mentioned that every time the ball came toward you from an opponent across the net, the question arose whether you were going to make a mistake, in staying focused, getting your racquet back, keeping your eye on the ball, turning your body, hitting the ball at its apex in a volley, hitting through the ball in front of you, bending your knees, on and on. A mistake could cost you the point or the game. Needless to say, however, it paled in significance to other mistakes that could be made daily in real life with most anything. The business of counterintelligence, spies, and spooks was a business that could not tolerate error. The end result of a mistake could be deadly either for you, a source or informant, or one of your team. Unlike tennis, a mistake here had no avenue for recovery.

With my combative street-agent mind-set, I got it in my head early that in New York it was necessary to not always play by the rules. A lot of leeway was given in internal security on everything, including kidnapping, for the definition of *internal security* was very broad.

We could do most anything within reason, or at times with no reason but imagination, in an effort to keep the Soviets off balance, scared, and intimidated.

To maintain surveillance on Yuri's automobile and Yuri himself, a bloodhound or Labrador was needed with a good nose. In the absence of something with four legs, I settled on an electronic device that was small enough to hold in my hand. All I had to do was figure out how to plant it on his car and where, which for me, with imagination, was simple enough. For an answer to this, I turned to our office tech people.

Legally, this meant installing a tracking device on Yuri's vehicle for use in surveillance, without a warrant and without going before a judge requesting permission.

To accomplish this I had to first borrow Yuri's car for at least an hour. I snatched it.

Borrowing or snatching a car is not like snatching a live body. Yet, it is still something that a man will not do in a spirit of groundless inquiry.

Snatching a live body required a great deal of planning and thought, unless we got the Russian to agree to be snatched. With defections this could happen, but it would raise a great hue and cry from the Russian government, which would not go along with the fact that such a disappearance of one of their KGB agents was with his or her consent.

Snatching a two-thousand-pound piece of rusting machinery like an automobile on the other hand was not something that caused a great deal of indignation even among the Russians or even with New Yorkers. Yet it still required some organization and planning to successfully accomplish it without being shot by some off-duty cop who thought that a car was being stolen.

Stealing is when something is done with intent to permanently deprive. Internal security allowed me to snatch the vehicle without technically "stealing" it. It was not our intent to keep the car permanently. Thus, this wasn't theft.

Since I was running the show, I picked the team. I assembled the usual suspects from my office to help me. There were four of us. There was Old Yeller, a six-foot-four Mississippi linebacker type.

When Old Yeller was out on a surveillance, his mind would often drift to what was then happening in the stock market or women. His social calendar was filled with arrangements for weekend dates. He was working on his MBA. He wanted to be somewhere else and looked at the bureau job as a stepping stone to some higher-paying corporate position.

Although he was on the team, he was never in the game. The Poet thought he should ride the bench. I left him on the team, for he was trustworthy and fun to be around. Besides, if the KGB cornered us in some dark alley, I was confident Old Yeller would have his mind focused on the task at hand. He was one I wanted with me.

Then there was Shenandoah, the Poet, the country boy and English major out of South Carolina, the only one of us who was married. He even had two kids. The Poet enjoyed three things, not necessarily in this order: drinking, gambling, and writing. I needed the Poet because he spoke three languages, including Russian. The Poet turned any situation into a witty, fun experience. Whatever the job, the Poet was wanted. He was flat-out great company.

Then there was the Knife, the Blade, like me a Chicago boy with a law degree, the soft-spoken, serious, dependable career bureau lifer, whom any agent would want as his wing man, just in case the cops showed up and somebody was needed to provide an explanation. Horses during races wear blinders to keep them from being distracted. When the Knife went out on a bureau job, he had on a pair of blinders. Nothing distracted him from the job at hand. He was set to face adversity totally focused. Also the Knife was an expert with a gun.

I remember the Knife in training class at the range in Quantico. There were scenes that were acted out and played with a .38 Special. The Knife turned his back to the target and started walking away. The revolver was holstered on his hip and some-times pushed lower until it was hanging western style, touching his right thigh. His face was serious and focused.

Then in a split second when a bad guy popped up in the window of a propped-up façade of a saloon twenty yards away, he stopped, quickly drew the .38, crouched, and wheeled around in one pretty motion. The revolver exploded with cracking sounds and deadly accuracy—one, two, three, with bullets spraying the center of the target every time. The instructor yelled out, "Through the chest, near the heart!"

There was applause from the rest of us as we sat around and witnessed this drama.

"Lift the son of a bitch and blow the smoke from the barrel!" one yelled.

The Knife had tremendous skill with a weapon. If it was necessary to have another agent shoot a hole in an apple perched on your head, 99 percent of the agents would pick the Knife to pull the trigger. No doubt about it. The Knife was good and he knew it.

We knew where Yuri parked his vehicle at night, and tonight it was on Seventy-Eighth Street, between Third and Lex. Old Yeller and the Poet were stationed outside Firefly's second residence. They were prepared to give us a heads-up if Yuri ventured out of his residence for a walk, which was out of the ordinary and not in line with his routine.

Also prepared to give us a heads-up was the doorman at Yuri's residence. He was one of my paid informants. His name was Sam. Sam was a World War II vet, who'd served honorably in a tank unit in the European theater. Owing to a service-connected injury that made him partially disabled, Sam had trouble finding work when he came home. With one bad arm and a bad leg, job opportunities were simply not there or were limited. According to Sam his choices included jobs like a security guard, doorman, or as an usher in a theater. So he took the doorman job. One day after covering Yuri, I stopped by and introduced myself.

"Sam," I said, "you've had a great career. We want you back in the service."

"What do you mean?" replied Sam.

"We need your help. Your eyes and ears."

"Like what do you want me to do?"

"There is a guy upstairs. One of the bad guys from another country. The enemy. We need you to help watch what he does, who he sees. That kind of thing."

"That's it?"

"Yup, that's it. What I want you to do is simply to keep me informed. What time of day he leaves. What time does he come in? Who is he with? That sort of thing. In exchange I'm going to give you expense money from the government."

"That won't be necessary."

"Sam," I said, "thank you. But for me it's necessary. One hundred dollars a month."

That was that. Sam became the man, the patriotic soldier who would fall on a grenade in your foxhole to save the rest of us, eager to help and assist on anything. As an informant Sam didn't want money, but I gave him money anyway, because I knew he needed it, and the last thing you wanted was an indignant disabled former tank commander having spent two years in France fighting Germans getting mad at you. The information he provided was priceless. He kept a written daily log of Yuri's comings and goings, the times he entered and left, what he was wearing, who he was with, packages he was carrying, conversations and contacts, which was useful in studying routines. It was when Yuri did things that were outside his routine that we knew he was up to no good.

In getting over to Yuri's vehicle to snatch it, and for deniability purposes, the Knife and I traveled in a rental car. Generally a rental car was never used unless the agency was a friend, a good friend.

As we drove over to Yuri's car, the Knife was driving. I sat in the front seat, watching out for police cars and potential witnesses to the event we had planned. The Knife was jovial and chuckling.

"You OK?" he asked.

"Well, my adrenaline is flowing and my pulse is one thirty. Does this mean I'm OK, or am I frightened?" I replied.

"Come on. In this job you have to be prepared to die. For America. You know the drill."

"Right," I said. "I know the drill, but I am getting second thoughts about whether what we are doing is really worth it. The Russians are not dumb, and in the next thirty days, they will probably do a routine sweep of Yuri's car and stumble on the device anyway, so why even bother with this?"

"Good point, but it's a little late to think about that now, isn't it? Let's stay focused on the problem at hand. What happens if you get in that car and you can't start the son of a bitch?" the Knife asked.

"Frankly, starting it is the least of my worries," I replied. "What is bothering me is if some city cop or off-duty cop sees us and thinks we are carjacking. He then decides to shoot first and ask questions later. Aren't we a little young to be sent in harm's way? When I'm lying in the hospital, or even worse, the morgue, what do you intend to tell my mother?"

The Knife was quick. "I suppose I would visit her personally over the holidays, give her an American flag and sympathy letter from the New York office signed by those agents who have enjoyed your company around the poker table, thanking her for your monetary contribution—sorry, strike the words *monetary contribution*—and years of service."

"My mom will appreciate that. This is the last time I'm going to suggest a carjacking. Seduction of Russian women and convincing them to give us information is more in tune with what our team would be good at, don't you think?"

"Well," said the Knife, "I'm not so sure we should have this discussion in a bureau car, even though it's rented."

I always viewed sex and espionage as going together. In training class I pictured spy work to require seducing women routinely. It was always interesting to me, whether I was on the tennis court, playing poker, or involved in a bureau operation where I was about to heist a Soviet automobile, that thoughts of sexual fulfillment entered my soul. Extraneous thoughts, and dilations within me, somewhat like stalking a fugitive and the thrill of the chase, brought about by the New York environment, filled, as it was, with many beautiful single women who often would give you that...that look. Even though working for the government, I felt some degree of debauchery in this intense, stressful, argumentative city had to be good. There had to be some pleasure that one could derive living in a gray city of woe, a place that housed every vice known to humanity.

Doing it was a necessary appendage of hard work and play, lifting the spirits, and reactivating a body, my own, which after a long, stressful day on the street suffered from lethargy and the blahs and couldn't always be relieved by simply sitting by myself drinking a Rheingold at six o'clock in a hot tub filled with rusty water. To say that I had little moral resolve was an understatement. But then, the Knife, as the FBI lifer and celibate with a chastity pledge, a goyim totally devoid of any affliction of the flesh, brought me quickly down to earth, with a warning to hold back.

"Never ever mix pussy and government work," said the Knife.

"You sound like a philosophy major. Why's that?"

"You always have to be on guard and careful. There are women, femmes fatales, planted by the KGB for sexual provocations. You go to their room. Two girls remove their clothing. You climb into bed, and the whole thing is filmed through a two-way mirror."

"Really," I said, feigning naiveté, for I was thinking about the army of pretty FBI office girls who handled so many of our office administrative chores. "What about dipping your pen in FBI and not KGB ink, every now and then? What about that?"

"You don't want to do that either," said the Knife. "Never shit where you eat."

I had trouble understanding the relevance or even the meaning of that piece of advice. I said nothing and simply grinned and thought about all of this. First of all, the Knife knew his stuff. It was common knowledge in the office that the Russians took great pains to lure sources of information, like tourists, businessmen, and engineers into sexual liaisons, and then confronted them with threats of disclosure unless they cooperated. On married guys that might work, but, hey, I was single. The likelihood of sex totally twisting one's sensibilities was to me very remote. Government gals at the office ought to be OK. I wondered if the Knife ever looked for love, but maybe as a bureau lifer, like Hoover, he didn't need love and didn't need or have the urge to even send out valentines. What he needed, I thought, was an arrow from Cupid to strike him in the ass every once in a while. Shapely young girls working for the KGB? In today's world man takes great risks for money, but even greater risks for sex. The knife was right, but it represented the old school of thought. If you are single and didn't give away any secrets, what difference did it make? You might be able to turn the girls and get them to work for you and not them. Yes, it was a diversion enjoyed by residents in an area of human degradation, but it was important to look at potential benefits.

I looked at the Knife. "Seduction by women in the spy world is really not the answer or relevant anymore. Surely you agree with that, don't you?"

"What do you mean?"

"I mean that today, it is all about greenbacks. Gathering secrets by seduction doesn't work. It's old and not in vogue in the world of spydom. Then again maybe some old Russian spy still thinks like you. They do have women."

"Yes, they do," said the Knife, "and they are beautiful."

"Perhaps what is needed is the right person to come along on our side to prove that seduction is still used by the Russians. Somebody has to expose these kinds of traps."

"Have anybody in mind?" asked the Knife. "I'll mention it to Charley."

"Ah, don't throw me in that briar patch of femmes fatales. Christ, I can't even pronounce it." Sexually provoked? I thought. Every guy in our office was dying to be sexually provoked.

"Deuce, there is one thing you are forgetting."

"What's that?"

"It's much more than being sexually enticed. These femmes fatales don't come in for simple casual sex. They utilize physical and psychological seduction, which leads to manipulation. They exist to recruit you. They are there to get you to fall in love with them. That way they can compromise you and control you. That's a standard classic Soviet tactic."

"Yeah?"

"Once they have you hooked, they report on you, keep an eye on you, and give the Soviets details on how you operate. By the way, who is that girl you are seeing, and how much do you know about her? I'm being serious. You know shit about her. She flies in. You never see her friends. She tells you she is from Little Rock and throws out some heavy reputable names. Then she leaves, and you don't see her again for a month."

"Hmm. Maybe I'd better run a background check." Actually I had already done that on C. Not a lot but some. I couldn't find much.

We tooled down Fifth Avenue. The cross streets were silent with nobody around. We finally spotted Yuri's vehicle. The actual insertion of this small dildo of a car into Firefly's parking spot took only a few minutes. I put on a pair of surgeon's latex gloves and got on the Motorola radio. "Apache, this is Alpha. How we doin'? You in place."

The voice of the Poet gave us a quick response. "We are Whiskey Foxtrot Tango. The package is quiet. Looks like a dead evening here, over."

"It's a go. God have mercy on such as us, " I replied. "We'll be in touch."

I exited the Knife's car and entered Yuri's vehicle, disconnected the odometer, started the engine, and drove ten blocks to the bureau garage, which took less than ten minutes. Heart rate up. Everything was cool. The space Yuri's vehicle had occupied was replaced by the Knife's rental car. The tracking device was a metal box about the size of a cigarette pack. When I got to the garage, our tech man Danny placed it near the gas tank.

I looked at Danny, who had purposely come in late to handle the installation. The garage was crowded with shelves and peppered with equipment. "Well, Danny," I said, "is this thing going to work?"

"It will work. I've got a wire from the device to the exhaust with a sensor. When the exhaust pipe gets hot, it will turn the device on. That way the battery should last. The Russians will find it eventually. You can't conceal it in a piece of steel. But, hey, if they find it, why, we'll just slip on another."

When activated, the device sent out a signal, and if the frequency was known, it could then be picked up by the receiving equipment. Distance could then be estimated but not the speed. But it would allow us to follow the car.

I then drove the vehicle back to its original site. Once operational the tracking device generated a beeping, which could be heard on earphones while sitting in another vehicle.

We ended this evening with a visit to Big D's favorite bar on First Avenue, called the Bishops. Sadly, even though our operation had gone real well, I felt I wasn't gaining that much ground on Yuri. But sitting in the Bishops, I was set to buy the rounds. Crowded as usual, the place was jumping and the beer flowed freely, as it would around the poker table, except this time it was filled with agents, including TH, Big Al, and Big Al's roommate Mad Dog.

On the menu were oysters. The stress of the entire evening made me lightheaded and happy. We had won one of the games, without a turnover, fumble, or any slipups. But it was midnight and everyone was hungry and thirsty.

I downed a few oysters. The Poet leaned over and said, "Deuce, when the aboriginal Americans ran into Ponce de Leon in Florida, they told him to never eat an oyster in a month without an *r* in it. Do you know what month this is?"

"Yeah," I said, "is this leading to another one of your shell games?"

"Before you get hit with diarrhea or abdominal cramping, we need to roll the dice to see who buys the beer. You familiar with ship, captain, crew?"

"Thanks, I am," I said, "but to save time, let me just get out my wallet." It was following this visit to the Bishops that Shenandoah pitched yet another poem.

BORN TO LOSE—PART II

The stars shown bright, the moon was full, the clouds had
    rolled away.

Deuce's heart was very light, the eagle having flown that day.

Yes, Deuce Ballou was confident; a smile played on his lip.

He whipped into the Bishops with three hundred on his hip.

His threads were of the finest cut; his shoes were lizard skin.

He obviously was not a man who'd ever order gin.

He spotted Mad Dog, Shenandoah, the Blade, TH, Big Al,

but keyed his gaze upon the babe who's only known as Sal.

Struck by her awesome glances, Deuce knew he had found real class.

She nonchalantly sipped martinis from TH's glass.

Then, suddenly, the music swelled; to Deuce Ballou a dove appeared, a symbol that this truly was his night for love.

As Sal ordered another drink, Deuce said, "Please let me pay."

She stirred him by the way she cooed in Brooklynese, "OK."

Charmed by this show of lightning wit, Deuce swiftly pressed her hand

then stared in disbelief; she wore a copper wedding band.

Deuce whispered, "Are you married?" And she nasaled, "He's a drag,

a queer, a junkie, alky, pimp, a fourteen-karat fag."

Deuce nodded, reassured, now knowing this would be his night.

He told her, "I feel better knowing your old man's all right."

TH and Al both told Deuce, "She's from the Cloud 9 band."

And Shenandoah then warned him that Sal had too much right hand.

The Blade said, "Cool it, baby!" But Deuce was hooked too deep.

He knew, with or without her, that this night he'd get no sleep.

So, like the Light Brigade, Deuce plunged into the battery smoke

(though slightly disillusioned for she now drank rum and
   Coke).
She swayed against him, and those angel tresses kissed his
   brow.
Deuce knew each man must love sometime and that his time
   was now.
The world's a stage, and Deuce now played one of his finest
   parts.
He said, "Let's hit my pad and have a friendly game of hearts."
Already out a hundred (he'd been buying for the house),
Deuce heard her say, "Blow, buster, here's my ever-loving
   spouse."
A clabber-headed bastard with two gold rings in his ears,
And Sal waltzed out with him as Deuce sat blinking through
   his tears.
The Blade was swift! He saw Deuce's mind was in that losing
   frame.
"Come on, Big Deuce, there's still time for a friendly little
   game."
Epilogue: Deuce did his best: you know the rest.

CHAPTER 16

EVALUATION OF A DEFECTOR

Wednesday, June 5, 1968.

THE MONASTERY OF OUR LADY of Mt. Carmel in Brooklyn is in a building that resembles a medieval fortress. It's a concrete, seemingly impenetrable, foreboding block house occupied curiously by passive cloistered nuns, who had little ability or motivation to rebuff or repel anything. Inside the marble walls, sounds from the Brooklyn streets were completely shut out.

Having attended Catholic grade school, including a short stint as an altar boy, I knew a little about the ferocious demeanor of nuns. What comes to mind is fear. A hostile gaze from a nun could cause a third grader to pee in his pants. The rules were, never cross them. Don't do anything to displease them. Remain quiet and look forward to recess or lunch, where a modicum of creature comforts would be dispensed.

Punishment from nuns for even a minor offense ran the gamut, from belts, paddles (with a large hole to make them move through the air faster before striking your behind) to a boxing glove, which a nun would don to smack you in the kisser.

The number of nuns living in this monastery was unknown. No one had ever been inside to take a body count. In fact no one at the office could tell me if any non-nun had ever visited the place.

What was known was that the Carmelite nuns were completely hermitical. They were isolated, rarely seen, lived in silence like fish in water except when they prayed together, and unlike beguines, totally looked for holiness in a monastic order under vows of chastity and lifelong celibacy.

They did not minister to the poor, the hopeless and helpless outside their walls. I thought to myself that they were too busy praying.

After speaking with Ricky, I arrived at the monastery to meet Firefly. I approached the place quietly and surreptitiously on foot, trying not to call attention to myself. The exterior of this concrete fortress was covered with graffiti and scribbles, like "It's a white man's world. That's why the world is fucked up." and "Leroy was here. Those who know him know him well. Those who don't can go to Hell." Vines hung above it. Within the vines was a sparrow's nest.

To get a glimpse of what I was getting myself into, I opened the door and entered the turn room on St. John's Place to scout around. Sunlight fell in a ten-foot-by-twelve-foot room. To communicate with anyone inside the monastery, a message or gift had to be sent on an oak barrel-shaped revolving cabinet. After placing an item in the barrel, it was then spun around so a sister in the room on the other side could retrieve it. Parishioners would often come in and place a bag of groceries inside the barrel.

I once met a priest who described these monasteries as the Big Leagues of prayer, a place where only highly serious, earth-shattering needs were taken under prayer advisement. Prayer was hard work. As a Catholic, I had no heroic religiousness or expectations. But I was convinced that the nuns were not behind the barrel-shaped cabinet wasting time.

The turn room was empty. There was a total deathlike silence. It was austere with an oak bureau, several oak chairs, a lamp, a picture of Jesus, a jewel box with paintings, frescos, stained-glass panels, and statues. Above the revolving barrel, a hand-lettered sign was visible: "In the house of God, talk of him, or do not talk of anything."

I exited the monastery and took a seat on an outdoor bench. A short distance away, I observed the Poet, parked, waiting in the bureau vehicle. I nodded to him.

The meeting here was secret. The Boss, the Poet, and I had concocted it. The monastery was picked for its extreme remoteness from Manhattan. Remoteness was better for Yuri. It gave him a lot of space to clean himself from scrutiny and surveillance.

The normal life for Russian spies was that they were watched, studied, and reviewed. To combat some type of potential future internal exam, I carried with me a good cover story for Yuri, if by chance he was questioned about his Brooklyn visit.

This was the story. The Russians had a mansion in Glen Cove that they used as a hideaway for its top dogs. A large number of Russian émigrés resided on Long Island. They were often approached by and met with Russian spies. Discussed was the homeland and their relatives who still lived there. Yuri's presence in Brooklyn reaching out to an émigré was one that we could make very innocent and convincing.

Soviet intelligence officers were taught to report contacts of any kind. If Yuri was for real and a bona-fide defector, the Poet and I expected that he would spend a lot of time cleaning himself to make sure he was not followed. To make sure he was not falling into a trap, he would have to rely on his instincts and years of training at spy school.

If he showed up, we anticipated that little would be accomplished in this first meeting. Each side would be doing some tire kicking.

Sitting on the bench, I went through all the finer points of what I had learned in training class in how to deal with the enemy. Successful interrogation was not simply controlling the situation, but patience was needed. It was necessary to understand the interviewee's background, his culture and the particular predicament he found himself in, in being willing to talk to you.

I also went over what Charley had said. String him along. If he is felt to be genuine, talk him into staying inside the mission. See what he wants in return.

What was most important was simple preparation. That required knowing everything possible about the person you were interrogating. I had done my homework, memorizing a lot of facts regarding Yuri's bio and work history. Cooperation and accurate intelligence should follow.

I leaned over and retrieved a two-foot-long stick shaped like a billy club, waved it at the Poet, and started slapping it into my hand, all the while grinning at the Poet, comically thinking that maybe this was what should be used on Yuri. The bureau (if I could forget about Alex) had never been an agency to deal in harsh interrogation techniques.

It was now well past noon. Still no Yuri. Then in the distance I saw a figure walking toward us.

I looked over at the Poet and nodded my head toward the figure approaching. It was Firefly all right, dressed for a wake or a funeral, with all dark clothes. As he came closer, his face appeared ashen and chalked. He could pass for one of the dead.

He stopped and turned around to look in shop windows.

I looked behind him to see if anyone else was visible. There was no activity. In a few minutes, Yuri entered the monastery.

I walked in and extended my hand to a stocky, heavyset man about five feet ten with close-cropped hair. He wore a dark gray suit, white shirt, and tie, like a US insurance agent making a call. He examined me with an unwavering stare. His egg-shaped face was unsmiling. He was visibly nervous. He shook my hand. He was out of breath, but he began to examine the turn room and paced around.

I studied Yuri and tried to read his mind. I thought of Nosenko and wondered what brought him here. Did he have marital problems? Was he heavily in debt? Was he a serious alcoholic or none of these?

I searched his face for answers, but Yuri only glowered at me like a lawyer might do to a client who arrives at the courthouse without having with him the agreed upon fee.

Motioning with my hand at the Poet's vehicle, I said, "Yuri, walk with me to the dark blue car parked over there, where we can talk."

In the vehicle, the Poet greeted Yuri with a smile and shook Yuri's hand.

When I first arrived in the New York office, I had participated in the transcribing of tapes of CIA interviews with defectors. I was familiar with their interrogation techniques. Coupled with our own techniques, I was confident we could handle Yuri.

What we wanted were the names and addresses of the KGB's sources of information, in the United States and abroad. We didn't expect to get a lot out of this initial interview, but still, gathering any low-hanging fruit was a start.

Meanwhile the Poet had his poker face on.

Yuri reached into his coat pocket and retrieved a pack of Winston Salem cigarettes. He offered one to the Poet and then to me. We both declined.

Yuri lit up and took a drag on his cigarette. I turned around, leaned over, and for a few moments we simply looked at one another without saying anything. I felt I was back in my law-school library, staring at an attractive classmate, sizing her up for a study group or a Saturday night get-together.

Without looking at the Poet or me and simply staring out the window, Yuri finally said something. "It was very difficult for me to come here. Things are happening at the mission. I've given this meeting thought for some time."

"Yuri," I said, "my friend here speaks Russian. Do you wish to speak in English or Russian?"

"English is not a problem."

"Fine. If we go on with this, there is no turning back. Do you understand?"

"Yes."

"Is this what you want to do?"

"Yes."

"Fine. Then why are you here? What can we do to help you?"

In preparing for this meeting, the Poet and I had decided to take a quiet and calm, unsurprised approach and to hear Yuri out, to let him do the talking and not hit him with a lot of questions.

Yuri paused, looked around, and then said, "I have a serious financial problem, one that I am not ready to discuss in full. Assuming you help me, I believe I can help you."

"What help do you want?" asked the Poet.

"Money. I'll break with my government. I want asylum. Are you recording what we say?"

The Poet looked up from his notepad. "Yuri, we have a portable recorder. We are recording this conversation."

"*Nyet*, if you please. I prefer no recorder," said Yuri, shaking his head. "This will have to be quick. I do not have much time. I spent too much time trying to find this place."

"All right," said the Poet, "I'll turn it off. I am going to take some notes. Continue."

We lied. The automobile had a voice-activated microphone concealed in the ceiling of the car tied in to a recorder hidden in the seat. The device was activated when we entered the vehicle. The Poet and I decided there was no way we were going to proceed with this interview without a record of the conversation.

"I am Yuri Popov. I am a colonel in the KGB. I have diplomatic cover and a diplomat passport and am assigned to the UN. You understand that there are directorates. I am assigned to the First Chief Directorate, North America, that works with agents in the US without diplomatic cover."

There was no way of knowing if he was telling us the truth, that he was a senior KGB officer, even if he had medals on his chest and was wearing a red flag with a hammer and sickle. Yet, if he was in a directorate overseeing the United States and illegals, such a defector would be a monumental coup.

Illegals who were residing and operating within the United States would not be US citizens. They often entered the United States through Canada. Finding such people was next to impossible. If this meeting played out and Yuri's statements were true, it could result in a major setback for the Russians.

Since the Poet and I both knew we would have to make a determination as to whether Yuri was telling the truth, we studied him.

There are two schools of thought to consider regarding interviews, one being body language and the telltale face. It was a great indicator of whether a person was lying. If a question was asked, did that person respond by looking you in the eye, or were his eyes averted down? It's a judgment call. Yuri wasn't averting his eyes. Yuri's eyes, mouth, and hands were expressionless. There was no trembling, no sweat, no rubbing of his nose. His arms weren't crossed. He was speaking calmly and objectively.

The other school of thought in judging a person's honesty was focusing on content. What is he telling you? This was the CIA's approach. We were nowhere close to assessing that.

As to body language, fidgeting or sweating, he was passing the test. Yup, I thought. Either he was telling us the truth, or from years of training, he was very, very good, with no visible indication of a hidden agenda. Since I had been covering Yuri for some time and had digested his complete file, I knew enough about him to separate most facts from fiction.

I thus decided to pay close attention to the CIA approach, concentrating on content and details. If a person is telling the truth, and not concocting a story, he or she will be able to provide you with more external detail of events and places, such as sounds, odors, the presence of other people. We wouldn't need a rubber hose to get this out. The final script of what was said would be the proof of the pudding.

I nodded at Yuri. "Go ahead."

"As I said, I have a serious financial problem. I'm in need of money. I wish to remain in the United States with my wife and child. We seek asylum, not right now but in the foreseeable future."

I looked over at the Poet, who lit a cigarette. We nodded at Yuri.

"I have run up sizable debts. Giving you reasons why I need money would take me too long to explain. I have six months remaining on my tour. I've been told that my tour is not going to be extended."

"Who told you that?" asked the Poet.

"My superior. I don't get along with him. He constantly belittles me. He says that I have not been productive. They want to bring over someone who…who…What is the word I want? Someone who is more aggressive and vigorous? They will send me to some remote, insignificant pasture. My wife will not be happy."

"Does she know you are here?" I asked.

"No. But she will know. We are happy here. Life has been comfortable and good, not like living in Soviet Russia."

Yuri paused. I continued writing notes. The Poet finally looked over and asked our first important question.

"How much money do you need?"

Yuri took another nervous draw from his cigarette and responded, "Fifty thousand dollars."

The Poet and I had discussed prior to the interview that to determine if Yuri was telling the truth, we would have to test him, not simply by what he told us but by actual deeds.

"If we get you fifty thousand dollars, how can you help us?" asked the Poet. "Give us specifics—something right now that we can take back to the office to persuade our superiors."

"I think you know we have people living here quietly in the US. Since I have been here, I have had contact with many of your Americans. I have interviewed several walk-ins, a few of whom being extremely helpful and knowledgeable with your military bases and weapons. I'm also assigned to agents in place operating here. I can supply you with names and addresses."

"How do you handle these American agents?"

"I have an associate, a junior officer that assists me. We arrange contacts at restaurants and other places. With documents, we insist on actual originals, not interpretations. We pay well. You Americans are greedy. Money is primary motivation. We look for those who are vulnerable, someone with ego or grudge or perhaps person terminated from one of your governmental agencies who feels he got a raw deal."

"You have access to files?"

"It's not like a public library, but I have ways of breaking security and copying."

"Yuri," I said, "we'll need something concrete now with legs."

Yuri looked confused. "What means legs?"

"Something credible. Something or someone we can pinpoint or identify."

Yuri looked down at his watch and then at me. "What about the money?"

"What about it?" I asked.

"The fifty thousand dollars I have mentioned. You will provide?"

"Fifty thousand dollars?" I said. "All right."

"You guarantee?"

"Yes."

"Thank you. I have confidence that the information I provide is worth it.

"A few agents I handle live Upstate. They have been here from some time. They live quietly, becoming acclimated to the US. They are not yet productive. We expect one to become employed in one of your defense industries. His code name is Lester. We also have one of your naval officers supplying us with information. I do not know his name. His code name is Locust."

"Where is the naval officer located? What base?" asked the Poet.

"His base is in New Jersey."

"What does he look like?" I asked. "White, black? Give us more details."

"I am not his handler. But he is a white officer, in his thirties."

I looked over at the Poet and smiled. The Poet picked up his pen. "OK, give us all of the facts that you know on Lester and Locust and your duties here. Then we are going to adjourn, come up with some kind of plan, and get back to you."

For the next hour, we talked and banged away at things happening at the mission. We discussed with Yuri the subject of protection and when he wished to defect and how much time he would need, what would happen if he did in fact defect, and the potential risks. We told him how we would contact him for meets. Yuri provided us with information regarding his living accommodations outside the Soviet mission and his role and job as a Soviet delegate assigned to the United Nations. If he was going to help us and gather facts, then it was important that he be around people who said things worth knowing. We thus quizzed him on his associations both in the Soviet mission and at the United Nations. We knew this delegation had diplomatic cover to work with their agents and American citizens who were providing them information.

Yuri was one of many Soviet delegates and as a delegate had certain duties to attend to, but for the most part, he was able, according to him, to come and go as he pleased; he did not believe he was being watched extensively. We knew the Soviet delegation had security officers, whose role was to police, cover, and watch the delegates and to report any idiosyncrasies, quirks, or indications that a delegate was tempted and appeared to be headed in a direction to stray over to the American side. Yuri confirmed this and outlined his role as a delegate, trying to cultivate contacts, attending trade shows, calling on Russian émigrés living in the United States, giving them news about their relatives living in Russia, and further utilizing indices on American tourists who frequented Russia and communist-bloc countries, and then calling on them for social engagements. We agreed to meet again and discussed arrangements. We wanted to meet soon and told Yuri we would have the money for him at the next meeting.

CHAPTER 17

RHAPSODY IN BU

Thursday, June 6, 1968

IT WAS THURSDAY, THE DAY after meeting with Yuri. I got to the office early. I went directly to my desk and wrote down as much of the conversation with Yuri as I could remember. I reviewed it with other investigative files to see if everything Yuri gave us was plausible.

The Boss finally noticed that the Poet and I were back in, jumped up from his desk, and came around his cubical.

"Hey! What is this? Let's have at it? What happened?"

The Poet and I entered the Boss's office; he sat down behind his desk, on which sat a large stack of FD 302s, weighted down by a New York Rangers hockey puck.

"Well, somebody begin. How did you two make out?" Charley asked, as he put his arms and hands behind his head and leaned back in his chair.

"Yuri talked and rubbed his nose a lot," answered the Poet.

"That means he was lying," said Charley.

I smiled. "What are we—human lie detectors?"

"Hey," said Charley, "with interrogation, it's like a carnival side show. You know the drill. We guess their height and weight. What do we have?"

"We've come across a gold nugget. If he is who he says he is and does what he says he does, then we are about to enter the holiest of holies," said the Poet.

"Meaning?"

"He handles and appears to have access to information on illegals."

"Illegals?" Charlie stood up and then began pacing. "He works in the branch of the KGB that oversees agents that have no diplomatic cover?"

"Yup."

"Jesus. How long has he been doing this? There's nothing in his file or anything from the home office that tells us that. Deuce, do you agree?"

I looked at Charley. "Nothing that I've come across. I was as shocked as the Poet when he started telling us about it."

"This is incredible. This could be a real coup, if of course it's true."

The Poet looked up. "It could get you out of here, Boss. You'll become a section chief. You'll get a promotion away from the city that never sleeps. You'll head down to the swamp in DC. Your wife will love it."

"You have four of those, right."

"What I don't understand," I said, "is how the CIA stumbled on this information. Why would they turn it over to us? This guy is too important."

"Have you asked them?"

"No, I haven't."

"Who knows what they know. Maybe they don't know anything more than we know," said Charley. "So why is Yuri doing this? Or is it just bullshit?"

"He needs money," said the Poet.

"Money and not disillusionment with the communist system? Did it occur to you that this could be all bullshit? Maybe the KGB sent the guy over to give us disinformation."

"Since he only mentioned money, it does look like he is only interested in a pension," said the Poet. "As to whether it is bullshit, Deuce and I didn't have our fingers on his pulse. But to me the guy is for real." The Poet looked over at me. "What do you think?"

"I don't know. According to Yuri, he's not viewed within the KGB as a guy that's productive. Yuri would be happy with any new American contact and information source. That would make him look good and perhaps extend his stay. We can probably help him there, and maybe that is the real reason for all of this."

"Where is he in the KGB chain?" asked Charley.

"High level."

"Did he give any actual reason other than money for talking to us?"

The Poet looked over at me and then back at Charley. "He wants to break with his government. We didn't discuss ideological convictions. We didn't have that much time."

"Any domestic trouble? What about his wife and family?"

"Nothing there that we could determine. He hasn't talked to his wife yet, but he thinks that she will not be a problem."

"Frankly," I said, "if the test of bona fides is the type of information he gave us, then we are off to a good start."

Charley now sat down behind his desk and leaned back. "OK. What good stuff did he give us?"

"Information on one of their sources," I said. "A US naval officer. In exchange for this information, I had to guarantee Yuri big bucks."

"Really. How much?"

"Fifty thousand."

"No kidding. Have you come into an inheritance?"

"Boss, promises are one thing. Paying is another. Frankly, I thought I could raise the money at the poker table."

The Poet looked over and grinned. "Deuce is getting better at cards."

"So what are the details on this naval officer?" Charley asked. "Identity?"

"Caucasian. A guy in his thirties. Works out of a base in New Jersey. They've been working the guy for two years."

"Really," Charley chuckled. "I bet I can tell you where they met?"

"What do you mean?" asked the Poet.

"The naval officer is one of our informants. Code name ANJOB. The file is top secret and being handled by an agent from DC."

"So what does this tell us?" I asked rhetorically.

"What it tells us," said Charley, "is that the Russians are giving us nothing we don't know. It's chickenfeed. They are probably on to ANJOB as a double."

"Which means?" continued the Poet.

"It means that Yuri is either being knowingly played as a disinformation tool by the KGB and is not bona fide, or he is simply out of the loop within the agency and a real defector. Either way this is not a good start because at the moment we've been given shit."

"Shit? As in nothing?" I asked.

Charley shook his head and looked at me. "Did he give us the names and particulars of the hierarchy in the mission?"

"No."

"Did he give us the locations of any dead drops?"

"No."

"Then I rest my case," said Charley.

"Wait a minute," I said. "What about Lester, the illegals in Upstate New York?"

"All right. What about Lester?" asked Charley. "What did he tell you?"

"He said Lester was expected to be employed in one of our defense industries."

"Duh," said Charley. "That's a nothing, right?"

The Boss was right of course. It was a nothing.

"Lester," said Charley, "is a giveaway, if they are not producing. Overall when you look at it closely, he has not given us much, and he walks away as a thief with our fifty thousand, which is probably just the beginning. That's not such a good deal, is it?"

The Poet nodded his head in agreement. "If we continue to talk to Yuri, he may give us more nonsense. We then have to check it out."

"Right," said Charley. "This will keep us busy and occupied and gobble up our resources chasing ghosts. That is what the Russians want. Look, the game we play here is difficult enough without wasting a lot of time. We have to think about the information being passed. What are their intentions? What's the bait? What do they want with us?"

"So what do we do with him?" I asked.

"We meet with him again, see what he gives us, and encourage him to stay put, on the outside chance we are mistaken. We feed him placebos. Every now and then, we give him something a step above. It will improve his standing with his bosses. How much time does he have left on his tour?"

"Six months."

Charley now stood up like a nervous horse smelling smoke and began pacing.

"Something else has come up. This past week we received a directive from our esteemed leader authorizing us to commence a counterintelligence operation called New Left, or COINTELPRO. We've known for some time it was coming. Its purpose is to infiltrate and disrupt domestic political organizations."

"What is that supposed to mean?" I asked. "Our job is Russians."

"You are right, but a lot of this flows together. We've got information from a Cuban informant that the KGB are going to pass money, perhaps two hundred fifty grand, to the Cuban mission for delivery to the Black Panthers to sow more dissention. It has to do with recruitment of agents and giving the Panthers funds, perhaps for weapons."

"So the Russians want to start helping the militants," said the Poet. "That information is not chickenfeed."

"Weapons and insurrection," I said. "It fits right in with everything going on."

"Right," said the Poet, "they are probably heading for Harlem?"

Charley peered over at us. "If they are successful, Harlem won't be quiet for long. We'll need to cover this meet between the Cuban and the Panthers. My instinct is to tell you to seize the cash. We now have evidence that the Soviets are trying to stir up American dissidents. It blends right in with the antiwar protests on the street."

"Yeah," I said, "but there are a lot of Americans donating money to the Panthers. We are not arresting them or seizing that cash."

"Yes," said Charley, "but this is different. You can't have the Panthers or any other new left group, like the SNCC or the Weathermen, operating as secret agents of a foreign power, accepting money from the Soviet Union. If this information is true, then the Panthers are legitimate targets of our counter-intelligence. No ifs, ands, or buts, we have to stop them in their tracks. We'll have to cover that Cuban meet. I'll get you the date. This new directive gives us a ton of leeway. When we are told to expose, disrupt, and neutralize these groups, it means we are going to be able to do a lot of covert shit. I'm going to give each of you a top-secret memo that came across my desk from the seat of government on the New Left and black-extremist groups. I want you to read it, initial it, and give it back to me by the end of the day. Deuce, I want you to get your team together and come up with a plan to seize the KGB cash—and for the love of God, no mistakes. Also I suggest you contact a few Panther informants to see what they know."

"We are ahead of you on informants," the Poet jumped in. "I have a Panther informant, and we will see what he has to say."

I left Charley's office, went back to my desk, and looked over Charley's memo. There were always a lot of unanswered questions on money. Where did the Russians park their money? Did they have bank accounts? I reasoned that they used money carriers from the Kremlin.

No one had to tell me that the black-extremist groups like the Black Panthers needed money. Publishing and advertisement costs required funds. This could not be satisfied with the sale of literature. One had to rob banks or develop international contacts.

I looked at the memo, which read:

Top Secret The Radical Movement Top Secret
The Black Panthers
Development of New Left Movement: Overview

There has appeared most notably among students and young intellectuals a leftist movement marked by violence and lawlessness and evidenced in riots and demonstrations. The catalyst for this movement is the Vietnam War along with the continual struggle for civil rights by blacks.

The youth movement is revolutionary and brings with it bloodshed, countless arrests, and the use of the National Guard and federal troops. The financial outlay, borne by state and municipal governments, universities, and private citizens, amounts to millions of dollars.

The movement manifests itself in numerous organizations. The Students for a Democratic Society (SDS) is the most vigorous and is led by Thomas Hayden and Mark Rudd. The SDS concerns itself not so much with civil rights as it does with the Vietnam War.

In contrast the black-extremist movement is designed to achieve identity and power. This movement is predominantly a college student movement, and this paper is focused on the black-extremist student movement and not organizations like the SDS. There is growing militancy, with campus rebellions and riotous demonstrations. Many student groups desire to be a part of the black-nationalist movement, which has been exploited by articulate individuals like Stokely Carmichael of the Student Nonviolent Coordinating Committee (SNCC), who has made statements that we must prepare for the confrontation between white and black, that he is for revolutionary violence, and urging listeners to arm themselves. The SNCC was founded as a nonviolent-protest civil-rights group but has moved toward the notion of black revolution. The SNCC has attempted to align itself with the Black Panther Party (BPP), but it has not yet materialized. H. Rap Brown succeeded Carmichael as national chairman of the SNCC. Brown has been found guilty of violating the Federal Firearms Act and has been sentenced to five years in prison. He is free on bond pending his appeal and resides in New York City.

The Black Panthers

This is the most violent black-extremist group in the United States. Eldridge Cleaver was its minister of information and spokesman. He is self-educated in large part due to the fact that most of his life was spent behind bars. Following his release from prison in 1966, he joined the Black Panthers and formulated disturbances and violence. Since revocation of his parole, Cleaver is now a fugitive. The BPP supports communist revolutionary movements. It advocates guerrilla warfare and seeks to exploit black college students.

The BPP are believed to be the superstars of the radical movement, considered heroes to some white college students and the "radical chic" social set. They constitute an army of approximately three to four thousand black militants, concentrating their efforts in Oakland, Seattle, New York City, and other cities. They have coined the phrase "Power comes from the barrel of a gun." Their platform calls for, inter alia, "financial reparation to the black man for centuries of robberies by the white man, full employment, decent housing, exemption of all blacks from military service." They are known to scream obscenities on street corners, exhorting blacks to kill whites and police. Their aim is to bomb public buildings, like department stores and train stations. Huey Newton is their supreme commander.

To staff organizations and publish materials and other advertisements requires funds. The black movement obtains money from the sale of literature, contributions, and occasionally through criminal acts. Several foundations in New York who are sympathetic have also been generous. The movement has also turned to international contacts. Many members have journeyed to Cuba, heaping praise on Castro and in turn receiving instruction on techniques in demonstration and revolution. They have been told not to identify themselves in any way with the communists or the Communist Party but rather to speak in terms of the better life that was in store once the revolution is complete.

Tactics to Be Used to Counteract

We must expose, disrupt, and otherwise neutralize the movement. We must frustrate every effort of these groups and individuals to consolidate their forces or to recruit new or useful adherents. The anarchistic activities of a few can paralyze institutions of learning, induction centers, cripple traffic, and tie the arms of law enforcement officials, all to the detriment of our society. Our goal is to prevent militant black-nationalist groups and leaders from gaining respectability by discrediting them to three segments of the community—the responsible Negro community, the white community, both the responsible community and the "liberals" who have vestiges of sympathy for militant black nationalists simply because they are Negroes.

The following plan and tactics are being recommended. Specific details have been orally communicated to each field office and for security purposes are not herein set forth verbatim, but they include and are not necessarily limited to the following: Focus on ways to deny funding. Concentrate on disruption and disinformation to curtail and disrupt Panther activity; promotion of internal party power struggles, strife, and ego-tripping; securing informants and infiltrators within the BPP; and doing whatever you need to do to enhance our knowledge of this group and keep rabble-rousers out of black communities, such as Harlem, by any means deemed appropriate.

I set the memo down and started to think about this. With apologies to Poe, words from "The Raven" came to mind. I pondered a title called "Rhapsody in Bu."

Once upon a law day dreary as I pondered weak and weary,
Over many and quaint curious Bu files of forgotten lore,
As I sat there dreaming better, typical agent go-getter,
Suddenly there came a letter, from the bureau's hatchet corp.
"New Left lawlessness," they muttered, "attacking at our nation's door."
Quoth the agents, "Evermore."
Bug, attack, and kick their ass, is what I felt we had in store. This was it and nothing more.

CHAPTER 18

TAMING THE CAT

—————◆—————

Friday, June 14, 1968.

AFTER OUR MEETING WITH YURI, the Poet and I spent a lot of time together going through a ton of files on the New Left, the SNCC, and the Black Panthers. We were interested in the funding and financing of these groups.

This morning I was seated at the counter of Thompson's restaurant having breakfast, drinking strong black coffee and reading *The New York Times*, when I heard a voice and felt a hand on the back of my neck. "Now don't move. This is not a cathouse but a respectable restaurant."

"A cathouse would be more to my liking," I said. I didn't bother to look up or even turn around.

Then another voice behind me said, "Every time I see this guy coming to the office, he comes in from a different direction. What does that tell you?"

The waitress was now standing in front of me. I looked at her.

"Ma'am, call security. I've got some homeless guys bothering me again."

I wheeled around and looked behind me to see the Poet and Big D. They then sat down and joined me at the counter. Like me they were two of the regulars who came in for coffee and breakfast. D flipped open one of the menus. I looked at D.

"I come in from a different direction each day to protect myself," I said. "Routines can be dangerous. You guys know that. Staying alive is important."

"Of course it's important," said D. "We don't want to get snuffed out at this point in our career, do we?"

"If I got snuffed out," I said, "who would you guys have to beat up on at the poker table?"

What was great about Thompson's was that the waitress was quick with the coffee, something important to the Poet, who, after leaning over for his first sip, immediately reached for and lit a cigarette.

Big D's eyes were bloodshot, and he was unusually quiet, which meant for me that he was suffering from a bad head, probably from lengthy hours at Bishops.

"The air outside is crisp; the sun is bright; what say you today, D?"

Big D took a sip of his coffee, paused a bit, and then murmured, "I have of late, but wherefore I know not, lost all my mirth."

"Could be an oncoming symptom of hemorrhoidal misery," I said.

"That's not it," said D. "It's more of a case of the continual blahs, not feeling good."

"The blahs are a disease of which I know every symptom. Happiness and gaiety are important. The loss of it probably means you are not drinking enough," I said.

"Yeah," added the Poet, "this city is a gigantic madhouse. Drink is medication and a worthy steed."

"And don't pay any homage to sexual abstinence," I added. "Always keep in mind that New York City could be worse. Do you remember when Captain Scott arrived at the South Pole? He wrote in his diary, 'Great God, this is an awful place.'"

"And it's the insufferable personalities of the people we must deal with on this island that is causing your problem," said the Poet.

"Present company excluded," I added. "We work to escape reality. Besides, you're a Southern boy. You're used to a slower pace."

"Seriously," said D. "Do you think that's what it is?"

"Of course. The pace of the city is fast. Your mood will pass. Give it time."

"Shouldn't take longer than a year or two," said the Poet.

I put my arm around D. "D, listen. All of us who work here experience bouts of anhedonia."

"Must be contagious."

"It is. But then the weekend comes. Pleasure resumes. Wine. Flirtatious girls. Song."

"You're forgetting the landscape," said the Poet. "Lush green courtyard, erotic playpen, thumpin' sounds...Every building, every stone, sans the desert and the sea, has a story all its own."

"Yeah, but I've been losing a lot of sleep. Bad dreams," said D.

"Losing a little sleep is not one of anhedonia's symptoms. What kind of dreams are you having?" I asked.

"Of being confined. Solitary confinement," said Big D.

"Thank God. You're just like the rest of us. You're trying to escape from reality," said the Poet, looking over and chuckling.

I looked at the Poet. "How about you? Did you have bad dreams last night?"

"The only dream I had included my informant."

"Who is your Panther informant, and where are we going to meet him?"

With a cigarette in his left hand and a filled coffee cup in the other, the Poet looked back and grinned. "His name is Luther, but his code name is Sweetness. He is going to meet us at the south end of Central Park in about an hour."

"What's he like?"

"Don't worry. You'll like Luther."

"Really, why is that?" I asked.

The Poet smiled and looked over at Big D. "Luther is sweet, gay, and may even be a cross-dresser."

My voice cracked, and I almost bounced out of my chair, with the Poet's cigarette ash all over me. I was laughing so hard I gasped for air.

"You have to be kidding. This is one of your tough informants from the extremist Black Panther Party, a violent revolutionary, a person who is supposed to be organizing campus sit-ins and disruption?"

"Yup. He's one of their tough guys. You don't think a guy smothered by his mama can be tough?"

"Oh, they can be tough. So how do you know he's gay? Is there a tattoo on one of his arms that says that?"

The Poet looked at me and repeated the question. "How do I know?"

"Yeah. That's what I asked. Did he come out of the closet?"

"More or less. I spoke to his mom. He was a precocious kid."

"That's not enough. What does a mom know? There must be more."

"There is. When I interviewed him a few years ago, he admitted it. But he's gone back into the closet."

"Maybe you are the magnetic core for the guy. So today, he's back in the closet, because he doesn't want anyone to know. Why would he do that?" I asked.

The Poet paused and took another drag off of his cigarette. "Probably because he is with the Panthers. They don't want someone that is soft."

"I never looked at the Black Panthers as a homosexual crowd. Hmm...Does the Boss know this? This informant sounds like the guy I was going to fix D up with."

"Yup, and he is still available for D."

I looked over at D. "So what do you think D? You have a chance to get out of your blahs. You can participate in a scientific study, as to whether sex between men is the same as female sex."

"I think I'll pass," said D.

The Poet smiled and turned serious.

"Listen now. According to Luther, his parents (a couple of militants) got him involved with the Panthers. They used their influence and gave a substantial monetary contribution to get him in. Maybe they wanted to toughen him up."

"A bribe will generally open a lot of doors and can get you into med school or law school," I said.

"Hey," said D, "not in North Carolina."

The Poet took another drag from his cigarette. "Luther's parents are probably trying to make him stoic, like some Christian waiting for the lions to be admitted into the arena."

"If Luther's parents wanted to toughen him up, is there something wrong with having him enlist in the marines?" I asked.

"He tried that. Got rejected."

"I'm anxious to meet this guy. We can toughen him up, or maybe we should introduce him to Alex Santoya and let him toughen him up."

I was surprised at this news from the Poet. Always we were told in training class that gay informants were not wanted. Could not be trusted. There were too many issues. The daily control of physical desires and passions sometimes led to loss of self-respect and humiliation. For many it could be overwhelming, leading to a lot of despair, frustration, loneliness, anguish, therapy sessions, and a regular intake of pills. Any one of these could lead to a willingness to concoct stories and pass along information that simply was not true, or so we were told. The problem with gay informants, just like occasionally dealing with the Boss, was separating fact from fiction.

But there was another side of the coin that I figured the Poet was exploiting. We needed more informants, particularly in the Panthers, and Luther was the man.

"How did you recruit this guy?" I asked.

"Deuce, espionage is what we do, right?" said the Poet. "I didn't confess to Luther the same longing, but I did mention that I had a brother that was gay, which was a lie. That showed sympathy and understanding. I also gave him some money, which relieved some anxiety."

"Jesus," I said, "you put a lot of thought into this."

"Listen," said the Poet, "remember one thing about gay guys. They are the best conversationalists and greatest cooks around."

"Maybe we can get Luther over to my pad the next time I have you and the crew over for fish."

The Poet and I left the restaurant and walked over to Fifth Avenue. I observed its usual bustle with black limousines lining the street waiting for many of the residents. In the distance as we walked south on Fifth Avenue, skyscrapers rose in the morning light like plants. Cabs were moving to and from their front doors like beetles feeding on them.

As we approached Fifty-Ninth Street, the south end of Central Park, the Poet leaned into me and nudged me in the ribs with his right elbow. I looked at him. He nodded his head toward a black man sitting on a park bench, looking in the direction of the Plaza Hotel, a large building located on the southwest corner of Fifth Avenue and Fifty-Ninth Street. From the bench where the black man was sitting, a pathway existed running northwest that took you into the interior of Central Park.

"There's our guy," said the Poet, quietly. "I'm going to introduce you as David."

From a distance, Luther looked boyish. It was difficult to tell his age. I took him to be late twenties or early thirties. He was leaning back on the bench, looking relaxed, with his arms crossed, resting. He was wearing sunglasses. His legs stretched out in tight trousers leading to shoes that looked more appropriate for a tango dancer than one who walked on city streets. He held a brown bag. I thought to myself that maybe he was waiting to feed the pigeons. We walked over. The Poet quickly made the introductions.

"Luther, meet David," said the Poet.

I gave his eyes a fixed stare.

"The white men cometh," said Luther as he looked up at us.

I nodded to the Poet, who spoke to Luther with a quiet voice and purring rasp.

Luther was smiling. He was a striking young man, with a handsome body, pomaded hair, and delicate almost feminine hands. His skin was smooth. His eyes were large like a deer in headlights. Eyes in front, likes to hunt. Eyes on the side, likes to hide. Luther was not a hunter. He appeared to be at peace with himself.

"You guys took your time."

"Been waiting long?" I asked.

"I never have to wait long for my friend here. Besides, the scenery at this hour is sizzling." Luther nodded his head toward Fifty-Ninth Street.

I looked over to see a leggy blonde crossing the street dressed in a blouse and a tight, flowered short dress.

"God don't like ugly. You won't find it on this corner," said Luther.

"Can we join you on this bench?" I asked. Without waiting for an answer, the Poet and I sat down next to Luther.

"You're the feds. Help yourself."

"So how are the brothers, Luther?" asked the Poet.

"The bothers are angry but doing well."

"They are always angry, aren't they?"

"That's because there is a lot to be angry about. Deal wit' it. It's a daily class struggle."

"Tell me, Luther, you guys aren't really planning to kill some cops and blow up Midtown stores, are you?" I asked.

"Who told you that?"

"We're the feds. Remember."

"All we want is to be free from the white racist establishment."

"The Panthers aren't racist?" asked the Poet.

"Look. It's the media that has made us look like racists. They never discuss the true nature of the struggle."

Around Luther's neck was a heavy silver necklace slave chain.

"That's a nice chain you have there. Where can I get me one of those?" I asked.

Luther put his hand under the necklace and moved it around.

"Paid cash for this. I have a friend who sells these on the street. The next time I see him, I'll pick you up one."

"Thanks," I said. "Luther, come on; it's a beautiful day. Let's take a walk in the park. We can go down and see one of my favorite animals, a panther, at the zoo. I get a hard-on for panthers."

Luther smiled. "I like panthers too. But I never get a hard-on."

"Really," I said, looking distressed. "Have trouble getting it up, Luther?"

Luther laughed. We got up and commenced walking toward the Central Park Zoo.

"Luther," I said, "my friend here tells me that you have a federal criminal case coming up. Some drug charge. Possession of cannabis."

"Yeah. They got me on some hash. They say it was mine. But it wasn't. All a mistake."

"No kidding. Possessing ten pounds of marijuana looks like delivery to me."

"Sure enough," said the Poet. "With that amount they're going to say that you were dealing in the stuff. What does your lawyer tell you you're looking at if convicted?"

"My lawyer is guessing. Maybe three," Luther said.

"Three, huh," I said. "With good time, maybe you can get out in two. Shit. The slammer is going to be tough. Rat infested. Broken toilets. It's that clunk of the steel door slamming shut behind you that will get to you, Luther. Then comes the horror of it all once you are in there with mentally ill gang guys. You become one of theirs. Fresh meat thrown to a pack of wolves who will sadistically brutalize you."

"But it was a mistake," Luther says.

"What's a mistake?"

"The hash. It wasn't mine."

"It may be a mistake, but if it's found in your possession or you are close to it, you own it. Guilty. End of story. Case closed."

"But I'm not guilty. I can't do time. I just can't."

"Sounds like a real tough case to me, don't you agree?" I asked, looking over at the Poet.

"You're not going to need a lawyer, Luther, to beat that charge," said the Poet. "You're going to need a magician."

"But I've been helping you guys. You said you would do something."

The Poet stopped and looked at Luther.

"Like what are you suggesting? Talking to the assistant US attorney. You looking for references on your resume?"

"Well, I have been helping, haven't I?"

"You've been giving us some stuff but nothing special. What am I supposed to tell the prosecutor, that you are giving us some general information about Rap, Stokely, and how the Panthers function? You gave us information about a planned hijacking of an interstate shipment. Then when we covered that, it didn't go down. You're going to have to do better than that. We need something much bigger with legs."

Luther stopped walking. His smile vanished.

"Suppose I were to tell you that the Panthers are receiving a package with a lot of money next week and I'm supposed to pick it up."

"Suppose we were to ask how much money?" I asked.

"Six figures."

"Where's this money coming from?" asked the Poet.

"Cuba. All I know is that the delivery is going to be made to us next week in Central Park. Someone from the Cuban mission."

"So where is Cuba getting this money?" I asked. "Cuba doesn't have a lot of money to give away."

"We talk to a lot of people. We don't care where the money comes from, but there is a guy I met that has offered some help."

"So who is this nice guy that out of the kindness of his heart wants to contribute big bucks to the Panthers?" the Poet asked.

"He's Russian. He was at one of our rallies. We met. We talked. He said it would be delivered by a Cuban from their mission to the UN."

"The Panthers now doing business with the commies, Luther? You all drinking from the same well?" I asked.

Luther didn't reply. We kept walking.

"What are the Panthers going to do with all of that money? Are you preparing for an offensive?" asked the Poet.

"Don't know yet," said Luther.

"Say it ain't so, Luther. Sounds to me like you are buying weapons to off the pigs," said the Poet.

"Hmm," I said. "You get money from an unfriendly foreign country like Russia, and you become an agent for that country. You on the Russian payroll, Luther?"

"Me?"

"Yeah, you? It's about security. You're a threat. That's why we bug your house and steam open your mail." I smiled.

Luther laughed. "That would be scandalous. Listen, we get checks in the mail from people, US citizens, all of the time. You are telling me that if we accept some dough from another country, that's different?"

"You got it," said the Poet. "First of all when you act as an agent for a foreign government, the law requires that you notify the US attorney or the secretary of state. Have you or anyone from the Panthers done that?"

Luther looked perplexed and said nothing.

The Poet looked at him. "That is something that to us is totally unacceptable and endangers the security of our citizens and the USA. Consorting with commies can be a serious offense."

"Luther," I asked, "when you and the brothers spoke to the Russian, what was he interested in?"

"He's talking about recruitment, about finding young people who want to work for the US government. He's also talking about helping the Panthers in organizing in Harlem."

"Harlem, huh," I replied. "Like doing something similar to what went on in Detroit and Watts?"

Beads of sweat appeared on Luther's face.

"Something like that, but it's only in the planning stage. No dates have been set."

The Poet looked at Luther.

"Let's see, Luther. It's like this. If you put us at the right place and the right time next week, so we were able to retrieve that package of money from the Cuban, and if you keep us closely posted from here on out about planned events taking place in Harlem, then David here and I will talk to the assistant US attorney about you. Right, David?"

"That's right," I said. "We would tell him you were instrumental in helping us resolve significant internal-security matters, and we needed you with us on the street. That ought to cause the government to cut you a lot of slack on your case and give you probation with no jail time. But if you say a word or talk about this to anyone, the deal is off. What do you think of them apples?"

"So what do we do to keep the brothers from getting uptight, when they don't get their money?" asked Luther. "My head could be on a platter."

"Luther, we are the FBI. We will figure something out," said the Poet, who extended his right hand to Luther.

Luther reached out and shook hands with the Poet. "All right. Give me the details and tell me what you want me to do."

"Luther," the Poet said. "Listen. You have to be cool. You have to be discreet. A closed mouth catches no flies. All of this has to go down correctly, and that money has to show up where you tell us, or all bets are off. Understood?"

Luther nodded. "Understood."

CHAPTER 19

A DATE IN THE PARK

———◆———

I FELT THE DAY WENT great. We learned a lot from Luther. He confirmed what Charley told us. He would help us. I was a foot soldier in an ongoing war, and soon we were going to strike.

I walked home to my cramped quarters, exhausted. I felt like a stricken diabetic or someone with MS. The good news was that the weekend was coming up in Manhattan. C was flying in. I felt curiously happy for a change and in a state of erotic arousal.

Regrettably, however, my sexual feelings, or lack thereof, were rendered physically insensible by thoughts of what we would have to do with the Cuban money man. A plan was needed with no slipups. My devotion to the cause of justice and doing good for America brought on thoughts of a need to stay focused, avoid perversion, and follow the celibate lifestyle of the Knife. Then I thought that a short delay in such thinking with perhaps a romp in the hay over the weekend would hurt no one.

The celibate lifestyle of the Knife was always a puzzle. The Knife somehow managed to avoid tawdry encounters and sleaziness in his personal life in Manhattan and remain chaste. I thought more about this after meeting an attractive female in a saloon on Third Avenue when she commented to me, "You guys coming here from west of the Hudson are accustomed only to necking." I began to wonder if it was the Knife that she was talking about. At the time, the only response I could muster was a very lame, "Ho-hum."

It was time for my blood to rise. A detour to my hot tub with a few cans of Rheingold was a necessity. As I soaked my body in my iodine-colored hot water, I figured that the Knife was probably again at home staying in the weekend reading another of his nonfiction books, keeping loneliness at bay.

Exiting the tub, a mist of perspiration clung to my skin, which allowed for easy shaving in front of my cracked mirror above the sink. I was able to see my wrecked appearance and blood-shot eyes and realized that my face wasn't getting any younger. Stress, a heavy workload, and New York City had caused my life to undergo a metamorphosis. I was losing it. Depression, like perhaps what D was experiencing, was not uncommon with New York City lives. Not even a dalliance could save it. The job and the city were doing me in, creating havoc with a once decent-looking human being.

Then I thought, forget it. This was the weekend, and nights out in New York City were exciting and could, without reading nonfiction, produce a tremendous amount of fun. There were always plenty of options, including meeting friends for conversation. Although the lack of a lot of money left me innocent of New York gastronomy, there was still an option of hamburgers and beer at a local pub or going to a concert or Yankees game, where I could badge my way in for a seat in the grandstand.

I looked again into the mirror. Taped to the bottom half were photos of the top ten fugitives, the toughest and most dangerous guys on the run and in hiding. I had placed the photos there, reasoning that if I stared at them long enough while shaving, I might remember their faces. I could get lucky and run into one of them on the streets of New York. I could make a solo arrest. It would mean a commendation. Money. A transfer to San Diego.

I frequented a lot of bars. The whereabouts of a fugitive named Mapps, believed to be employed somewhere as a bartender, had always intrigued me, although many of the agents thought the guy was dead.

I finally gave C a call.

"Granada here," I said over the phone. "What are you doing tonight?"

"Today you're Granada? Why don't we get together? I don't fly out until Sunday."

"Super."

"What shall we do?" asked C.

"Well, maybe we could start out at Max's and finish at the Bishops."

Max's was another bar scene, a small place on Park Avenue South, the interior of which looked like a set for a movie, frequented extensively by musicians and artists, twenty- and thirtysomethings, pretty boys using a lot of cologne, and only occasionally an assortment of goons. The downside was that it was a bit expensive, but what attracted us to it, like Bachelors III, was that it was a great place to go to, not to be seen, but simply to anonymously look and listen. For a glimpse of the underground and drug use, we could find it at Max's. We went in unknown, undiscovered, and simply became flies on the wall. Super art was displayed all over the place.

"Max's has great art. According to Picasso, art washes away from the soul the dust of everyday life." I had just read that comment in the New York Times and thought that might impress C.

"Deuce, you say the nicest things."

"Well, a good liberal arts education will do that."

"I want my dust washed away." said C, "What's happening at the Bishops?"

"D wants us to meet him there for drinks. He wants to introduce us to Jake Lamotta."

"Who is Jake Lamotta?" C asked.

"C, Jake is the king, the bull, the middleweight champ. Like, sweet Sugar Ray, pound for pound, one of the best fighters ever. He is a friend of D's. This will be fun."

"What shall I wear?" C inquired.

"How about leg warmers over leotards. You can go as a dancer. I'll be right over. I'll pick it out for you."

I jumped in a pair of jeans and threw on a light navy pea jacket, and some clear glass spectacles.

C was staying at an apartment complex on East Fifty-First Street, sans a doorman. To get there was a lengthy walk, but to save money, a walk was the only way to go. I rang the downstairs bell and quickly heard C's voice.

"Who is it?"

"It's Freddie, the masseur, sponge, and bath guy, who relieves aches, pains, and stress. Therapist, sex-crazed maniac, man for all seasons...Can I come in?"

The buzzer rang, and I bounded up three flights of stairs to C's apartment. I opened the door and stuck my head in.

"Hello," I called.

From the bathroom I heard a whisper. "Freddie, is that you. I'm over here. There is a bottle of Mateus in the fridge. Bring two glasses."

I located the Mateus and saw that the level was down to the label. It was unusual for C to drink wine. She preferred Scotch. I located glasses, filled a kettle with ice, and walked down the hall to the bathroom. I pushed the door open, poured two glasses of wine, sipped one, and found C relaxing in a bubble bath, with her right leg hanging over the tub.

She turned her head and looked up at me, smiling, with her mouth a little open.

I leaned over and gave her a kiss.

"I was surprised you called. Thought you would be working."

"Couldn't resist seeing you. Are we celebrating something?" I asked.

"Yes, a six-month anniversary of going out together. Freddie, could you start with a sponge on my back? I need to be rubbed and kneaded. Do you see anything new?"

"In that bubble bath, I can't see anything. The foam is up to your neck. What is it, a piece of jewelry, your hairdo?"

C lifted her right foot. On it hung a rather thick, black braided bracelet. "I got it just for you," she said.

I reached over and removed it from her foot, placing it on my wrist. "Gee, thanks. It's beautiful. A wonderful gift. I can't think of anyone who deserves it more. Luther has one of these."

"Who's Luther?"

"Oh, just a friend."

"You look bedraggled. Jump right in, why don't you?" C beckoned.

"Ah. Relieving tension is what I'm good at, and I need to relieve some of my own. It might be a lot easier to work my magic hands if I did that."

I undressed, dropped my Levi's, climbed in the tub behind her, and lowered myself into a mass of foam. I handed her a glass of wine. I wet my finger and slowly rubbed it around the rim of her glass, producing a high-pitched sound.

"Not bad. Huh? It's the key of C. Opens doors to hearts."

"Thank you. Sounds beautiful."

I leaned my head back and closed my eyes. The steaming water made me feel totally relaxed. At last, I thought, my crippled body was starting to heal. Despite the fact that I began to sweat profusely, sitting in the tub filled me with the erotic promise of an approaching tryst, something I hadn't been able to experience in at least a week, with all that was on my mind. To put it bluntly, I was filled with lust and a state of excitement, not an uncommon thing living in Manhattan, despite its motorized angry horrors. After a day of stress, worrying about how I was going to handle the Cuban money man and all that cash, I felt this to be my just reward. It wasn't about the money. C woke me from these thoughts.

"What are you thinking?"

"The usual demented fantasy."

"Am I in it?"

"Very much so and your response should be, 'Oh, darling, yes.'"

I would be a liar if I told her I didn't get horny and experience a primal attraction when I was around her. It was after all part of the New York scene. On these occasions when I had not seen her for a while, I decided that, rather than simply lifting her up and carrying her to bed, I instead would control my emotions, until I just couldn't take it anymore. So I sunk down again into the water, hoping beyond hope that she would say something like Madame Bovary, "I'm yours. Take me, Deuce, take me; have your way with me, right now. Oh, I can't wait any longer." But when such conversation didn't come, reality always asserted itself.

"I believe my stress today is dissipating," she announced. "I feel relaxed, terrific, and horny."

"Gee, I love it when you talk dirty."

"More wine?" she asked. With the tip of her tongue, she licked the bottom of the glass, and then lifted the bottle of Mateus.

"Yes, ma'am, I'll have another, and thank you for being horny."

"Deuce, have you ever been shot at or had to kill anybody?"

"What brought that on? Why do you ask?"

"I worry about you."

"You should. Every day could be my last. Reason enough why you should make love to me every chance you get."

C smiled.

"A bulletproof vest would help." This was something my mother wanted to get me. I resisted because she had no money and would have to raise it through garage sales. Somehow with C's questions I felt the promise of an approaching tryst was vanishing.

"The answer to your question is that I've not yet been shot at; nor have I had to kill anybody. But next week may be different."

"Next week. What's going on?"

"Have an operation. You want to know the details. Right?"

"Yes."

"Sorry. I can't give them."

"What about the Russian?"

"What about him?"

"Who is he?"

"Why do you want to know? Why do you always ask me that?"

"Curious. Don't want you getting hurt. What do you do if someone gets shot?"

"That happened to me once. I was with two other agents chasing a fugitive, trying to arrest a thirty-year-old gangbanger. One of the agents ended up shooting the guy, after he pulled a gun. He was lying unconscious in a pool of blood, with a few slugs in him and part of his brain on the pavement. As you stand over him, the question arises, how bad is he hurt? He appeared to be dead. I checked his pulse. It was beating fast under my forefingers. An ambulance arrived. No blood pressure. The guy needed to be in an operating room if only to harvest his parts for heart and liver transplants. It was definitely not my theater. About all I could do was hold his hand and try to comfort him. He expired at the scene. It's a hell of a way to go. They put a tag on his toe. Off he would go, to the morgue."

"Doesn't that bother you?" she asked.

"What? That we shot him? That he died? What?"

"Both," she said with a grin.

"Not really. The idea with law enforcement is to get the fugitive or bad guy off the street. What difference does it make if he ends up alive or dead?"

"What do you mean?"

"What I mean is that the goal is to have to chase as few fugitives as possible. It's a revolving door. They keep coming. But if we eliminate them faster than they come, then we win."

C looked puzzled. "You may win, but then you would have nothing to do."

"Not exactly," I said. "We could spend more time on other cases of importance, instead of running down leads chasing bad guys."

C was not smiling. "I think I'm beginning to get it. A bad guy leaving the streets by death is OK."

"Exactly. If he ends up dead, it was his choice. For some, the only game they know is do or die. When a person—someone you are trying to arrest—draws a weapon on you, it's an invitation, an automatic invitation to shoot. Well, not necessarily automatic, because in a split second, before you shoot the son of a bitch, you have to decide if he is going to use it or does he just want to flash it, telling you simply to leave him alone. If you do shoot, it is always with the intent to kill, not injure or maim. So to answer your original question, no, it doesn't bother me, even if I had to pull the trigger."

C gulped down her wine. We wrapped ourselves in towels. I took her hand and walked her from the bathroom.

"Don't worry. There is an element of danger in most anything that you do, particularly when we live as we do in this city. My job doesn't involve fugitives but Russian matters. There are risks. But it could be worse. I'm OK with what I do."

"What do you do with the Russians?"

"C, don't go there. Can't discuss it."

"You like this macho business, don't you?" she asked.

"The thought of being shot doesn't appeal to me. But in this business, even if something isn't dangerous, you can still get hurt. Fortunately, I've never had my nose broke."

C started to laugh. "That could destroy the gentleness of your face."

"Thank you. I'll keep that in mind the next time I'm in a fistfight."

We walked to her bedroom. I sat down on her bed, watching her. "OK, do you really want me to pick out what to wear?"

"Yes," C said. "What I like about you is that you notice a woman's appearance. Most men are not that way."

"Clothes conceal your body but reveal your soul. Obviously, you have never read the proverb concerning a harlot's attire."

"Which is?"

"Clothing worn to attract men's eyes and excite the lust of their flesh."

"Oh, stop it," said C. "I don't wear stiletto shoes and black leather skirts."

"Well, at least remember that when you get dressed, you make a decision on what you will be doing all day."

"Meaning?"

"If you have to do some running or serious walking, you do not want flip-flops. Let's see. Dress like me."

"Like someone who put his clothes on in front of an airplane propeller?"

"Exactly. The rumpled, wrinkled look is in"

Looking into her closet, I pointed to jeans.

"For starters, how about jeans, the ones with your fabric bottom. We don't want to look like we have money. Then add boots, black wig, no makeup, small leather tan Hermès tote (just kidding), Chap Stick, some cash, no identification. I've got my credentials, cash, gun, two paper cups, and the rest of the wine."

I looked over, and C was sitting on the bed, bending her leg and pulling up her boot.

"Beautiful leg there." Her leg was a beautiful specimen, flexing in her tight jeans, and then she stood up.

"Well, how does this look?" C announced as she bent forward, poking out her magnificent buns.

"Actually your posterior is probably more impressive than your legs. C, let's leave. It's time to disappear and get lost in the city." I looked down at my watch. "But we do have a few minutes."

"To do what?"

"Fool around."

C fell back on the bed, laughing, and then hesitated and looked at me. "Maybe later. It's something I look forward to."

"Yeah, right." C was a beautiful love machine, who would give back twofold what you gave in love to her. There was no low libido in C's makeup. While other couples we were with would occasionally discuss being perfectly adjusted sexually, that type of communication or disclosure would never come from C, who preferred to have whatever we had together a hidden secret. Whether it was the glue that held the relationship together, which I doubt, we never seemed to run out of fuel. The relationship didn't get tepid. It just got hotter.

As we walked out of the building, I looked over at C.

"Well, you do look cute. Stylish. You dress nice. Must have something to do with the person who picks out your clothes."

"Where to now?" she asked.

"Let's wander down to the park and then on to the Bishops to meet D."

"It's a beautiful night, isn't it?" And it really was with a slight breeze. The day was winding down.

"Very and we're in the coolest town in the world."

C turned to me. "You have nice friends."

"Yup, a good crew to have fun with. They do crazy and eccentric things. The city makes you a little of each."

Actually, for many years I tried to cultivate a reputation of being atypical and unconventional. To acquire such a reputation of eccentricity is not easy and takes a great deal of thought and labor. Weird, bizarre conduct is often not enough. Somehow, one's total personality is examined to come up with that type of assessment, which is something the Poet pointed out to me.

With C, our eccentricity, if I could call it that, involved disguises and disappearing acts. She was a most happy camper participating, for as she explained, it was like being onstage in a theater. She knew I did not want to be identified by anyone from the office, or any number of the sources, informants, I'd been in contact with and that the unrecognizable appearances, the masquerading (if you could call it that), produced a smoke screen and freedom of movement, enjoyment, and happiness. We were both happy losing an identity and assuming another.

I concluded that the roles we were in fact playing were live. For lack of a better definition, I called it Stanislavski's system. Stanislavski was the Russian actor and director who developed techniques for acting. I thought it fit well with the Russian cases I was working on.

In the shadow of a lone tree protruding out of concrete, C stopped, put her hand in my hand in my coat pocket, looked up at me, and said, "Deuce, I think I like you."

"Is it because of my money or the magnetism of my charm? My guess is that you are intrigued with my stringent attitude toward sex."

"Well..."

"Do you realize that there are at least a thousand women living in the Sixties on the East Side that have carnal plans for my body?"

"Stop it. Let's take these mother—"

I looked down and quickly interrupted her. "It's motherfuckers? That's supposed to be my line. But in the words of my Italian informant, I'm wich you."

We strolled holding hands and walked north and over to Fifth Avenue, which along with Park Avenue was the richest of all neighborhoods. The warm evening was descending with a nighttime breeze. The tall illuminated streetlights ran south like a string of pearls in the direction of Fifty-Ninth Street and the Plaza. It was the cocktail hour. It was getting dark. So much of life in the city was now invisible, all contained in buildings behind walls.

The avenue was beautiful, contiguous as it is to Central Park. The street was deserted, with light from the apartment complexes on one side and darkness and quiet on the other. At this hour few of the socialites, retired bankers, and power brokers were out and about, for the avenue was winding down, with traffic sparse. Residents were returning home, carrying bags after a day of shopping, and there was a changing of the guard of doormen and bellmen, all clad in their charcoal-gray jackets, with their steps echoing on the empty streets, and in their pockets the dreaded screeching whistles that drew cabs, upsetting the quiet and penetrating apartments and your body like a knife.

The whistles, however, at this hour were silent. I reasoned that maybe the upshot of living on this gilded isle was that the time of day had come to be spent inside talking about death and money, or maybe even counting it. The area here was packed with wealth, with more money in one block than in many midwestern small towns.

It was a place loaded with *twis*, an expression and word not found in a dictionary, but coined by a pretty antique dealer friend of mine and a Newport, Rhode Island, designer. A *twi*, pronounced "twee," she explained, was a person with very little empathy, displaying extravagance and pretentiousness, old and fancy. "You don't want to be a twi, believe me," she said.

We found a park bench. C climbed onto my lap and curled up into my arms. I took out the wine and filled two plastic cups with rose from a flask. A flask was a necessity in Manhattan. We sat there casually sipping, watching the traffic. A few horse-drawn carts went by. I closed my eyes.

I rarely got drunk sipping wine. For that matter I rarely got drunk period. Around the poker table, we drank a lot and looked at it like oil lubricating a machine. It kept the machine operating smoothly, settling the nerves and slowing down the usual aggression and tension. At the poker table, a discussion generally centered on current events and what it took to survive and get ahead in New York. To get ahead took a fevered hustle and a necessity to keep up mentally. Reading *The New York Times* daily cover to cover was a start.

Normally I carried *The New York Times*. We would sit together and sift through the news, but it was getting too dark for that now.

The problem with New York was that it offered too much. There was too much going on at any time during the day. It could be overwhelming. It came down to the fact that unless you got out on the street, you felt you were missing something.

I began to wonder if Yuri felt the same way. It was seven o'clock. What was he doing? Was he having dinner or out hustling and getting into trouble?

C poked me in the side. "Where are you?" she asked.

"New York City. On a park bench. Somewhere on Fifth Avenue."

C smiled. "I know that. But you are not with me. You are always doing something in your head. What are you thinking about?"

"I was thinking of twis."

"They are attractive, aren't they," C added as she cocked her head back and stared up at a large chestnut.

"Well, I wouldn't know. Most of them at the moment are indoors."

"What are you talking about?"

I looked at C. "Actually I'm dreaming one of my demented fantasies. But to make a dream come true, you have to stay awake."

"What did you dream?

"I don't know. I dozed off and slept through most of it."

"OK. What was it?"

"I'm daydreaming. Look around. Don't you think this scene is like something out of Fitzgerald's Gatsby?"

"How do you mean?"

"I mean that many people in the buildings down this avenue acquired their wealth through inheritances, complete with bootleggers and shady deals. You have to see through the mist. It's all an illusion. You've read Gatsby, right?"

"Yes."

"I've read Fitzgerald too but not with such intense interest that I reserve for Warren or Styron. Anyway, in his book, Fitzgerald talked about a night scene painted by El Greco with several men in suits walking along a sidewalk carrying a stretcher holding a drunken woman in an evening dress. Her hand dangles over the stretcher. It sparkles with jewels. No one knew her name and no one cared. This is what I'm talking about. The people that live on this street, they party and do things to excess, and we're left cleaning up their mess. Wouldn't you rather live in a place where your conduct is founded on something other than money?"

"Well, it's fun and fascinating for me for now."

"True. When you go home for the holidays, you realize how much you miss it. At least I do."

"But my point is that if we were married, I don't think we would be feeling this way or doing what we do now. I mean, really, if we were forty or fifty years old, would we be going out and gallivanting around, visiting Irish bars or concerts disguised or dressed like hippies or even sitting on this park bench drinking Mateus?"

The answer from my perspective was yes, because I got a kick from Mateus, just as much as if I were drinking Dom Pérignon.

As she said that, I heard voices. I looked up and noticed the shadows of three persons coming out of the park approaching us. Out of instinct, training, or street savviness, I knew right away where this was heading. I lifted C and put her beside me on the bench.

"C," I said as I stood up, "sit tight. If something happens in the next few minutes, I want you to run as fast as you can across the street into that apartment building over there and find somebody you can trust."

"Like a guy wearing khaki pants and a striped Brooks Brothers shirt," she said. "What's wrong?"

"We have company. Tell the Brooks guy to call the cops, OK?"

Coming toward us adjacent to the park were three young, medium-height Hispanic or Puerto Rican heavies with muscular arms.

"Hey, gringo!" one yelled, as he was about ten feet away. "You need to pay rent if you use that park bench."

Here we go, I thought. The weight of my revolver in my coat was reassuring. I looked over at C. "Hey, remember what I said."

"Hey, man, do you think I'm joking? Do you think this is some kind of game?"

As the first one came within an arm's length, I reached into my jacket with my right hand and pulled out my five-shot Smith & Wesson. With my left arm, I reached forward and grabbed the Puerto Rican by the front of his shirt, pulling him forward, knocking off his baseball cap in the process, shoving my gun into his neck. I could smell the liquor on his breath.

"Amigo, listen to me. I'm the heat. FBI. Don't you guys know that crime doesn't pay? We feds don't pay rent when we sit on park benches. None of you move. *Comprende!*"

There was a long moment of silence as we all stood there. The other two Puerto Ricans stood back, motionless, saying nothing.

Finally, one said, "Hey, man, everything is cool. You keep that bench. We'll be going."

I shoved the middle Puerto Rican away and lowered my gun. "Really. Just like that? We're not done yet. Have you anything to offer before the sentence is passed?"

"What do you want, man?"

"Take everything out of your pockets and lay whatever shit you got in there on the sidewalk. Take off your shoes, and you"—pointing to the middle Puerto Rican—"you also take off your pants. *Ándale!*"

I looked at C, who just sat there wide-eyed while the three Puerto Ricans sat down on the sidewalk, emptying their pockets and removing their shoes. The third unbuckled his trousers and dropped them to the ground.

"OK," I said, "now listen up. We're going to play a game. It's called the hunt. You start running north into the park."

They stared at me, nodding their heads.

"Politeness requires that I give you a fair start. So I will wait ten minutes. Then, I'm coming after you. Once I catch you, I'm going to beat the shit out of you."

The three shoeless Puerto Ricans stood there saying nothing.

"Don't worry. Where you will be running you will not be abused by coyotes. Now go, before I change my mind and haul you to the slammer."

The three Puerto Ricans took off running and disappeared into the darkness and the woods. I sat down on the bench, put my gun away, reached for C's hand and the rest of the wine. Finally, she looked over, smiled, and squeezed my hand tight.

"You don't take prisoners. Do you?"

"They are delinquents under eighteen. What's the point?"

"It would give them a record."

"One way to stop this foolishness is with birth control. Besides, if I hauled them in, it would ruin your evening and mine, what with the paperwork and all."

"Well, Deuce, I can't wait to tell my flight crew about this."

"Don't. When you survive a frightening experience, there is always the tendency to exaggerate the danger, and we don't need that—do we?—because this was a nothing." It was after all a nothing. I was prepared to kill them, and it would have been done by instinct, like being a point down and shooting a basketball from the top of the key with only a few seconds left on the clock.

C looked dumbfounded. "A nothing? Are we going to call the police?"

"C, I am the police. An incident like this is commonplace and routine in a city this size. They needed a little money. I was prepared for something worse. Besides, never take all of your woes to the nearest police officer."

"You don't trust them?"

"I trust them. They are New York's finest. It's the paperwork and explanation, particularly since I ran these Puerto Ricans off without their shoes and a pair of pants. Think about the dispatcher putting out a bulletin. Be on the lookout for three Puerto Ricans running through Central Park, one with no pants. I think we both need a few more drinks at the Bishops." As I stood up, I kicked the Puerto Ricans' shoes, pants, and everything else off into the grass. "Come on."

I grabbed her hand and started fast walking south toward the Bishops. "Let's get out of here, before they return and bring a shitload of their friends back." I looked over and winked at her. "I've only got five shots in my revolver. And, C, please look at me and listen. What happened tonight—it stays with us. You and me. OK. Don't tell a soul."

C and I hustled down to the Bishops, which was Big D's favorite watering hole and was a place that C and I often visited. Bishops occupied a building on First Avenue in the Fifties that was sizzling with neon, but devoid of lowlifes and pimps. It was generally crawling with businessmen, banker types, and young people with money who worked on Wall Street and lived in Midtown Manhattan in the Forties and Fifties. As we approached the front door of the tavern, I could hear booming music and the pulsating rhythm of "Hold on, I'm Coming," by Sam and Dave. We were comin', all right, walking with a fast step to get inside, pulse rates up from a close Puerto Rican encounter, and I wanted to be comin' but hoped that that would come later.

Inside, the place was hopping, packed, congested, with a crush of people and couples so dense it was difficult to get through it. It was throbbing like a bee hive, with the draft beer flowing freely and everyone lit with a buzz. The tavern had a wooden floor, a long bar, booths where couples could sit eating quarter-pound hamburgers, flashing lights and a place to dance, which was already filled with young men and girls all in casual attire. A large mural was against one wall, depicting a scene from the roaring twenties, with flappers and long-legged teasers doing the Charleston. I looked down at C and winked. She was laughing and looked gorgeous. I put my arm around her and asked, "OK, ready to kick some ass?"

Across the room, sitting at the bar, I could see Big D motioning for us to come over, and he was sitting next to Jake, who was hunched over the bar with body language that read like "Leave me alone." The bar was facing about twenty feet of mirrors.

As we approached D, C was turning a lot of heads. We were, at least I thought, an attractive, if not odd and perhaps eccentric-looking, couple. I leaned down to C and whispered in her ear,

"Don't look to the right. You are being ogled." The guys in the bar were ignoring their own dates and were undressing C with their eyes.

C looked up. "Should we give them something to talk about?"

"Not yet," I said, "I want you to meet Jake."

Big D was laughing. He looked a bit hungover. He wheeled around and said, "Deuce, C, meet Jake LaMotta."

He turned around, grinned, and faced us while sitting on a barstool. I shook hands with Jake, who smiled. He still had all of his teeth and was the tough-looking, stocky fighter I'd once watched on TV, but shorter than I thought; he looked like he was staying in shape, not like a boxer gone to seed. Everyone was having a good time, but the music was so loud it was impossible to talk. Jake didn't say much, and even if he would have, I couldn't have heard him.

C and I took a few seats at the bar next to D. I looked at D and was struck by the incongruity of it all, sitting here with D and C and a guy who was familiar to me as a very combative Italian slugger.

D scraped the foam off a mug of beer with his forefinger and then drained a quarter of the beer from the mug with one swig. He looked over at me, smiling. He curled his finger around an imaginary trigger of a gun and fired a shot in the air.

"With all the noise in this place, we could assassinate some-one, and nobody would even know. So what do you think about next week, Deuce? You OK with everything? I'm looking forward to it."

"D, when I'm with you, the Poet, and the brothers, I feel we can pull off anything. Seriously. We are going to take care of business." I looked past D over at Jake, who was sitting facing the mirrors, with both elbows on the bar and a tall Budweiser in front of him. I nodded my head toward Jake and looked at D.

"Does he know you are a spook?" I asked.

"No," D replied. "Like you, I never discuss business, but I've been coming in here a lot, and we have been spending a lot of time together. He has lot of stories about boxing. He's made money hand over fist."

"That's what a boxer is supposed to do, isn't it? So what do you drink with this guy? Tell me it isn't punch."

D grinned. "Always beer. He's a great guy, fun. But he never asks me what I do. If we close this place, Jake has an after-hours place over on Forty-Eighth Street that he'll take us to. I've been over there with him. The place looks like an old speakeasy. Jake knocks on the door. They know him, so they let us in."

"Open after curfew? Somebody from the PD must be cutting them some slack. Who is in there?"

"Hoods. Wait until you see the bar girls. They all carry stilettos."

"Hmm," I looked over at C who was grinning. "Stilettos, huh. That ought to be interesting. I wonder why they carry them. There has to be a reason for it. Is it just for show or to get more dough?"

"Maybe both, but more probably for protection," said D. "The guys in there are all hoods or look like hoods."

"Jesus, D, it's because it's mob connected. You better get off Russians and work for a while on the pizza squad."

I got up from the barstool, grabbed C's hand, and headed for the dance floor. Before I got there, I turned around and yelled back at D, "And take something along more deadly than a stiletto."

After we left the Bishops, I walked C to her apartment. She was acting strange.

"Anything wrong?" I asked.

"I don't feel well. I've got a long trip planned, and I won't be around for a while. I love you, Deuce."

"I love you too. Take care."

We kissed. I went home and went to bed.

That was the last time I saw C.

CHAPTER 20

TAKING IT TO THE STREET

Monday, June 17, 1968

I DIDN'T SLEEP WELL. I lay awake thinking. I started to think about C. Toward the end of the evening, it'd seemed like she was in some jagged depression. Then events at the office rolled over in my mind. How should we handle the Cuban money man, while protecting our sources? Luther and Yuri were my concerns. We had to take care of business. I thought about Alex Santoya's comments to the mob. "Today we are on your street. But tomorrow you are on our street." The Cuban money man was going to be on our street and we had to hit him hard.

The weekend passed quickly. I spent time in the office Sunday, going over files. Monday morning, I got out of bed early. I strapped on my Smith & Wesson and took a five-mile run at Central Park, came back, took a hot shower, and decided that today I would dress totally in black.

It reflected my mood and the anticipated meet. I was ready. Along with the Smith & Wesson, I also carried the small Browning .25-caliber automatic, which on special occasions I felt brought me luck.

At the office, the Poet, the Knife, Old Yeller, TH, Big Al, and Big D were all tucked away, chattering and vociferous, in a private, smoke-filled windowless office, sitting around a table drinking black coffee. They were waiting for me.

Today they did not look like pallbearers at a funeral, although I may have. The Poet, oblivious to the noise, was completing the *Times* puzzle. Everyone looked pumped, alert, and ready.

"Gentlemen, gravel crunchers, and brain-dead ex–football jocks," I said, standing at the head of the table, banging a water glass with a spoon. "Did I miss anybody? Could I have the pleasure of your absence?"

D turned around looking at everyone. "Quiet please."

I continued. "Tonight we have a Cuban representative delivering a large sum of money received from the Soviet Union to a representative of the Black Panther Party. This is heavy stuff. Charley has given us the go ahead to seize the cash, but we need to do it in a fashion that nobody will know that the FBI was behind the seizure. This is not going to be an operation where we can afford a mistake."

All heads turned but with the usual noticeable grins.

"The hour of performing great deeds for America is fast approaching. The Russian bear is on the prowl," said TH.

"Yeah," said the Poet.

"And he be hungry and looking for meat," said D.

"What kind of meat he be looking for?" said TH. "There is white meat, red meat, minced meat—"

I banged the spoon again against the glass.

"Given the fervor of the Russians to provoke militant unrest, are we to carry on our relationship with them in an atmosphere of politeness and mutual consideration?"

"No!" they yelled back.

"Politeness is the product of an agrarian society," said TH.

"Good point," said D.

"There is a meet coming up, spelled m-e-e-t, not a dead drop or a brush, and a large sum of money is going to be delivered by a Cuban rabbit, which we must seize and retrieve."

"That it should come to this," cried D.

"A frontal assault to seize the cash is not going to cut it. We need stealth and cunning."

"You will have it, my lord."

I looked at the Poet. "When football teams roll in to Death Valley to play an adversary, what happens to them?"

"We kick their ass," said the Poet.

"And"—looking over at D—"when the Tar Heels are down ten points at half time, what do they do?"

"We tighten up. Grapple them unto thy soul with hoops of steel," cried D.

"I thought you treat them like mushrooms and blow out the lights, or is that at Duke?" said TH.

All of this was too much for the Knife and Old Yeller, who doubled up with laughter. "OK, did anyone bring a deck of cards, or is it too early?" said the Knife.

"Guys, we have got a mission. It's time to get serious. It must be daring and aggressive."

Old Yeller looked up. "Does this mean we must abandon our gentle nature?"

"Precisely," I said. "Charley has left the details of how we accomplish it to us. But we have to be disciplined. No wildcat tactics. No one gets killed or hurt. No blood. Once the sum of money is delivered to our Panther informant, we seize it."

In discussions with Charley, we'd agreed that Cuba was a morass. Their intelligence was poor. They were guided by the

Russians. The likelihood that they suspected anything was remote.

"And," said the Poet, "we have to protect the informant, because he is my informant."

"The plan is simple. We do not want the Russians to expect we know anything or that we are involved. So we stage this as an assault and robbery by thugs."

"Thugs?" said Big Al. "Hey, I like that."

"Thugs," I said, "as in purse snatchers and robbers of which the city has plenty."

"No assassination?" said Big D.

"*Assassination* is not the word you want," said the Poet. "Assassinations are reserved for people who are in public office. There are executions and murders. In this case, assuming we chose to do so, it would be an execution, because we would be fulfilling our public duties of protecting the internal security of America."

I took a sip of water and looked at D. "Don't mess with the Poet when it comes to words. Hey, with this mission, no one gets killed or hurt. We don't hurt the Cuban or Luther. We hit them when they are inside the park. Luther will walk the Cuban in to the park. The Poet and I will be there to seize the package. It's a robbery. We mess Luther up a bit, ever so lightly."

"I'll tell him in advance," said the Poet.

TH chuckled. "Let's roll over them. Hit them hard. But no roughing penalties. What do we need to carry?"

"I suggest that we each carry mikes and ear jacks, so we can communicate to one another. We dress like hoodlums and wear ski masks. I know. So what's new? Right? Oh, one other thing: Charley has arranged for one of us, probably Big D, to occupy a dental office after hours across the street from Central Park, to monitor things."

"So what about weapons?" asked the Knife.

"Hopefully," I said, "we won't need or have to use weapons."

The Poet pulled his pearl-handled revolver. "I can't imagine that I'll need something more than this, since I'll be at point with Deuce."

"Could we all stay serious for a moment?" I suggested. "As far as we know, Luther is to meet only one Cuban deliveryman. The Poet has arranged everything with Luther, and Luther knows what we are going to do."

Big D looked over at the Poet. "So what does Luther do in real life? Can we trust him?"

The Poet grinned. "Well, he doesn't go to the office. He works part-time at the local YMCA and also part-time as a nurses' aid at a local hospital. Yes, we can trust him."

"He's very shy—the kind you have to whistle at twice," said D.

The Knife looked over. "What happens to the money we seize? We count it, inventory it, and turn it in to Charley O?"

"That's the plan," I said. "Could be a big payday for Luther, probably in the range of five thousand dollars, depending on how much is there."

"He knows that if all goes well, he'll get a cut," added the Poet.

"He's like a lawyer," said the Knife. "He gets a percent."

With that we spent the rest of the day on details, going over to the park in pairs, studying the terrain, and then meeting again in late afternoon, to make sure everyone knew their assignment and what was expected of them. The Poet contacted Luther to again give him details on what to do.

The Poet suggested we each carry two guns, just in case a problem arose. I felt this to be a bit much but went along with it anyway. Shoes or hiking boots with laces were important. If you kicked somebody, it was important that the shoe stay on your foot. It was the little things that could ruin the day.

The evening came quickly. In the park the Poet and I took a seat on a bench.

I finally stood up and looked over at the Poet.

"D by now should be in the dental office. I see TH, and he is walking his black Labrador up and down Fifth Avenue. Looks like we are set."

Here in the Nineties, the park was densely wooded with over-arching limbs of chestnut trees protruding over the sidewalk. The Knife was with Old Yeller in a parked vehicle next to the entryway to the park. Everyone was in position.

I got on the horn. "Yankee to Foxtrot. How we doin'? See anything?"

Big D responded, "There are more things in heaven than are happening here. I see Sweetness. Things are quiet."

I walked to the entryway to the park. Down the street, I could see Sweetness, sitting on a bench, hunched over, looking at his feet.

I looked over at the Poet. "Well, I'm getting worried. The road to success is supposed to be paved with preparedness. Is there anything more we should be doing? Where the hell are they?"

"Patience," said the Poet. "We're OK."

On the radio, I heard the Knife. "How long do we wait? This may be a no-show."

"Give it time," I responded. "Maybe the package had a late dinner. Thirty more minutes and we go home."

When waiting for something to happen, time is like a watched pot that never boils. Everything seemed to pass so slowly.

It brought back to me memories of an earlier case where we'd had approximately eight agents involved in arresting a fugitive bank robber at a motel. The plan was to simply wait him out, to arrest him after he exited his motel room. Agents were stationed in adjoining rooms. I was in a stairwell, with another agent, a Cherokee Indian from Oklahoma. We sat in that stairwell for hours, bullshitting about food, girls, and life, until finally the fugitive came out of his room carrying an overnight bag. He was completely surprised and arrested without incident.

Suddenly, the voice of D came over the radio. "OK. We have company. The package is with us. He's following Sweetness to the designated site."

The Poet and I were approximately twenty feet from the entryway of the park. We donned our ski masks, squatted down, and positioned ourselves near the entryway. My adrenaline was flowing, with my heart throbbing in my ear. I felt rather pleased with myself that I wasn't nervous or frightened. I just wanted to get it over and get out of there.

"I'm going to hit the Cuban with a serious body block, Death Valley style," I said as I winked and grinned at the Poet. "When he is on the ground, I'll search him for weapons. You tell Sweetness to hit the turf. We grab the bag and get out of here. OK?"

The Poet looked over. "When this gets over, let's split with the troops for beer and poker. This day has gone far too long."

I looked at the entryway to the park. I could see TH in the background with his Labrador, tied to a parking meter, ready to lend assistance. Luther was now side by side with the Cuban, who was about five feet ten, thin, and in an overcoat. In his left hand, he carried a briefcase. As they walked past, I looked at the Poet, gave him a thumbs-up sign, got up from my squatted position, and ran the fifteen yards toward the Cuban in what felt like 4.5/40-yard speed, hitting the Cuban from behind with a body block and roll that lifted the Cuban about three feet in the air. I looked over to see the Poet push Luther to the ground. The Cuban was lying face-down. With my left hand, I shoved his face firmly into the grass, frisked him for weapons, removed his wallet, emptied it on the grass (taking the cash), grabbed the briefcase, and ran through the entryway with the Poet. It was over in seconds. In an alleyway across the street, we observed the Knife's vehicle. The Poet and I darted across the street. We climbed into the backseat, laughing like hell, and eased down the alley to conclude a successful mission. Everything had gone down so smoothly. We drove the bureau cars back to the garage, dropped off and inventoried the cash I'd taken from the Cuban and the briefcase, but not before looking in it. The cash was there, a lot of cash, which we all decided to inventory together and count in the morning.

Everyone was in high spirits. I was sky high with emotion and wanted to hug these guys. I looked over at everyone and handed my apartment key to the Poet. "OK. Let's go play some cards."

"Indeed," said D. "It's only ten o'clock. I'll call Louie and see if he wants to join us."

"I'll meet you guys at my apartment. I'll stop by Moe's for beer and sandwiches."

CHAPTER 21

KEEPING HARLEM QUIET

Tuesday, June 18, 1968

THE NEXT MORNING, THE POET and I joined the Boss in the conference room. The boss beckoned us to sit down and, after uttering a few complaints about traffic problems on New York City streets and getting to the office, came directly to the point.

"Two hundred fifty thousand dollars—wow, it's all here. Just as the Cuban informant said it would be." He laid out all of the bills on the conference table.

The Poet and I were sitting across the table. We looked at each other and grinned as Charley went through all the bills inventorying everything in a plastic bag. The Poet had checked on Sweetness, and everything was cool at his end. A nice payday for Luther was approaching.

"I'm thinking," said Charley as he looked at the Poet, "that Luther—Sweetness, or whatever you call him—deserves at least five thousand and maybe more. This is a major haul. Why don't you plan to make arrangements to get him that soon, OK, and help him with his drug case, for Christ's sake. Speak to the AUSA. This guy is an asset. We need him on the street."

I thought to myself that while Luther might be happy, the Russians were not going to be amused by this chain of events, losing $250,000 in some reported heist. It seemed likely that the problem of the Russians causing civil unrest by funding the Panthers was not over. Surely they would try again.

Charley leaned over the table and now grew serious. His eyes narrowed, and his head began to bob up and down. Even through my fatigued eyes, after a night of poker playing, I could tell he was coming up with something.

"Let's discuss this a bit and think about what we have here. The Russians want to sow dissent."

"Well, that's what the money is for," I said.

"Remember this," said Charley. "What is important is not who fires the gun, but who pays for the bullet."

I looked over at the Poet. Charley was getting philosophical. This was an interesting statement by Charley. In theory if someone hires a hit man to rub another person out, they are both culpable and would be charged with murder by the assistant US attorney. But the person doing the hiring, the one who initiates the scheme, is considered more culpable than the one who fires the gun. He'll get the longer jail sentence.

"Well, in our case the Russians are paying for the bullet," I said.

"Right," said Charley, "and the Cubans are making the delivery and firing the gun."

Charley now stood up and began pacing. He started to talk like a criminology professor to college students.

"Hmm. So why are they paying for the bullet? What neighborhood in the New York City borough of Manhattan would the Russians like to see erupt with violence and get over a thousand people either injured or killed, four thousand people arrested, and have billions of dollars in property loss like they had in Watts?"

The Poet grinned. "Is that a question you are asking us or yourself?"

"Hey, I'm asking you."

"Harlem," responded the Poet.

"Exactly. Harlem. A cloud in the sky may be small, but it can portend a storm, and as I see it, a storm is heading for Harlem, don't you agree?"

"It's a-comin'," I said.

"We have only one major black cultural neighborhood, and to date Harlem has been quiet. Can you imagine what would happen if Harlem were to rise up?"

I looked at Charley. "I agree. I guess it is time for some activity and action there."

Charley, the Nervous Norvus, now sat down, leaned back in his chair, raised his arms, and rested them behind his head.

"So what do we do? You guys read that memo from DC. We can't just sit here, bullshit, and do nothing."

The Poet lit another cigarette and looked over at me. "The way to keep things quiet in Harlem is to keep the rabble-rousers like Rap and Stokely out of there. Maybe it's time to make a house call on Bumpy. Bumpy controls Harlem."

I looked over at the Poet and laughed.

"Bumpy? Let's see, you mean the Harlem racquet king, the ball-buster, the Harlem Godfather, the Robin Hood of Harlem, the—"

"Enough," said Charley.

I was laughing and Charley was too; he looked over at me and winked.

"There is only one problem with making a house call on Bumpy," I said.

"What's that?" said the Poet.

"It would be difficult to interview a corpse. We would have to go the cemetery."

Charley looked at the Poet.

"Deuce is right. He's been dead for over a year. There hasn't been a lot of news out regarding his death. But you are on the money. Ordinarily, Bumpy would be the man to see, if—if—he were around."

Bumpy was a man filled with contradictions, but there was no question he was or had been the lord of Harlem. If we needed assistance, he definitely would have helped. Prior to his death, he partied and gambled a great deal. The last lap of his joy ride was made in a hearse.

"With Bumpy gone, there is only chaos," I said. "The place needs Italians."

"So who is the landlord?" asked the Poet.

Charley said nothing for a moment, seemingly in thought before giving a response. "Probably his second in command. We may have to settle for his protégé, Frank."

For a minute everyone was quiet. "Frank?" In my mind I did not think this would be a good idea, but I didn't say it. The problem with talking to Frank was that nobody knew much about him, except that he committed all kinds of crimes. Bumpy was a pimp but a standup kind of guy, even though he wore a lot of gold and encouraged unsafe sex. You could count on him in a time of need. He would never fool around with women if it hurt his business. With Frank, we wouldn't know what he might say or do.

"Frank will be OK," Charley said. "These guys are mobsters. They make their mark by rising up through the ranks. Once they are on top, they are king of the hill, and we can talk with them."

"He's definitely king of the hill," said the Poet. "Harlem is his private kingdom. Everything there is his."

They were in fact mobsters. They learned a lot from the Mafia, which was about shielding the guys at the top from the shit that took place on the ground. At the bottom rung of the ladder were the street guys, and at that level, it was all business and economically driven. They—the lower-rung guys—had to produce.

I looked at Charley. "So how do we handle Frank? What can we offer him to keep Harlem quiet?"

Without waiting for Charley to answer, the Poet cut in. "Look. We don't give him money. First we scare him. Then what we do is cut Frank some slack. We tell him we give him a free ride and leave him alone on certain things like gambling, drugs, and prostitution in exchange for some help."

"Maybe we should add extortion, fixing prizefights, and knocking off people. Is there anything else evil that he doesn't do up there?" I asked.

Charley looked across at us. "Hmm..." He started laughing incredulously. "As wicked as this guy sounds, why hasn't anyone put him in jail?"

"Probably," said the Poet, "because he's good. Also he has power and other people doing his work for him, and those people won't talk and be witnesses. So even though there's a lot of criminal activity, we and the NYPD can't put a glove on him."

"Well," said Charley, "if we want him to help keep Harlem quiet, we don't want to lay a glove on him, right? That's the point, at least not yet."

"I say we do what the Poet suggests. In exchange for keeping the Panther's out of there, we tell Frank we will cut him slack on numbers, bookmaking, prostitution, and drugs," I said.

"OK," said Charley. "But we can't cut him slack on drugs. If that got out, our ass would be grass. But gambling and prostitution we can live with. Those vices are tolerable, at least when you measure them against the alternative of Harlem burning and billions of dollars of property loss. I'll discuss Frank with the chief. We would also have to clear things with the New York PD. This may take some time, but I'm sure it will be a go.

CHAPTER 22

IN THE LAND OF THE WEARY BLUES

Monday, September 9.

AFTER OUR DISCUSSION WITH CHARLIE, I knew that a trip to Harlem and a visit with Frank was a fait accompli and would eventually come. As it turned out, it happened. There was simply too much riding on keeping Harlem quiet and free of violence.

Chaos, political turbulence and civil unrest had vastly increased. Bobby Kennedy was assassinated in Los Angeles in June and Hubert Humphrey was now the presidential candidate for the Democrats. Their convention held in Chicago in August was a disaster. Thousands of protesters including the SDS took to the streets. The police responded with mace, tear gas and beatings. Frustration and rage over the war were growing, along with demonstrations.

It was with this background that the Poet and I headed to northern Manhattan to speak with Frank. We weren't convinced that we would be able to get the job done with Frank and had doubts about his reliability, so we also worked on plan B, just in case Frank didn't pan out. We decided to locate and speak with Allah, who headed the Five Percenters, a local gang of rowdies and toughs in Harlem with no headquarters, who simply hung out, freelancers in a life of crime, looking for opportunities for mischief and lawlessness, which to them were normal and routine events in a typical day. We felt that the Five Percenters would be an appropriate fallback control group to keep Harlem quiet. They were tough. They would take on anything and were strong enough to keep the peace, we thought, in exchange for money of course.

The Five Percenters were also known as the Brotherhood of Allah and got their name from the 5 percent of the Harlem Muslims who smoked and drank.

Harlem was the largest neighborhood in New York, stretching from about 116th Street to the river and was a place that still boasted some of the best venues for food and jazz, and every vice imaginable.

When visiting Harlem, there were certain places—the mean streets—filled with gamblers, hustlers, and gangbangers, which were best to avoid and not recommended for a casual stroll at any time of day. In fact, there were sections that would not be wise for even a foreign power to invade. Certain places could be very violent and nasty and was a war zone already, where people would get rid of you with the wrong blink of an eye. For the guys at the office, including myself, we were content and willing to let it stay that way. We avoided Harlem, unless a visit to catch a fugitive was absolutely necessary.

Russian counterespionage, which was my shtick, did very little business there, for there was nothing existing or living in Harlem that was attractive to them from an espionage point of view to glom on to for sustenance. To remain permanently in the city and not get recalled to Moscow, food and good info was important to Russian spies.

The square to shun or dodge in Harlem was Fifth Avenue on the east, Seventh Avenue on the west, 130th Street on the north, and 120th Street on the south. This was a neighborhood within a neighborhood loaded with squalor and muscular, explosive soul, stray cats, dust, litter, filthy oily puddles, and massive potholes large enough to find refuge in, created according to the Poet from maybe a missile or two from an enemy battery. What was needed were some retired, conservative, angry, churchgoing ex-military folk with rifles and handguns to keep the place calm.

There were nice renovated houses, but when approaching the front and venturing into that quadrant, with its high-crime rate, it was paramount to pack heat and perhaps a supply of sulfa powder just in case you got wounded, and the Poet and I had plenty, including the Knife and Old Yeller as back up. The Poet and I were again each carrying two guns. I had my lucky Browning .25-caliber automatic strapped to my shin and my small five-shot Smith & Wesson in my right trench-coat pocket. The Poet and I both felt that a trench coat was needed for an interview with Frank to give us an edge. The weather was cool. The coat had an intimidating military bearing that we thought would be useful. Probably every agent in New York had a London Fog trench coat in their wardrobe. Mine had shoulder straps and D rings.

The plan was to talk to Frank in Mount Morris Park, in the morning, in the open, where the Poet and I were visible to our backups. Morning was a time when we felt things would be quiet and peaceful and not alive or bustling with families and gangs with handguns.

Mount Morris Park with its 20 acres had a lot of wooded terrain that would be suitable for artillery and guerrilla warfare training or survival courses, but we didn't have time for that. We wanted to get in and get out.

To meet Frank we gained the assistance of an informant from the Mafia, who set up the time and place for a meet and who advised Frank that it was a matter of the utmost importance. Frank was asked to come alone. We did not expect that, so the Poet and I first did a little recon, driving around the park a bit, checking it out, just to see what was out there and what we might be getting into, and sure enough the park appeared to be empty except for three big black guys a football field away from the street.

I parked the bureau car and checked in by radio with the Knife to see if he and Old Yeller were nearby and in place. It was one of those crisp days that would be more enjoyable sitting in Central Park with a date, a blanket, some wine, and an afternoon and evening with the promise of sexual fulfillment.

I looked over at the Poet. "Well, it's a perfect day to take a walk in the park, but I can think of other places I would rather be."

The Poet said nothing. He had picked up a pair of field glasses and was peering out the window.

"What do you think? Is that Frank over there?" I asked.

The Poet nodded. "That looks like him. Look at his clothes. I think he is the one standing. Here, take a look." He handed me the glasses.

The Poet started singing, "I had ma clothes cleaned, just like new. I put them on, but I still feels blue."

I put the glasses down. "You OK?" I asked.

"Deuce, when you visit Harlem, you have to read up on Langston Hughes."

"No time now for Langston." I focused in with the glasses. "Nice loud duds. He looks like an out-and-out pimp. The only thing missing is a pearly vest, pearl spats, and a cane. He must be making money off women."

"Duh. Nothing wrong with that," said the Poet.

"Hey. It looks like they are talking. Their lips are moving." What I noticed was a lot of gestures being made, but it was impossible to tell what was being said. "How are we going to handle this? Should we knock him out and then show him our creds?"

The Poet smiled and looked straight ahead.

"Let's do this. The first thing we need to do is to get Frank alone. Our discussion should be with him only."

"I'll go for that. Deniability, right, if things go bad?"

"Hey," said the Poet, "things are not going to go bad. This is a great move for America and beats the alternative of a Watts riot."

"Yeah, but does Frank have the power and the balls to carry it out?"

"He's got the power," said the Poet. "We don't want to be his friend, but we show him respect and scare him a little, and I bet he is scared right now, wondering what this is all about."

"Bumpy would have been a better target."

"Probably."

Bumpy had been hired by the Mafia and protected their operations up here. Frank was now doing some of that. This was one time I thought that we'd be on the same side as the Mafia.

"Let me do the talking," said the Poet.

"That's fine with me," I said. "I'll handle the introductions."

With that the Poet and I exited the car, and we started to walk the one hundred yards to where Frank was standing.

Frank was about forty years old, and everything we knew about Frank suggested that he was moving heavily into drug trafficking. To feel safe and to control loyalty, he surrounded himself with family and friends, many being from his hometown in North Carolina. They handled the distribution and were the go-betweens. Heavy surveillance on Frank, to document and detail how he spent his time, would probably reveal nothing, except his style of dress and living, which showed that Frank had money, plenty of money, but how and when he got it and from whom remained a mystery, which was why Frank was able to still roam the streets freely and not be in the slammer. We needed an informant, an inside guy, some kind of defector in place, like Yuri, who could provide us with information on Frank's operation, but there was no one yet that we had in mind that could undertake such a role because Frank was cool and smart, limiting his contact to close family members and friends.

When we are about ten feet away from Frank, I called out, "Frank! Long time no see. How are you getting along?"

Frank looked over, a bit surprised by this greeting, nodded, and didn't say anything. Frank had on a pinstripe suit and silk pocket square. All he needed for a ride was a pimpmobile. His face was expressionless. He didn't look happy.

Finally, he said, "What is it you want? What can I give you?"

"We've heard that business is good and that you are doing well. Bumpy would be proud of you." I extended my right hand and reached down to locate his and shake it.

"Frank, we're with the FBI." I quickly flashed my credentials. "How about if the three of us take a little walk? We are not going to go far, and we are not going to stay long. You OK with that?"

Frank looked over at what appeared to be two of his family members to see if they had any problem. They nodded. Frank glanced back. "I'm OK with that."

I extended my left hand in an "After you" gesture, and the three of us started walking farther into the park.

The Poet didn't waste any time. "Frank, we are talking to you for a reason. I think you know that."

Frank said nothing but nodded.

"We know what you are doing and what's going down."

"Like what?" asked Frank.

"Like numbers, policy slips, extortion."

Frank looked surprised. "Extortion, numbers?"

"Like eating potato chips, Frank, can't stop at just one."

"Yeah. When people owe you money, what do you do?" asked the Poet.

"I turn it over to a collection agency."

"No kidding."

Frank looked genuinely puzzled. "Am I supposed to hire a lawyer and go to court? People up here don't have the money for that and don't like to deal with nonsense. We encourage people to pay up," said Frank.

"So you make them worry and understand that there may be some pain," said the Poet.

Frank stopped and looked at the Poet. "Am I bothering you guys? I support my family and make a decent living, not hurting anybody. People up here need a little recreation. They like numbers, make a few bets on the Jets and the ponies."

"Frank," said the Poet, "slow down. We're not up here to catch you making your rounds at night."

"Then what's the beef? Why this meeting?"

"It's about America, Frank. It's about Harlem. We have some serious issues being raised down here. Potential demonstrations. Violence. We need assistance."

Frank paused. "No kidding. You are up here asking for help. That's a switch. There's a lot of anger on the street. Our people need help." He looked at the Poet. "Up here we take care of our people. Money we spend, we spend in the community. What kind of assistance you want?"

"First, we need to know if you are interested."

"I'm not looking for trouble. I'm interested."

"If you are interested, it's between you and us. It doesn't go further than you and us. National security. If you can't accept those terms, we're outta here."

The Poet stopped and looked over at Frank, who nodded. "This is something we do not want anyone else to know, cops or anybody. Understood?" Frank again nodded. "So if somebody starts asking, you lie."

I listened to this and could see the direction the fisherman Poet was heading. What a guy like Frank wanted was money, hot babes, and a fine set of wheels, and he knew that we could not only take that all away from him but throw him in the slammer as well, so he was going to do anything he needed to do to keep it. The Poet had thrown out his pole, dangling a hook above the water, and like some curious fish looking up at it, Frank was becoming impertinently curious about something yet unrevealed. And there was still no bait on the hook. I studied the expressionless face of Frank, and finally he looked at the Poet and nodded.

"Frank, if we find out otherwise that you are discussing this arrangement with others, then we are going to come down unmercifully hard on you. My friend here may even come up to Harlem with a ball bat and break your fucking kneecaps. Are you still interested?"

But for the seriousness and earnestness of the Poet and the moment, after that comment I nearly cracked a smile.

Frank looked over and again nodded.

"All right, Frank, what we want you to do is simple. It's about keeping Harlem quiet and free of demonstrations, violence, and riots. We are looking for assistance from somebody strong that can maintain peace and harmony. We wish Bumpy were around, but he's not. We think you are the go-to guy. It's about preventing another Watts from happening here on the East Coast. That would be bad for America and bad for your business. Am I right?"

Frank again nodded.

"So for starters, we are asking you to do what you need to do to keep certain people out of this neighborhood. We don't want anybody from the Black Panthers or guys like Rap and Stokely coming up here stirring up a lot of dust. You can handle that, can't you?"

"I know the players. We hang out. I treat them with respect, and they treat me with respect. That's why you are here?"

"We want things up here to be cool. When the summer heats up, people need something to do. A few numbers, bets, women. If this is what people need to be happy, we have no problem with that. Understand?"

"The days up here do get hot and exhaustin'. Everyone looks for a little amusement. Copping a thrill. You know."

"Amusement and money," said the Poet. "Everyone has to earn a living. You keep the neighborhood cool. We leave you alone. Are you with me?"

The hook was now lowered with a tasty morsel that I was confident no hungry, greedy fish could resist. And he didn't.

Frank paused, looked over, grinned, and extended his right hand. "Gambling and women, right? Should we draw up papers, or will a handshake do?"

The Poet extended his right hand and shook Frank's. "We are in a hurry; a handshake will have to do."

"Thanks," said Frank. "I'll take care of it."

As the Poet and I were walking away, Frank called out, "Hey, is there a way to make an adjustment on this deal?"

I looked back at him. "Adjustment? What kind of adjustment?"

Frank paused. "I can handle what you want done. But it's a large undertaking. How about sweetening the pot?"

"Like how?" I asked.

"You know," said Frank.

"No, I don't know," I said.

"Give me carte blanch on everything for a while. Let me fill in the blanks. No conditions."

The Poet jumped in. "If you are thinking of having us extend this arrangement to cover narcotics, no deal. Can't do that."

Frank looked at us and smiled. "Yeah, but maybe I can make it worth your while if you used your influence. Give you some candy. That sort of thing."

I smiled. "Do you have room for us?"

"I've got room," Frank shot back.

The comment by Frank was clear enough. The only way traffic in drugs paid off was if law enforcement and the police were paid off. That was the key to making money and survival on the streets, and there were a lot of cops on Frank's payroll. I could see the blood now rising in the Poet's face.

"Frank," he said, "we are going to pretend we didn't hear that. Attempted bribery of a public official can be real serious. The deal covers gambling and prostitution. Any other questions?"

"I was just kidding. Just testing you guys. I'm happy with the arrangement, and as I said, I'll take care of it."

"Frank, listen to me," I said. "Certain people have serious misgivings about what we are doing."

"Yeah," said Frank.

"Yeah. If there is the slightest outbreak of violence, burning, or bloodshed up here, we'll take that to mean that there is something wrong with this arrangement and that you can't deliver. Understand?"

Frank nodded.

Frank's words—"I'll take care of it"—hung with me, all the way back to the bureau car. As soon as the Poet got in, we both burst out with uncontrollable laughter, giving each other high fives.

"Jesus," I said, "I can't believe we just made a contract with the devil. This is historic. Did you see Frank's face and how serious he was? It was like asking him to help raise the American flag on Iwo. He is ready to follow us into battle. I honestly think Frank is going to take charge and help us, don't you? Fuck the Five Percenters. We don't need them."

The Poet looked over, smiling. "You bet. It's all about human nature. When the chips are down, and it's about America, the Mafia and the drug lords are ready to stand tall and pitch in. When we see Charley, we give him only a thumbs-up and put nothing about this visit in writing. The contract is between us and Frank. Let's hope we both stay alive, if we need to enforce it. Hey, let's contact the troops and celebrate tonight at the Bishops."

CHAPTER 23

IT'S NEVER ENOUGH

Thursday, September 12, 1968

IT WAS THURSDAY MORNING. THE Boss was beaming over all of the good news.

"We're on a roll. First we get our hands on a possible defector. We grab two hundred fifty grand of cash destined for the Black Panthers, and now we save Harlem from becoming a battleground."

Charley paused and looked over at me. "I was hoping that one of you guys would fuck things up, so I could kick your ass out of here."

It was not often that the Boss used foul language, but around this crew it was clearly the only way to make yourself understood.

"We're trying to make the bureau proud, Boss," I said. "It's about pride and tradition."

"Well," said the Boss, "maybe we are the best."

I looked around the conference table at the Poet, the Knife, and Big D, and all were grinning, for Charley was pacing around us, excited and going nonstop. "All this good news is going to lead to my promotion. If I'm not careful, I'll be packing my bags and heading for Washington, DC. Damn. Then I'd have to leave you guys."

"I don't know what we would do without you, Boss," said Big D. "The place would fall apart."

"Yeah," said the Poet, "but the Russians would be on their knees, saying, 'Thank you, Lord.'"

"It's a plot," said the Knife. "This good news was hatched and given to us by the Russians in order to get Charley off their backs and out of town."

"Now, listen," said Charley. "I'd love to get back into the field with you guys, but that's not an option. For that I'd need a demotion and not a promotion. You have the best of it. Me—I'm just a desk man. But let's not let everything go to our heads. With the bureau the grass is never green enough which is why they are always miserable."

Charley sat down with a pleased look on his face and sipped his coffee.

"Gents," said Charley, "don't lose sight of the fact that we work to please the seat of government. They are not concerned about the mob right now. They worry about the same things Congress worries about, and right now they are worrying about the Russians. They are also worried about violence and riots in the cities and whether the commies are promoting unrest. We stay concentrated on Russian agents. It's time to have another meeting with our mole, Firefly. The Russians have a mind. Get in it. Then massage it and manipulate it. Be tough. We need to generate more cases and more good news. Meet with him at Limestone. Pull out all the stops. If we are going to give him political asylum, do whatever you need to do, short of beating him with a rubber hose, to get more information and see if he is legit."

I looked over at the Poet and winked. We both knew this was not going to be easy. Finding out if Yuri was legit could never be sorted out with absolute certainty, and it would be tough to form concrete beliefs on anything. Limestone was our designated safe house on East Fifty-Second Street, a two-bedroom apartment rented by one of the agents and only periodically used. Although he wasn't telling us directly what to do, Charley was giving us a signal. Do whatever you needed to do. That meant breaking the rules if necessary.

It was not the time to be in a conservative mold. We had to be liberal. From a defense lawyer, I once learned that a liberal was a conservative who had been arrested and sucked into the criminal system. Our crew didn't have to be arrested. Here in New York City we were all liberal and willing to stretch things to the max.

I was very much feeling my oats. It was not important that Charley understand or know what we were doing. They were the desk guys. They didn't want to know. To the Poet, Big D, and me, it was all personal. It was protecting America. I knew that this was what we intended to do.

Having a defector in place inside the Soviet mission was a real bonanza. I took the first step by sleeping on this event and twirled around in my mind several thoughts about human behavior. Most people generally have behind their action or inaction one major motivation that supersedes everything else. Yuri had to have a reason to defect. If in fact he were bona fide, how would a KGB spy who wants to defect behave, particularly if he is still in place working and spying for us at the mission?

As I reflected on this, I concluded that the reasons for Yuri's defection could be (1) disillusionment with the Soviet system. But we didn't have enough information to make that judgment call. (2) Money—he said he needed money. Or (3) his failure to rise to a certain level in the agency—this could not be a legitimate reason.

If Yuri stayed in place, what kind of conversations would he have with his superiors? If he was bona fide, he'd want to keep the ruse going, to keep himself secure and behave in a fashion that did not let on to others that he was about to go over to the American side. Thus, I reasoned that such a person would want to go on with business as usual, but that if we supplied documents to Yuri, we could perhaps give him a boost within his inner circle, to show to his superiors that he was productive. Give him placebos but every now and then throw in some good shit.

To prove or disprove that he was legitimate, the Poet and I had a plan to get to the bottom of things. Capers and dirty tricks were always excellent ways to obtain truth.

CHAPTER 24

MOTHER'S LITTLE HELPER

Thursday, October 10, 1968.

IT WAS ABOUT NINE IN the morning when the Poet and I arrived at the safe house on Fifty-Second Street pursuant to instructions from the Boss. Today we had arranged another meeting with Firefly.

Limestone was a six-story apartment complex, located in the residential area of Midtown Manhattan on the east side. The building was situated on a quiet tree-lined street, where the noise of buses and cars and the babble of human voices were nonexistent. All of this encouraged intimacy. Discrete residents with quiet retired money oozed in and out of these buildings, but they mostly stayed inside. Life was lived indoors in unrestricted privacy. I was seduced. The area belonged in the South somewhere.

Utilizing a brush pass, we had slipped to Yuri a piece of paper with Limestone's address on it. We expected Yuri to arrive about noon. Within the building the accommodations, like the outside street, were very private. The outer door had no doorman. Once inside there was a well-lit high-ceilinged vestibule, which led across a marble floor to an inner door that had to be opened with a key, unless someone buzzed you through. We took the elevator to the fifth floor and entered the safe house.

This particular safe house was simply a large two-bedroom apartment that was leased by one of our agents who posed as a writer. To avoid daily commutes from his home on Long Island, he actually lived there during the week, but today we asked him to be out all day so that we could meet with Yuri.

We walked in. The blinds were slightly drawn, allowing some light to seep through, which revealed a living room that, owing to governmental budgetary restraints, was appointed with furniture one would find in a small-town mortuary, dark mahogany stuff and well-worked secondhand sofas. There was an odor of mildewed books. There were heavy curtains adjacent to the blinds that could be pulled if a need was felt for total privacy. We pulled them.

The Poet and I were told that the place was rigged with a large amount of audio equipment, including a hidden tape recorder and microphone. I walked over to the kitchen and opened the refrigerator.

I looked back and smiled at the Poet.

"Hey, looks like we are set for party time."

The refrigerator was filled with enough food for a banquet. The liquor cabinet was stacked with beer, Scotch, and vodka.

"What time is the good doctor going to arrive?" asked the Poet.

"He ought to be showing up any time."

"This is going to be interesting," said the Poet. "What do you know about the doc?"

"He comes highly recommended."

"Yeah. By who?"

"CIA spooks. He's cool, knowledgeable, and board certified. He is also Russian and earns part of his living as a translator and reviewing documents. He's also on the payroll of the CIA."

"Charley knows nothing about this, right?" asked the Poet.

"I didn't say anything. The only other person who knows we are here is Big D, who will be monitoring the transmissions."

"Good," said the Poet. "If it's a success and only if it's a success will we break the news to Charley. Agreed?"

"Agreed."

No sooner had we removed our coats, when a man's voice came over the intercom. I walked over to the intercom, pressed the button, and spoke into the metal grate. "Granada here."

A voice came back: "Good morning. The doctor has arrived."

"Doc, what's the name of the college where you did your undergraduate work? And give me your major," I said.

"Carlton and the major was biology."

"Come right up, Doc. I'll mix you a Bloody Mary. Take the elevator to the fifth floor. Turn left. It's the second door on the right."

I walked to the apartment door, opened it, and went out into the hallway. The elevator opened and out stepped the good doctor, carrying a large black duffel bag, looking relaxed and smiling. He paused for an instant and looked around, as if to get some feel for a possible escape route. He didn't say anything. He had an expression that I noticed with other agents. Someone resigned to do their duty. He was a large man, heavyset, fifty-ish with a beard and gray electrified bushy hair reminiscent of Einstein. He then came toward me, with a noticeable limp and with his right hand extended.

"Hello, Deuce, or should I call you 'Granada' today?"

I extended my right hand and shook his. "Granada will do just fine. Come on in. I didn't know doctors still made house calls."

"Well, we're starting to behave like plumbers."

"Except you don't charge like plumbers, right?" I motioned him in front of me and followed him inside the safe house. "And meet Shenandoah." The doc and Shenandoah shook hands.

"Bum wheel, Doc?" I pointed to his right leg.

"It's not the leg. It's my right hip. Degenerative problems. I've got all kinds of mobility issues, but I'm OK. What time does the patient arrive?"

"He'll be here in a few hours," I said.

"That's good. It will give us a chance to talk and give me a chance to set up. I'll explain to you what I'm going to do and how it will work."

"So how do you feel about this?" I asked.

"Good. I'm enthused and excited. It's not something routinely done, but I'm confident we can accomplish this without any complications. Where's that Bloody Mary?"

"The Poet is our chemist." I looked over at the Poet, who was shaking his head, chuckling, and walking to the refrigerator.

"One thing we have plenty of in this apartment, Doc, is vodka and tomato juice," said the Poet as he proceeded to mix the doctor a drink.

"I can see that this is not going to be a gathering of spies, languishing and eating Spam sandwiches. You know, when I was practicing medicine, I never used to have a cocktail until five o'clock. But all that changed when I became disabled and started drawing disability. Pain from arthritis comes early in the day."

"What are you on, social-security disability?" I asked.

"No. I'd been paying for a disability policy for over twenty-five years, and because of my right hip and leg, I got a friend to write me a nice medical report. He declared me disabled—unable to stay on my feet all day. It was enough to get the policy to kick in. Ended up quitting the practice. I started drawing disability payments."

"Shrewd move, Doc. So this business today is a side light?"

"Yup. This and other things I do for your sister agency. Gives me something to do and the pay isn't bad. Who is the patient?"

I motioned for the doctor to sit down. The doc walked into the living room and settled into a stuffed armchair. The Poet handed him a Bloody Mary. I looked at him sitting there and felt good and confident that this mission was going to be accomplished.

"The patient, Doc, is a Russian KGB intelligence officer. With espionage we deal with people we need but cannot trust."

"Hmm. I have a lawyer like that. What's his name?"

"His name is not important, but if this operation is successful, it's going to deliver a major blow to the Russians. What is your precise plan?"

The doc took a drink of his Bloody Mary and grinned. "What I will be doing is a little cutting behind the ear."

"I know that. But do we need to do a proctology exam of this guy before we ascend to the ear. That wouldn't pay dividends, would it?" I smiled and asked.

"Probably not, unless he's hiding something. But, frankly," he said, grinning, "I don't wish to go there. We are not trying to hide a recording device up his ass, and we are not trying to find one there, are we?"

The doc paused and took another sip from his drink. "No, we will focus essentially on the ear."

"I thought you dealt mainly with the nose and throats," said the Poet, laughing.

"Yeah, but the ear is close enough."

"Fine, but we'll have a big problem with our boss if you make a grave mistake and the EMT guys have to wheel him out of here."

"Don't worry. Whatever I do here, the patient will live."

The doc for about thirty minutes explained the framework of the ear and then discussed the bug. "The key is the transmitter. Battery power is needed, unless he's bald and white, in which case we could implant a solar cell is his scalp. Think of hearing aid batteries. It will last a week or so in a voice-activated circuit. There is going to be a radio frequency, and if the guy is in an embassy or mission, I'm sure someone will pick it up."

"Doc," I said, "we're way ahead of you on that. That's something we will deal with. But, I'd like to know, what's your feeling generally on what we are doing?"

"Well, you don't know if he is a legitimate defector, right?"

"Right, we don't know, because it's almost impossible to know whether his private thoughts and political convictions differ from those of the KGB," I said.

"Well, if someone sees me about a headache, there generally is no way of knowing whether the person is telling the truth that he has a headache or not. You either believe him or you don't. That's probably what you have with this guy. Communism has not necessarily made life good for most people. I would think that if you have a Russian spy defecting, it would have nothing to do with whether he is a true believer in Soviet communism or not. Don't you agree?"

The Poet nodded his head. "Probably. So what are you suggesting?"

"That his reason for doing this is something personal," said the doc. "So, what's the upside of what we are doing?" The doc was asking himself the question. "The upside is that what you overhear from the transmitter will probably be the key to his true intentions, and it should reveal if he is in fact bona fide or a schmuck. What you hear may also expose valuable Soviet secrets."

The Poet and I were now sitting next to the doc. We were both drinking champagne, cheap champagne, trying to get convincingly drunk to celebrate Yuri's anticipated defection.

"Doc," I said, "that's not totally what Shenandoah and I are asking about. Assume he is legitimate. But assume that after he defects, he shortly thereafter becomes disenchanted with the American way of life, for whatever reason—misses his homeland, becomes an alcoholic, has an unhappy marriage—and redefects back to the Soviet Union, despite our wishes to the contrary. Defection ranks right up there as a ten in personal trauma. To save his own ass from being executed in the Soviet Union, he then goes on national TV and states that he was drugged, kidnapped, tortured, and interrogated by the FBI, until he was finally able to escape. Then he states, 'The bastards even planted a listening device in my head, without my consent.' All of this obviously causes great embarrassment to the government with the end result being that Shenandoah and I are interviewed and brought before some congressional committee as rogue cops to explain." I looked over at the Poet. "Did I miss anything?"

The Poet nodded. "That pretty much covers it."

The doc leaned back and just sat there thinking.

"So let's see, today you are defending America, and tomorrow someone may decide that you are a criminal. Where does that put my ass in the chain? I'd like another Bloody Mary."

The doc started to grin as he handed his glass to the Poet, who got up and walked to the refrigerator.

"Look, you guys are making too big of a deal about this operation. There's no health consequence. The bug would show up on an X-ray. It's not that intrusive. It's not torture. It's a simple procedure that won't leave this guy with any disability. It's like putting in a pacemaker. If in fact such a scenario happened as you just stated, you could always say that the guy consented. Keep in mind that I could be in trouble too since I'm the one doing the operation. I'm not worried about it."

The Poet handed the doc another Bloody Mary.

"Not worried, huh? I'll bite. Why?"

"Frankly, I don't give a shit about congressional committees. Politicians are a bunch of feckless numb nuts. This is America, and I don't do anything that is not in the best interests of the USA. This guy is dirty and probably a killer. The upside is more important than the downside."

I looked over at the Poet, smiling. I raised my glass and leaned over to click the doc's raised glass and then the Poets.

"Doc," I said, "my sentiments exactly."

"Let's move on," said the Doc, "and talk about what you are going to do when he gets here. How do you want to handle that?"

I was hunched over, sitting in front of the doctor. "Well," I said. "He's going to have to be unconscious for about thirty minutes, right, for you to do what you need to do? What do you suggest?"

"Go ask Alice," said the Doc as he grinned again and now leaned over, opened his duffel bag, and began sorting through instruments and drug bottles.

"Go ask Alice?" I laughed and looked at the Poet. "Wasn't that Jefferson Airplane?"

The Poet said, "One pill makes you larger, and one pill makes you small, and the one that mother gives you don't do anything at all."

"True," said the doc, "but we want him chasing rabbits. There are a lot of options. To knock him out, Benadryl combined with a lot of vodka might do the job."

"Alcohol has always been known to preserve everything except secrets," said the Poet, looking at me and grinning.

"What else, Doc?" I asked.

"There are barbiturates like pentobarbital, a short-acting sleeper. The old Mickey Finn of chloral hydrate is a bit archaic. I suggest we use mother's little helper, valium, which, when added to a good dose of vodka, should be effective to put him in la-la land and make him ten feet tall, chasing rabbits in his head."

Handing me a small plastic container of valium, the doc said, "Here, I've brought all that you need. You knock him out and I'll do the rest. Once he's out with the valium, I'll give him pentothal, which will give him retrograde amnesia. He won't remember anything when he wakes up. If he feels soreness behind his ear, tell him he took a tumble. He fell hitting his head, and you carried him to the couch."

"I don't think we will have a problem getting the guy comatose, do you?" I said, looking at the Poet.

"No," said the Poet, now standing up and carrying food from the refrigerator to the dining-room table. "This will be a banquet. We have a lot of vodka, smoked salmon, and beluga caviar."

I looked over at the table and nothing appeared to be spared. There was fresh toast and dishes of butter, along with a few bottles of champagne.

"We'll make like it's a celebration," said the Poet. "After he passes out, I'll clear off this table, and we can do the operation here."

"That will do. Look, I have to go to the john. I'll wait in the bedroom. Call me when you need me," said the doctor as he stood up, lifted his bag, and limped into a bedroom, closing the door.

I felt my pulse rate go up. The Poet, across the room, looked unnerved. "Perhaps you ought to put your coat on to hide that sidearm," he said.

"How's this?" I said, as I removed my .38 snub-nose from my belt and taped it around my ankle.

"That'll work," said the Poet.

Just then, another voice came over the intercom.

I walked over to the intercom and pressed the button. "Can I help you?"

The distinctive voice of Yuri responded. "I'm here to make a delivery."

"Come right up," I said. "Get off on the fifth floor. I'll be in the hallway."

When Yuri exited the elevator, he looked edgy but was dressed like a lawyer, wearing a white shirt and tie. He was carrying a brief-case. I greeted him, smiling, and extended my right hand. The Poet came out, and we ushered Yuri into the living room. On the cocktail table was a tray of caviar, herring, crackers, and bread.

Yuri walked into the kitchen and peered around the apartment, saying, "These are nice quarters." The Poet motioned Yuri toward a couch, and Yuri sat down.

Yuri looked over at us. "The criminal activity in this city is growing."

"Growing?" I said. "It's mushrooming, quadrupling."

"The Cubans were unable to deliver their package to the Panthers," said Yuri. "It seems that their representative was mugged."

The Poet was now sitting next to Yuri. "It's a tough city. We of course are sorry to hear that. But today is a cause for celebration. We are going to be able to bring you over. We have to work out some details. How much time do you have today, before you are needed at the UN?"

"I have a few hours," said Yuri. "I signed out early to familiar-ize myself with more Manhattan streets. But I need to tell you something."

"What's that?" asked the Poet.

"I want to defect right now. I don't want to go back."

"What?" I exclaimed. "Right now? Can't do it. We are not ready for it. Has something happened?" In my mind this struck me as completely bizarre. Here we had a Russian spy who had met with us only once. He had a family that we hadn't really talked about extricating. He came to us alone, carrying very little, and announced that he wanted to defect immediately. As Big D would say, "Something is rotten in the state of Denmark."

Yuri looked over with a concerned expression on his face. "I guess I'm getting nervous doing this. The KGB have a lot of sources."

"Doing what? This is only the second time we've met. Yuri, you are becoming paranoid. Let's talk about this," I said. "But first let's have a drink."

The Poet got up, holding an empty glass. "How about a drink? Vodka?"

Yuri nodded. "I need one. In Russia, it's never a long time until lunch."

The Poet looked at me. "Granada?"

"Yes," I said.

The Poet returned with three glasses filled with vodka, neat. Lifting his glass, he said, "Gentlemen. Nostrovia!"

Like a true competitive Russian, Yuri lifted his glass, tossed back his head, and drained the contents as if it were water. He now sat back in his chair and appeared more relaxed. The Poet immediately handed him another fresh cocktail.

"Yuri," I said. "What are you talking about? What brought this on?"

Yuri sat down on the sofa and looked over. "Things are not going well. My tour is ending. I've been told that I am one of those on the list to go home because I haven't done enough."

"Yuri," I said, "we have something to give you that may help."

Yuri looked up. "I hope it's the two hundred fifty thousand dollars."

"The money, Yuri, will come on our next visit with you. Today, we have something different." I handed him a brown envelope, which he opened and began to sort through. The envelope contained about two inches of documents labeled "Top Secret," concerning an abandoned missile system designed for US naval warships. The content of the documents was manufactured, but the fraud was not going to be easily detected, and we reasoned that the material would not only help Yuri in his quest to produce, but it would keep the Russians occupied and busy sorting through and trying to come to grips with whether the material was genuine or worthless. Misinformation probably had some value to the other side and thus was not totally useless, for at a minimum it gave them an indication of what we were thinking about, but the beauty of it was the workload it created.

"Why are you giving me this?" Yuri asked.

"With all due respect, think about it as pabulum for an adolescent mind."

"What do you mean?"

"It will make you look good. It's good stuff, and the people you report to will love it."

"You do with it as you wish," the Poet said. "Here's the cover story. An unidentified US naval officer approached you at the UN. He handed you the envelope and said he could supply you with more documents, but that he needed money. Future contacts with this person would be away from the UN."

"I see," said Yuri.

"Yuri," I said, "most—shall we say seventy-five percent?—of the secrets we protect really closely in this country are known to your side, and by the same token most of the secrets your country guards very closely are well known to us. If your agency and ours didn't observe these pretenses, we would both be out of business, wouldn't we?"

"Good point."

"Consequently, while we continue with what we are doing," I said, "we want you to stay put. We need time to arrange for your eventual departure. What about your family?"

"They will be coming too."

The Poet and I spent several minutes discussing the arrangements for defection, and finally Yuri agreed to the plan. The Poet and I both knew that Yuri was much more valuable in place, providing secrets. We did, however, wish to proceed with the implanted bug to have that play out and see if it bore any fruit. We further knew that our CIA friends would have to get involved in the debriefing process, someone fluent in Russian who was familiar with counterintelligence areas of interests abroad. The men and women there were bright, polished, and Ivy. What they lacked in street savviness, rapport, and bullshit with strangers, they made up for with intelligence and strong interrogation techniques. But with Yuri right now, it was too soon to bring them in.

We spent thirty minutes to an hour bullshitting with Yuri about life in the Soviet Union, until finally I got up to have yet another drink and excused myself to go to the bathroom. Yuri showed no signs of being drunk. No bloodshot eyes or slurred speech.

After a few minutes, I walked back into the room. I observed the Poet sitting in a chair calmly smoking a cigarette. I walked over to the sofa. Yuri was sprawled out, lying on his back, either dead or asleep. I leaned over. His mouth was open a little. I was thankful he was still breathing. His face was pinkish. I touched him. His head was warm, so I knew we weren't dealing with a corpse, yet I felt like a buzzard hovering over a dying animal.

"Did you hit him with anything, like your fist or a club?" I asked the Poet. "Or did the doc's potion finally kick in?"

"The only thing I hit him with was a lot of vodka," said the Poet.

"Well," I said, "it looks like the vodka, along with mama's little helper, has knocked him into a coma." I knocked on the bedroom door and then opened it. "Doc, I think we are ready."

The doctor came out, carrying his black bag and looking like he had just taken a nap. He limped over to where the Poet was standing, hovering over the remains of Yuri, who was now lying unconscious but looking very peaceful with his arms and hands folded as if he were ready to be placed in a coffin. I touched his forehead, and it was warm. Yuri's appearance was one of a guy sleeping off a bad drunk, of the type I had witnessed many a week-end night at my college frat house. I reasoned that Yuri would be none the worse for wear, but I admit I was still concerned.

"Doc, do you think he is OK?" the Poet asked.

The doctor peered down at Yuri. "He's OK. He's in a Stoli coma," he added, chuckling as he said it. "With all of the vodka this guy probably drinks, his liver is exposed to a greater danger than what we are about to do. Let's get him on the operating table."

The Poet, the doc, and I lifted Yuri's heavy carcass over to the dining-room table. We placed him on his back on the table. He looked helpless and lay there like a human sacrifice. The doc stood over the body, fanning the air. He was either trying to blow away the Poet's smoke from his cigarette or making a futile attempt to levitate the body.

"Smoke bothering you, Doc?" I asked.

"No. In a situation like this, I'm used to it."

"What about blood, Doc?" I asked. "Do we need to bring in towels?"

The doctor now looked at me while putting on surgical gloves. "No, that won't be necessary. With surgery there are only two things you need to know. All bleeding stops eventually, and everyone has to die sometime."

"Thanks, Doc. Incredible what you can learn with these operations. I'll have to attend these more often."

"Don't be concerned about bleeding. The only vessels in the skin of the ear are small."

The doctor leaned over Yuri, moving his head to the side, and examined the back of his head. He then fumbled with his bag, removed a few instruments, and placed them in an organized fashion on the dining-room table. The Poet and I stood around the table looking like medical students, observing a professor about to cut and saw on a cadaver, except this cadaver was not repulsive or smelling, but rather had moving muscles and bones.

I had never witnessed an operation on a live body. I had viewed an autopsy in a makeshift morgue chilled to forty degrees. I had also witnessed an execution, but that was different and involved no cutting, rather, a little cooking in a chair.

Rolling up Yuri's shirtsleeve, the doctor picked up a needle and inserted it into Yuri's arm. "First I'm going to deliver an intravenous anesthetic dose of pentothal and the neuroleptic agent ketamine, which should give us a few hours of unresponsiveness without suppression of his heart or respiratory functions. As I mentioned, the beauty of pentothal is that it will give him retrograde amnesia. When he wakes up, he won't remember anything."

The doctor then appeared to prep a quarter-size area behind Yuri's left ear. "Now," said the doc, "I shall inject xylocaine with epinephrine here to minimize bleeding and to eliminate any undo stimulation. Do you see this?" he asked, pointing to a portion of the ear. "This is the tympanic membrane that separates the external ear from the middle ear. I will now play the odds and make a one inch incision here at the hairline."

Jesus, I thought to myself, play the odds? What was that supposed to mean? I didn't ask and didn't say anything. We were too far along, and we weren't going to turn back. I just trusted that the doc knew what he was doing. This wasn't supposed to be the most ticklish of operations.

The doc now took a scalpel and made a neat little cut behind the ear and then peeled the skin off the bone in a small flap.

"Hand me that instrument please," said the doc, pointing to small drill lying on the table. "I'm now going to use this three-eighths-inch drill to enter the mastoid cavity, which will provide us about one cubic inch of space." The doc, like some carpenter, was now bent over, peering into the area behind the ear with a tiny surgical telescope; he drilled a small hole while removing small bits of thin bone as he opened up the mastoid cavity. With my fingers, I picked up and removed the little pieces of bone that came out of Yuri's head and placed them in my pocket, thinking to myself that it was best to hide the evidence.

"Well now," said the doc, who was bent over, focusing a small flashlight on the inner portion of the mastoid cavity, "this is rather interesting. Hmm..."

I waited for over a minute, expecting something more to come out of the doc's mouth. "Doc, what is it? Problems?"

"No problems for us. But a problem for Yuri. Looks like a brain tumor of some sort. The mastoid is separated from the brain by the narrowest of bones. See this."

I leaned over and peered into the small cavity but saw nothing.

"There's a growth there," said the doc. "Could be malignant. It could also be benign, like a glomus tumor or even cholestea-toma. I'll take a small piece, and we'll have it examined. Let's get on and finish what we are here to do. Hand me, please, the wireless transmitter."

I handed the doc the small marble-size transmitter, which the doc took with his right hand and slipped into Yuri's mastoid cavity.

"As soon as I close this incision with a couple of dissolving Vicryl sutures and Dermabond glue, the deed will be done, and we can break out more vodka." In minutes the doc had completed the task. With his left hand, he grabbed Yuri's face, squeezing his cheeks, and moving his head back and forth. Then with his right hand, he lifted Yuri's head. Yuri's eyes were closed.

"Is he alive?" I asked.

"He's not ready for a hearse. It's too bad we can't question him right now, while he is asleep. I'll bet there is much that he could tell us about his life." He then let the head go back softly.

I looked at the doc. "If I didn't think Yuri could help us, I might be ready to consign the guy to a coffin."

"Yeah, but that would defeat your original purpose. Dead men tell no tales."

"True."

"Well, what do you think?" the doc asked wearily, looking down at the finished product.

I lifted Yuri's head a touch and examined the area behind the ear. I could see no sign of the surgery. "Not bad. When he comes to and sees your bill, it may give him a heart attack."

"The area back there will be a little sore when he wakes up. Maybe a little popping noise. This procedure is sort of the basis of cochlear implants or special implanted hearing aids, but it won't be defective. The Food and Drug Administration won't even know about it. Look at your watch. How much time did this take?"

I looked at my watch. "Thirty minutes," I said.

The Poet now went into the kitchen, came back, and handed the doc another Bloody Mary. "Well," he said, "you now have a device in a Russian spy that will transmit radio-frequency transmissions, but again you have to be careful when you use it."

"Doc," chuckled the Poet, "the Russians would regard any microphone or bug on their premises more as an opportunity than a menace, even if they discovered that it was in the ear of one of their agents. That way they could feed us disinformation."

The doc grinned and took a long sip from his Bloody Mary. "I must say that I never really looked at it from that perspective. All of this really is a game, isn't it? Deuce, I'll get back to you regarding that tumor."

Yes, it was a game. The Poet of course was right, for if the Russians did actually suspect and then find the implanted device behind Yuri's ear, they would probably let him still function normally with it, without doing anything, for it would give them the opportunity to pass more deception and bullshit over to us, to keep us off the trail of some target or merely to keep us occupied and busy. The Poet and I and all the guys around the poker table—we all felt that the FBI home office, the guys who sat at their desk all day, had an inflated view of the Russian espionage agents that was unrealistic, when in fact the KGB agents in many ways were a bunch of bumbling schmucks, who simply wanted to be in America to enjoy the good life, shop, and make money. We intended to send Yuri right back into the mission.

The doc left Limestone, and in a few hours, Yuri woke up feeling none the worse for wear. The doc was right about the pentothal and retrograde amnesia. Yuri remembered nothing. In fact he asked if he had fallen and hit his head. We told him he did and attributed it to too much vodka.

He left the apartment for the United Nations with only a headache, but he was extremely pleased about the "Top Secret" documents. We assured him that we could reach him if he felt he was in danger. On my part, I was merely grateful that Yuri had come to and was alive. The stress of the job and the inner soul searching I was experiencing as to whether we were doing the right thing was starting to gnaw at me. It all seemed so easy—too easy. We now had a walking, indoor plant coming and going at will from the Soviet mission, and we had the ability to pick up all of his conversations, at least for a short time. In the annals of spydom, this had to be a first. The insertion of a bug into the mastoid cavity of an honest-to-goodness spy was sure to produce dividends. I was anxious to sift through and obtain the fruits of our coup.

CHAPTER 25

THE SPY THAT LOVED ME

—————

AFTER LEAVING THE SAFE HOUSE, the day was done. I went back to my apartment. I really needed a drink, something with pop, and some female company. I had a pang of homesickness and loneliness. What puzzled me was that I had not heard from C for some time. I was supposed to meet Big D and the troops later at the Bishops. I was looking forward to it. I was preparing to jump in the tub when the phone rang.

"Deuce, hi; it's me."

"C! Where have you been? Are you back in town?"

"I'm not in town. I'm out of the country. Can't say where."

"When are you coming back?"

"I won't be back."

"What's that supposed to mean?"

"It means I love you, but I can't see you anymore."

"What's going on?"

"I'm not who I told you I am. I've been working for a foreign government."

"Oh, come on, C. You're joking with me, right?"

"I'm so sorry. I'm not. I'd like to tell you everything, but I can't right now. It has to do with my parents, money…family in Russia. The government helped me. They got me a job with the airlines."

"Who's they?"

"I don't really know. They told me it was a country in Europe. They wanted me to get to know you. They have a file on you. They told me you spent a lot of time at the zoo, around the seals and sea lions. I was told to plant myself there and try to meet you. That it was very important. So I did."

"Meet me? To do what?"

"Information. They said you were young and would make mistakes."

"You're putting me on, right, or am I just a gullible waif?"

C didn't respond.

"You're saying that Central Park, our meeting...all a setup?"

C didn't respond.

"You told me you loved me. That was a nothing?"

"I do. I do. That's why it's so hard."

For several minutes I said nothing. I was speechless and didn't respond. I wanted to say something, but words were not flowing. "C...I...I..." My voice started to crack.

"I have to go now," C said. "I'm sorry." She hung up.

I put the phone down. I sat down devastated. After several minutes, I put on my jogging shoes, left the apartment, and ran out to Central Park for a long jog around the reservoir.

By the time I got to the Bishops, traffic that night had slowed to a crawl. It was Thursday night, another raucous night on tap. My brain was totally occupied with C. Depression was setting in. How was I going to explain this, and should I even talk about it? Funny, I was not thinking about C's revelations and its impact on FBI cases or Yuri. It was all about me and someone I loved. I needed something that would knock me cold.

In my mind I recalled my last year in law school. At the end of the school year, I drove a classmate home to Chicago. He had been dating a girl for several years. She had just broken up with him. He was riding shotgun in my car, sobbing uncontrollably. Tears were rolling down his face. At the time, I could count on one hand the number of times I'd seen guys crying. His crying touched me, but I was perplexed by the sheer magnitude and extent of his grief. It had gone on for over one hour.

"Deuce, don't you understand? I loved that girl. I loved that girl. I can't live without her," he cried.

At the time, I thought in my mind, Get over it, man. If you bottled all the tears that have been shed by guys in love, there would be enough saltwater to fill many Olympic-size swimming pools. There are a lot of fish in the ocean.

Now, however, I was beginning to feel how he'd felt. I really loved C and was still trying to figure out what had happened. I was hoping Big D could help.

Young people around Bishops were out in mass, Upper East Side singles. The place was humming. Although we were months away from the Christmas holidays, the bar, both inside and out, was a fantasyland with colored and twinkling lights. As I approached the front door, I could hear the *thump-thump* of Jimi Hendrix and "Hey Joe." I wasn't going in to shoot my old lady.

Inside Big D was guzzling Budweiser beer, and surprisingly he was in a booth, next to impossible to get, unless he'd been in there for hours, which he had, and he was waiting for Carol, a girl he had just started dating, a friend from back home in North Carolina, now living in New York City. She was separated from her husband and going through a divorce. Relationships were becoming dizzy.

On a table in front of Big D was a half pitcher of beer. Big D was capable of drinking enough for three or four guys. Downing twelve cans of beer at one sitting in front of a six-inch TV was a nothing for the D man.

I sat down in the booth. "I'll say one thing for you, D: if I ever go through an operation, I'll bring you along so that they can use your blood to sterilize the instruments."

D peered up and gazed at me for several seconds. "You look down, beat up, Brother Deuce. Where's C?"

"Don't know."

"Has the Russian bear been stalking you?"

"It's worse than that. What I have to tell you may be the grist of a future novel."

I poured myself a glass from D's pitcher of beer and guzzled half of it.

"Let me guess," said D, "you've taken a vow of chastity and abstinence like the Knife. Sex no longer has become your consuming obsession. You're suffering tremendous guilt. You've started to look at sex as the glucose of sin."

"No, that's not it," I said as I took another slug of beer.

"All right," said D, "I'll go in a different direction, which is probably more likely. You're restless and on the prowl. Your commitment to sexual bliss when you leave the poker table and drift off to the street of dreams has resulted in your getting a new piece of ass every day, and in consequence, instead of getting the clap that might torture the membranes of your genitalia, you've come away simply exhausted, worn out, and bent out of shape."

"Jesus, since my gums have been bleeding, I thought I had a dental problem." The thought of the clap had never entered my demented mind. I looked at D, who was laughing, and thought to myself that numerically speaking, even in a place like New York, such a conclusion that a person could operate daily as some type of alley cat was way off base.

"Your imagination, D, is getting the better of you. That's not the problem either. I'm not sure I should even tell you."

"Jesus," said D, "it must be serious." He lit a cigarette.

"The Knife was right."

"The Knife is smart and always right. What is he right about this time?"

"Women. Femmes fatales, planted by the KGB for sexual provocations."

"Female spies are a rarity," said D. "It's always been a masculine world. These days it's all about money."

"Maybe it's changing."

I went on to explain to D my phone call from C and our entire relationship from the time we met in Central Park and the fact that I loved the girl. When I was done, D paused and calmly said, "Don't worry about it."

"Don't worry about it?" I asked incredulously.

"Yeah," said D, "she knows nothing and got nothing from you except how you operate. What could she possibly report back on?"

"How I live and eat and who we are. I was used."

"The only thing that got hurt was your pride. Get over it," said D. "Nothing relating to Yuri or anything else has been compromised. Furthermore, you have nothing to establish that what she is telling you is true. Correct?"

On that point D was right. I'd never met her roommates. Basically, I'd accepted as true everything she told me. Maybe she was lying on the phone and just used her explanation as an excuse to break up.

I looked at D and said nothing.

"So forget it and let it go. Don't discuss it with the bureau or anyone else. They will haul your ass to DC and spend a month debriefing you. Then they will transfer you out of here. Probably to the Dakotas. My guess is that C will call again. If that happens, maybe we can use her."

I sat there thinking about this and didn't say anything.

"What's happening with Yuri?" asked D.

"The dude's dirty. I know it. I'm going to prove it."

D was scanning the menu, mumbling, "You're getting a bit hawkish, aren't you, Brother Deuce?"

"I'm in an attack mode. Where are the rest of the troops?"

"On their way. To be or not to be, that is the question, and the further questions are whether I should eat, and if so, how much."

With that comment, Carol walked in and sat down next to D.

"Carol, meet Deuce."

Carol was tall and good-looking. She wore a sweater and dark North Carolina blue skirt. Her hair was parted in the middle and hung straight down.

"Are you sure you want to be with this guy?" I asked.

Carol looked at me inquisitively.

"You mean you haven't seen him without his clothes?"

Carol shook her head.

"He works out endlessly with weights and is enamored with his body, which is a work of art. His upper torso has muscles over muscles. Women are captivated with his pectorals."

"Wow," said Carol as she put her arm around D, "I like it."

"D, take your shirt off and show the lady," I said.

D, looking embarrassed, responded, "I'm not sure the bar owner would appreciate that."

The truth was that D did work out a lot, spending hours of free time on weights and pushups.

"He also eats a lot and drinks a lot," I said to Carol.

Carol looked over at D and remarked, "I thought you told me that you wanted to lose weight but that something happens to you every time you see the Golden Arches. I don't see any Golden Arches. So don't order anything."

More beer arrived in a large pitcher.

"D, the lady doth protest too much, methinks. Why don't we all get cheeseburgers?"

"Excellent suggestion. You know, Deuce, sitting around with you, here and at the poker table, I've come to the conclusion that you need a mind sweeper."

"Analyzed? You mean by a shrink?"

"Exactly. Living in Manhattan will make you go nuts. Look at you. You're too intense and uptight—working twenty-five hours a day—and you're in here all worked up, embarrassing my date."

"D, no one can be benefited by analysis. You'll become spent, like a flower that has lost its bloom. Maybe I'm just not cut out for the Russian game or for that matter the city."

D looked over at Carol. "Deuce has been in the spook house too long. He wants to save the world. He's a hustler and worries about this and that."

"That's right. I'm paranoid. Spies and criminals are everywhere."

What I didn't tell them was that I felt that I was a coiled piece of machinery. I was getting to the point that I preferred sitting on a park bench with C, drinking wine. My park bench of choice was the one in front of the Plaza on Fifty-Ninth Street. A lot of activity there. Yet, C had been right. I did a lot of worrying, and to that extent, maybe I did need to be analyzed. For me it was a question of finding myself.

"You're neurotic, Deuce," said D.

"All right, I'm neurotic but I am urbane." I lifted my beer mug in the air and clicked glasses with D and Carol. "To New York," I said, "a place where there is so much going on that you don't have time to worry."

CHAPTER 26

FRUIT OF THE POISONOUS TREE

THE NEXT MORNING, AFTER AN early morning jog around the reservoir, I walked down to Thompson's restaurant for breakfast. I found the Poet and Big D occupying a back booth. Over coffee it seemed like a perfect time to map out a strategy in handling Yuri. We agreed that the Poet and I would monitor and record the conversations we picked up by car when Yuri was outside the mission. When Yuri was in the mission, Big D would take over.

"So what do you think, D?" I asked. "Will we get any significant tasty fruit when he's inside the mission?"

"That depends where he is, once inside. The Russians have secure rooms and offices, where we probably won't be able to pick up anything. They are double walled and soundproof. But the Russians do not like to use those rooms."

"Why is that?"

"They are poorly ventilated; makes them sweaty and uncomfortable."

We agreed that anything that we laid our hands on would be reduced to a typed transcript. We decided not to monitor any conversations of Yuri at the United Nations. We were interested in, among other things, conversations concerning the "Top Secret" documents we had given Yuri and illegals.. In that regard we felt that the best information would come from the Soviet mission, the admonitions of the doc notwithstanding. We reasoned that we could get away with this, unless we did something stupid. But, with Yuri, we all agreed that we had to be extremely careful not to do something that would alert the Russians that they had a mole in their presence.

The following week, we again met with Big D to go over the transmissions. There would be tapes to listen to, but it was not always possible to tell who was talking. The Poet and I put on two sets of earphones and together, in a small, windowless conference room, listened to transmissions between Yuri and an unidentified Russian (X) within the Soviet mission.

TRANSCRIPTION OF CONVERSATION BETWEEN YURI POPOV AND UNKNOWN SUBJECT (LISTENING DEVICE LOG) TRANSLATIONFROM RUSSIAN

X: So, comrade, I hope you have been working hard and not just drinking coffee. Did the Americans take the bait?

Yuri: Like a sturgeon.

X: Are we ready to start having caviar?

Yuri: Soon. They were excited about the naval officer.

X: He was giving us little, which means he was one of theirs. It is no loss.

Yuri: We will continue contact with the officer, comrade general, to make it look like we know nothing.

X: I see that our money destined for the Black Panthers did not reach them. Some kind of holdup or mugging took place. Must I teach everyone in this building how to work?

Yuri: The Americans are good people. But it is all about material wealth. Greed. There is much crime.

X: That is true, but the nondelivery is unacceptable. We send out a delivery boy with two hundred fifty thousand dollars with no backup? The Cubans are weak. It was a mistake to use them. I would blame it on the Cubans and poor planning. You have followed *The New York Times*. There is much tension across the US. Belov wants the delivery of money to the Panthers to be made again soon. We want Manhattan to burn.

Yuri: The Kremlin will have their wish.

X: They have decided that we should make the next delivery. You have been chosen to do it.

Yuri: Me! I would be honored.

X: If something were to happen and you were arrested, you have diplomatic immunity. The US would declare you persona non grata and send you home. But nothing must happen. Understand? You will be covered and given support.

Yuri: How much money are we talking about?

X: One million American dollars.

Yuri: One million dollars? Never in my wildest dreams did I—

X: Enough. Don't question, Yuri. This is a decision made from the very top. It will pay dividends. Make all the arrangements. You can obtain the money from Aleksandr.

Yuri: I understand. KGB training is good.

X: Your tour here is coming to an end in several months, Yuri. It is totally within my discretion to retain you here or not, do you understand that?

Yuri: Yes, I do. I am raising the money.

X: I will need the fifty thousand dollars in American money. Cash. Within thirty days. I will then take care of things to help you.

Yuri: You will have it.

X: Good. Now who is this new American that you have made contact with?

Yuri: He is a naval officer. We have given him a code name, Walrus. He approached me at the UN and handed me a brown envelope with "Top Secret" documents. They relate to the operation of Minuteman missiles. He refused to supply me with his name and background but told me that other documents of a similar nature would be forthcoming. I gave him a number to call. He will contact me.

X: These documents that he supplied, did you review them with our maritime analyst?

Yuri: Yes. The information is excellent, and it's being transferred by diplomatic pouch to our home headquarters. Walrus is demanding a lot of money.

X: They are all alike, these Americans. It is all about money. How much does he want?

Yuri: One hundred thousand dollars for each delivery.

X: We need to talk again. Visit with the analysts and see how good these documents are. If they are good, we will pay it. In the meantime, you will need to assist Vladimir, who is meeting with Locust, our other American naval officer. We will see if contact with Locust continues or if he is arrested by the FBI. Vladimir could be out of the country if he too is arrested.

The Poet and I spent several hours listening and then relistening to portions of the tapes and making notes. The conversations were in Russian. For this I had to rely on the Poet. We put the earphones down, and I looked over at the Poet without saying anything because it was obvious from the conversations that these were interesting developments and a bit ambiguous in many ways.

CHAPTER 27

BAD NEWS FOR YURI

Friday, October 18, 1968

IT HAD NOW BEEN A little over one week that the bug was installed and this morning, the Poet, Big D and I were again at Thompsons, taking a booth in the back, where I started to review my notes from the tapes.

No doubt about it. The bug in Yuri's mastoid cavity was paying dividends. It appeared that Yuri was a plant, or did it? It could all be a ruse by Yuri. What about Lester? The tapes revealed that Yuri was up to no good and was possibly playing both sides. It was all about money. This could be exploited. He asks for money so that he can pay off his superior with an apparent bribe to allow him to stay in the United States. This was something he never mentioned. Now he would receive another hundred thousand dollars for the fictitious naval officer we handed to him. Then there was the one million dollars he was going to deliver.

I looked over at the Poet, who was smoking a cigarette and appeared to be deep in thought. "You know this guy is greedy, corrupt, and dirty. What do you think, D?"

"Well," said D, "we need to squeeze his nuts. He's being threatened to return home. He has to raise fifty thousand dollars for his boss. They are all corrupt."

"Yeah," said the Poet, "but there are other things to consider. Yuri will receive a hundred grand from the KGB to give to a fictitious naval officer we have established, which he will be able to keep. It means Yuri will be rolling in dough. We can use this. We could pressure him to defect and pressure him for information regarding illegals."

"Work him and manipulate him," I added. "I like that."

"Look," said Big D, "I've been covering these guys a long time. Yuri is not a Marxist. He's a swindler."

"I think that's true," I said. "Wait until Charley hears about the one million dollars going to the Panthers."

The upshot of all of this was that the Poet and I and even Big D decided that we needed an immediate meeting with Yuri. We prided ourselves in being street savvy and astute agents with no penchant for self-deception. We did not want to be taken in by a con man who either remained loyal and under the control of the KGB, and was paying bribes to his superior, or was simply a money grabber like Frank in Harlem.

Even with the message from the tapes, it was still in the realm of possibility that Yuri was playing both ends and wanted to defect. A lie detector would have been helpful. Every defector like Nosenko was given a lie-detector test, but nothing was foolproof and certain, including the results of lie-detector tests, which were only as good as the operators, and if more than one was given, it could lead to conflicting results, like two doctors who arrive at opposing views on the diagnosis and prognosis of a patient.

With a polygraph, wires are hooked up to critical points on a person's body. Operators claim beating it is difficult. Yet, with any defector who takes the test, they may be telling the truth that their defection is legitimate, but they also may be lying about other discretions or wrongful acts personal to themselves, which can result in their flunking the test.

As we sipped coffee at Thompson's, our attention led to the brighter side—namely, that the planting of the bug was a success and that we were getting some terrific stuff, including information on a few illegals codenamed Lester. Locust was another matter. It also looked like the Russians were not giving up on getting money over to the Panthers.

We walked back from Thompson's to the office. We decided that it was time to visit with Charley to bring him into the mix and make him current on what was happening. When we got back to the office, I was handed a telephone message. It was a message from the doctor, saying to call him immediately.

I picked up the telephone and put a call in.

"Doc, Granada here. You called?"

"Yes," said the doc calmly over the phone. "I have some news about that tumor."

"So the jury is in. What's the verdict?" I asked.

"The verdict is not good for Yuri. It's malignant."

"And?"

"For Yuri, it's potentially fatal."

"Explain that please."

"Because of its proximity to important vascular structures, the jugular vein and carotid artery, a tumor can erode into a vessel."

"Leading to?"

"Leading to fatal consequences. I'll leave it to you guys to handle this in whatever fashion you choose."

"What you are telling me is that he needs surgery, right?"

"Well, he needs some serious diagnostic tests and perhaps surgery."

"Would that fix the problem?"

"Perhaps. The surgeon would know more once he got in there."

"What they found could kill him. Correct?"

"That's right, but then…" The doc's voice paused.

"But then, what?"

"Everybody dies sometime."

"Thanks, Doc," I said. "Enjoyed it. Send us your bill." I hung up.

I motioned over to the Poet and Big D to head to the conference room, where we debated what to do.

"Well," said D, "he's your man. What do you want to do?" He was laughing as he said it. "This to me is an interesting and amusing turn of events."

I smiled and thought to myself that this really was no laughing matter. Yuri was a con man, dealing on both sides. He could not be trusted and maybe had taken part in the killing of one of our own agents.

I looked at the Poet with dead seriousness. "The issue is one that I can lay on the table in rather simple terms." I paused to just let it hang out there.

The Poet took another drag of his cigarette and then let some of the smoke curl up his nose. "Well," said the Poet, "before we die."

"It's a way to kill him without getting into trouble," I said.

"Schadenfreude," said the Poet. "The guy has a death-threatening tumor."

"So we just don't tell him or anybody about it," said D. "Let's see, as I recall from law school, we have only a moral responsibility."

"It's a rather callous position to take, but think suicide," said the Poet. "If this guy or someone you hated was going to kill himself and even attempted to do so in your presence, well—"

I interrupted, "Well, you just walk away, ignore everything, and let him do it."

"That's right. There is no criminal culpability there," said the Poet." Feelings are not actionable. Someone down the road—"

"Like his wife," I said.

"That's right, like his wife," added D, "might condemn you for your callousness, but who else is there?"

The larger question was whether I could live with myself—later. Figuring that, in this business, one had to be a scoundrel at times, I decided without hesitation that I could.

CHAPTER 28

GOING FOR THE JUGULAR

———◆———

AFTER LEAVING THE CONFERENCE ROOM, we saw Charley in his office alone, studying a file. We went in for a visit.

Since the results and the data we were getting from the hidden microphone were excellent, we figured that this might be the opportunity for the Boss to take his promotion, a bump in pay, and all of his expenses paid for a move to Washington, DC, not that the Boss wanted a promotion because both he and his wife loved New York City, and a trip to DC, particularly if it was permanent, was a step down for them both socially and culturally, for the Boss's wife had been born and raised in the city, was an extremely wealthy lady, and the Boss's government salary on their joint tax return amounted to peanuts. In fact the lady was connected and wired to several not-for-profit boards, which brought them perks, such as invitations to many cocktail parties and benefits, and since all of this would be gone if the Boss and his wife moved to DC, we speculated that maybe the lady would stay in their East Seventy-Second Street condominium with the Boss commuting back and forth to Washington, DC.

Charlie looked up from his file and said, "Sit down, guys. What's the latest?"

We took the Boss through everything we had done the last few days, and as expected, Charley was excited about everything.

He liked being aggressive, and he liked it when we were aggressive. It was the chase and thrill of the hunt. It was the sight and smell of Russian blood, speaking figuratively of course.

He liked it even better when the results from all of this aggressive activity were good, which they were, and were produced without a mishap. Charley couldn't care less about any promotion because the Boss's state of mind, like our own, was one that he wanted to stick whatever he could up the Russians' asses and win. It was like a lawyer telling you that the work is not about money, but justice. Every now and then, a statement like that was actually true.

I finally closed by taking Charley through the entire surgical procedure and the news about the malignant tumor. After this, the boss just sat there leaning back, staring at the ceiling and saying nothing.

When we had completed our long narrative, Charley paused, put his feet up on the desk and his arms and hands behind his head.

"Hmm. This is all very interesting and would be the makings of a great novel. I find it incredible that you did all of this without even talking to me. I'm impressed by your imagination, courage, and vigor."

"Since it turned out well, we knew you would be, Boss," I said, smiling.

"Yeah," said the Poet.

"Well," said Charley, looking at me, "the dude is dirty. Isn't he? He's playing both ends. How much time we got?"

"Time?" I asked. "Time for what?"

"The tumor, chief."

I looked over at the Poet, grinning. "Do you see feathers on my head?"

"Deuce," said Charley, raising his voice, "is the tumor slow growing, like a prostate tumor, or something rapid? How much time do we have before he's dead?"

I looked back at the Boss. "I don't know. The doc didn't say. Yuri never complained about headaches in our presence. The tumor can't be too far along, if he has no symptoms."

"The tumor is a verifiable serendipitous fact," said the Boss. "His bona fides, however, remain a suspicious concealed fact."

"Wonderfully put," I said. "Spoken like an expert headed for the lecture circuit or perhaps a job with some DC think tank."

"Gentlemen, it's time to go for the jugular."

"The tumor is headed for the jugular," said the Poet.

"Well, this is what we do," said the Boss. "We either go for his jugular or his nuts. It's time to put the screws to him."

I looked at Charley. "I believe the Poet and I would prefer the jugular. It's right near his mastoid cavity, which we both are familiar with."

"Whatever," said Charley. "We turn the tables on Yuri. We give Yuri reasons to cooperate. I think you know what it is, and if he doesn't…. well."

"OK," I said, "we'll meet again with Yuri and give him a—"

The Poet cut me off. "A tracheotomy of sorts," said the Poet. "Something that wouldn't kill him."

"That's good," said Charley. "With Yuri his motive is money. Give him another reason to cooperate. Squeeze his nuts. We have enough on him to put his head on the block in Moscow. Don't mention anything yet regarding the tumor. That will be our ace in the hole. Meet with him and tell him we want the illegals and to turn over Locust. If we are going to be successful, we have to think like Napoleon. Surprise."

Fuck Napoleon, I thought. He was never one of my favorites.

CHAPTER 29

THE END OF THE GAME

———◆———

Thursday, October 24, 1968

THE POET AND I ARRANGED for another meeting with Yuri at Limestone. Both of us knew this was not going to be pleasant. We were going to take off the gloves.

When Yuri walked in, he was visibly nervous. He walked over to the window and peered through the blinds.

"Yuri," said the Poet, "let's sit down." He motioned to the sofa, and Yuri took a seat. "Care for a drink?"

"No thanks," replied Yuri.

Yuri's face was filled with gloom. He settled back, put a Marlboro cigarette in his mouth, and lit it with a Zippo lighter. I thought to myself, how Americanized can you get?

"I think it's time that we cut the bullshit," I said.

"Yes, I agree. I am Yuri Mikhail Popov. There is much more you need to know."

"We're listening," said the Poet.

"After I tell you, you may feel I have an inflated view of myself."

"Hardly. Nothing we hear from you would come as a surprise," said the Poet.

"If you grant me asylum, it will amount to the most serious defection Mother Russia has ever experienced. I know too much. They will hunt me down unmercifully. They will try to either weaken or downplay the seriousness, saying that my leaving is a nothing and that I knew nothing and was not informed."

"Or," said the Poet, "they will simply say that you always had an inflated view of yourself and take another view."

"We know the way the game is played," I added.

"Yes," said Yuri. "It's also possible that they will come out publicly and say that my defection is devastating, hoping that you will thus conclude the opposite. They will do their best to convey an impression that I am insignificant or even a plant."

"Well," the Poet asked, "are you insignificant or a plant?"

"Neither, and most assuredly, I'm not a plant. Once you see what I have to give you, you will be paying me well for this information."

"We expected that," I said.

"This is business," said Yuri. "Your government pays corporate informants well. Think of me as a canary."

"All right," said the Poet, "start singing."

"I can give you a large string of illegals, how we communicate, short-wave radio operation, invisible writing, our codes and ciphers, encrypted Morse code messages, our countersurveillance measures. How much is this information worth?"

"You tell me," said the Poet.

"For the names and locations of five families of illegals—they operate in pairs, you know—I will need two hundred fifty thousand dollars for each, deposited in a Swiss bank account. I will provide you with the account number. My wife and I intend to secretly relocate. We will need a change of name and American passports."

The Poet was now standing up, pacing around, just like something Alex would do. "You're greedy, Yuri. It's all about money, isn't it?"

"Yes, I'm greedy. We like the same things you Americans like. Money. Comfort. A nice home. Look, we both know what this game is about. We have illegals. We want to know and get access to what is strategic in your country. You want to know who they are and what we are interested in and what we know and don't know about you. It keeps going. Am I right?"

I looked over at the Poet. Yuri was right, all right. He had overlooked a few things, however, that didn't necessarily put him in the driver's seat.

"Look, Yuri. We haven't granted you asylum yet. Moscow wouldn't be too happy with you if we passed the word that you were helping us and gave them the Swiss account in your name."

Yuri sat down, leaned over, and placed his head in his hands. He then looked up. "This is very dangerous for both me and my family. I know I'm playing both sides. To stay in the US, I've got to deliver fifty thousand dollars to my superior. Otherwise, I am gone. It's the corruption that is eating at me, and, yes, I know that I am part of it. So what should we do? How do we resolve this? What do you want?"

The Poet looked at Yuri. "This is what we want. Before we tell you, I want to play you something."

I figured that this was coming. To gain cooperation and accurrate intelligence, Yuri had to know that we knew everything about him.

The Poet walked into the kitchen and retrieved from a cabinet a small tape deck. He then brought it into the living room, plugged it in, and played the conversation Yuri had had inside the mission. Yuri sat there, transfixed, saying nothing.

Finally Yuri leaned over. "You are very good. I won't ask you how you acquired that. Our conference rooms are totally secure and cannot be penetrated by bugs."

"Yuri, we arrange to meet with you and your family in several weeks. We want every document you can get your hands on from the mission, contacts, illegals. You bring with you names, records, and the one million dollars in cash destined for the Black Panthers. After that you will disappear. Understand?"

"Yes," said Yuri, "I believe it is finally time."

With that we shook hands and Yuri left.

EPILOGUE

Thursday, December 19, 1968

WEEKS AFTER OUR LIMESTONE VISIT, the Poet and I met again with Yuri in an underground garage in Midtown. Yuri was with his family in a rented car. He opened the trunk, and the Poet and I removed boxes of documents, which we transferred to a bureau car along with a suitcase containing $1,000,000 destined for the Panthers.

After this transfer, things moved fast. The documents provided were a treasure trove of material devastating to the interests of the Soviet Union.

We handed Yuri American passports and enough docs to create a new identity. We gave him an envelope containing $250,000 in cash, informing him that $1,000,000 more would be transferred to his Swiss bank account upon review of the documents. Meanwhile, we quickly moved Yuri and his family to a quiet place south of Ludington, Michigan, along Lake Michigan, where he could hole up with his family and wait. Our plan was to review all of the material and then meet with Yuri to discuss with him the other subject of importance—namely, the tumor.

The documents were of such importance that they led to the arrest of several illegals. The $1,000,000 was transferred to Yuri's Swiss account. We informed Yuri he needed a medical exam and CT scan of his head without giving him reasons why. We set up an exam with a government-paid neurosurgeon, explaining to Yuri that after the exam he was on his own. We never saw Yuri again and were advised that he moved to Switzerland with his family.

I often wonder about Yuri. I believe I will encounter him again. He was a guy educated as a spy, who cultivated the habits and practices of deception. He was a swindler and a scammer, somebody who lied to get money. He now intended to go straight? It was not going to happen.

The biggest problem that arose at the office and for me personally occurred after our meeting with Yuri in the underground garage. I was out with Big D. We were having coffee when he casually asked me if C had ever given me anything. I said yes and removed my black braided bracelet from my wrist, handing it to him. He began examining it closely with a pen from his pocket.

I was about to ask him what was going on when he put a finger to his lips. He set the bracelet down on the table and motioned me to step outside the coffee shop at a place where we could visually see our table and the bracelet through the window.

D smiled. "Looks like your girlfriend gave you a bracelet with a bug or miniature listening device. Take a close look when we are back inside. The little thing is sandwiched in between the braids. How did this gift come about?"

I went on to explain the circumstances of the gift and C's dangling it on her leg over the tub and that I'd been wearing it ever since. D took the bracelet with him. Later in the day, he came over to my desk. Handing me back the bracelet, D explained that he'd shown it to some tech people but did not explain to them how he'd come upon it. He was told it was a very crude, antiquated bug that was totally lifeless and dead. He ended the conversation telling me not to worry.

"D," I said nervously, "some of our shit may be compromised."

"Nah," said D, "even if it was operational, it had a very limited distance and useful life. The Russians have always been way behind us in technology."

For me that was not reassuring. We agreed to talk about this over the weekend at the Bishops and concluded that the only operation the bug might have had an impact on, assuming that it had been functioning and operating correctly, was the assault on the Cuban money man. If the Russians knew that the assault was coming, would they have allowed it to proceed? As for C she was probably not aware of what she was giving me.

My relationship with C bothers me more than anything. I know I'll hear from her and will see her again. If I don't soon, my intent is to take a leave of absence and find her. I believe I can track her down.

Meanwhile, the election is past, and Nixon, never one of my favorites, is heading to the White House. The year—1968—was a tough one. King and Kennedy were shot, but we saved Harlem, even though arson and looting occurred in other cities. Frank appeared to be doing his job. The Democratic convention in Chicago, with its televised spectacle of the police beating antiwar demonstrators, was disgusting. Our guys around the poker table and even Alex Santoya would never do that. Next year should be interesting.

To be continued...

47250286R00185

Made in the USA
Lexington, KY
02 December 2015